NO RETURN

A GONE SAGA STANDALONE NOVEL

Stacy Claflin

www.stacyclaflin.com

One

RUSTY CALDWELL FIRST learned of Mandy Oates's suicide while standing in a grocery store line on a sleepy Tuesday evening. He put his energy drink on the conveyor belt and stared at the local newspaper headline, unable to read the article.

His mind spun the harder he concentrated, making it appear that the words danced before his eyes. He couldn't have read it right. It had to have been a mistake.

Hometown local, Mandy Caldwell Oates, dead from suspected suicide.

Rusty stepped out of line, stumbling, and left his drink. Gasping for air, he glanced around.

He needed to sit. There weren't any chairs in sight.

Benches—there were some just inside the entrance.

He made his way over to the nearest one and collapsed. He surely looked like one of the drunks he spent his nights towing.

Rusty's heart raced against his constricted chest. He took slow, deep breaths. It didn't help.

How could his sister be dead? Surely it was joke. A horribly cruel one.

"Are you okay?" asked a familiar feminine voice. "Rusty?"

He snapped his head up. It was Alyssa Mercer, a friend he hadn't seen in a long time. Rusty shook his head.

She sat next to him, placing her hand on his arm. "What's the matter?"

"I…" He couldn't even bring himself to say it. His sister was dead. How was it possible?

Alyssa's dark eyes widened. "Talk to me. You were there for me when I desperately needed a friend."

"My sister." Rusty gasped for air. Maybe if he didn't say it, it wouldn't be real.

"Is she okay?" Alyssa pulled her long, dark hair behind her shoulders, still giving him the look of concern.

He shook his head and braced himself. "Suicide."

Alyssa's mouth dropped open. "Oh, no. Rusty, I'm so sorry. Were you two close?"

Rusty nearly snorted. They couldn't have been further apart—estranged years earlier. He shook his head. "I always thought we'd... you know, make up one day."

"What do you need me to do?"

He stared at her. What could Alyssa possibly do? What could anyone?

"You probably need to go home. Can I give you a ride?"

How ironic was that? He was the one who drove people home for a living.

"No. I'll drive myself. I can't leave the tow truck here all night, anyway."

"Then let me follow you—just to make sure you get there safely."

"I can't ask you to do that."

"You're not. I'm offering, and I don't mind. I'll just call my friend and let her know I'm going to meet her a little late. It's not a big deal."

"Are you sure?"

She nodded. "I definitely owe you."

Rusty relaxed. At least he wasn't alone. Even though his whole world spun out of control, he had a friend keeping him grounded.

A family walked by with two kids screaming.

Alyssa rose. "Let's get out of here."

Rusty forced his feet to comply. His legs weren't very steady, but they would get him to his truck.

"You sure you're okay to drive?"

He took a deep breath. "Yeah. We're not far from my place, anyway."

"I'm still going to follow you." She pulled out a phone and texted. Then she glanced at him. "Is there anyone you need to call?"

"Nothing's changed since I last saw you. No next of kin." No new girlfriend or wife. No more kids.

He couldn't open himself up to that kind of pain again.

They walked out to the parking lot. "I'm over there." Alyssa pointed to the right. "I see your truck. I'll just follow you."

"Okay, but I'll be all right."

"You didn't leave me alone when I told you the same thing, did you?"

He thought back to the night she had been alone and drunk in a bar she didn't belong in. She'd been wallowing in misery she had every right to. And she never would have made it home safely. "No, I didn't."

"See you at your place."

Rusty nodded a thanks and headed for his tow truck. It took three tries to pull the keys from his pocket. Maybe it was a good thing Alyssa had crossed his path.

Once inside, he radioed into the office of his small towing business.

"Hey, boss," came Andy's voice. "Where you towing to?"

Rusty took a deep breath. "I've had a family emergency. I might have to fly out of town. Think you can handle things for a week or so?"

"Yeah, whatever you need. Is everything okay?"

"Death in the family."

"I'm sorry, man. Anything I can do?"

"Thanks, but no. I'll check in tomorrow."

"No, I got everything covered, boss. Just take care of your family."

"Thanks, Andy." Rusty turned off the radio. It was hard to leave his business, but Andy could easily handle it as well as Rusty. He knew all the ins and outs, and all the drivers respected him.

The only thing that no one replaced was Rusty's personal mission. The one that had gotten him into the towing business to begin with, and that was towing drunks home before they became another statistic. After losing his own family to a drunk driver, he didn't want anyone else to go through that kind of pain. Not on his watch, anyway. That's why he hung out at bars every night, giving free rides to people without designated drivers. All on his dime. All because he didn't want anyone else to lose a family. Like he did.

Alyssa's sedan pulled next to him. He waved and then started driving, staying focused on the road and not allowing his thoughts to drift to Mandy. Not yet.

Somehow, he made it to his house. Alyssa pulled up beside him and got out of her car.

He cut the engine, got out of the truck, and locked it, which he didn't usually bother to do. Who knew how long it would sit there? He would likely fly out to see Mandy's kids and husband.

"Well, I made it safely." He tried to smile, but failed miserably.

"Are you sure you don't need anything else?" she asked. "Something to eat?"

"I doubt I could eat if I wanted to."

She nodded. "I get that."

"I know you do," he said. "But I don't want to keep you from your friend."

"She's fine. Are you?"

"Yeah. Well, I will be." Rusty ran his hands through his hair. He'd just had it cut, and the new barber had gone too short. The familiar curls were missing. "I need to get inside and call my parents."

He closed his eyes. That was a conversation he wasn't looking forward to.

"You've got my number, right?"

Rusty nodded and opened his eyes. "I think I have it somewhere."

She pulled out a business card. "Call me if you need anything. Day or night."

"I might have to fly out of town."

Her eyes lit up. "Then I'll keep an eye on your place."

"You don't have to. Don't feel obligated."

"I don't. To be honest, I've always wished I could pay you back."

"And I was just glad to help. I better get inside."

"Sorry. I don't mean to keep you. Call if you need anything."

"Okay."

Alyssa climbed into her car and waved.

Rusty waved back and made his way to his front porch. He watched her drive off, and then he sat on his swinging bench. The cool, night air felt good in his lungs. The stars were out bright in the cloudless sky.

He closed his eyes and stretched his arms out across the top of the swing. In his imagination, his wife—his late wife—Lani sat next to him and snuggled close, nestling her head against his. Then their two boys climbed up onto their laps, cuddling with them.

Rusty enjoyed the moment as long as he could hold onto it and then opened his eyes. He was alone on the bench. No matter how much he willed them back, they never returned.

And now he had to deal with the loss of his younger sister, along with the guilt that he'd never made the first move to restore their relationship. He'd known that their parting had been because of her drug usage, not her. The real Mandy would have never acted the way drug-Mandy had. She certainly never would have said the horrible things to Rusty that she had.

He took a deep breath and stood. It was time to face the music—his parents, more specifically. He needed to speak with them to find out how to contact his sister. Even though Mandy had refused contact with any of them, their parents had kept tabs on her. They knew when she got married and had her two kids. It was a form of self-torture since they'd destroyed their relationship with her.

Not unlike Rusty's solitary existence. Making himself pay for his own mistakes.

His chest tightened at the thought of going inside and making that call. But he needed to. There had to be more to the story than just the suicide. Sure, they were in a pretty small town, but for his sister's death to make a headline… it had to have been more than a death. He had to have missed something.

If he'd been able to read the smaller print—anything beyond the headline—he would have surely found out.

Rusty slid the key into the deadbolt and unlocked it, his hand shaking. Then he unlocked the knob. He took more deep breaths and opened the door.

The empty house hit him like a slap on the face. He had barely changed a thing. It was exactly as it had been when his family had lived there. Even after so many years, he still expected to hear feet running his way when he got home.

He closed the door behind him and locked it. Then he went to his office and sat in the swivel chair, staring at the screensaver of pictures from happier times.

His cell phone rang. Rusty jumped and picked it up. It was his parents.

"Hello?"

"Did you hear?" his dad asked.

"I saw a headline. How long have you known?"

"We heard the news a bit earlier. Your mother has been drinking all afternoon, and finally passed out."

"Wonderful," Rusty muttered. "And how are you taking it?"

"I always told Mandy drugs would get her killed."

"Right." Dad would stay angry for a while before allowing himself to feel anything. That was typical. "Do you guys have her husband's number?"

"Why?"

"I'd like to see if I can do anything to help."

"Doubt he'd take it from any of us. Mandy no doubt made us all out to be monsters."

"In times like this," Rusty said, "he may be more willing to hear from us."

"Or find more reason to blame us."

Rusty shook his head. Was it any wonder his sister had fled? Their family was incredibly messed up. Rusty was lucky to have had as normal of a life as he'd had before the accident. It was also a miracle his parents hadn't disowned him, too. He'd nearly lost his house after turning to alcohol and pot in the wake of losing his wife and kids.

"Can I just get his information?" Rusty asked. "What's his name? Chris, isn't it?"

"Yeah. I'll text you." The call ended.

"Let's hope he's more pleasant than you," Rusty muttered.

The text came in. He added the number to his contacts and called his brother-in-law.

"Hello?" asked an exhausted-sounding male voice.

"Is this Chris Oates?" Rusty asked.

"Who's asking?"

"Rusty Caldwell."

Silence.

"Mandy's brother."

"I know who you are. What do you want?"

Rusty's stomach twisted in knots. "I'd like to help out however I can."

"How so?" Chris sounded suspicious, and for good reason, no doubt.

"I know what it's like to lose a wife. I've never had a chance to meet my niece or nephew—or my brother-in-law."

"You want to fly across the country? You still near Seattle?"

"Yeah. All I have to do is pack."

Chris sighed. "You know, Mandy never really had much bad to say about you. She wished you guys could have made up, but she was afraid to call. She never forgave herself for whatever she put you through."

Rusty ran his hands through his hair. Tears blurred his vision. "Yeah?"

"Yeah. If you want to fly out and help, I won't refuse you. My kids are going crazy, and the police—don't even get me started."

"Sure, okay. Is this your address?" He glanced down at his phone and read off his dad's text.

"Yep. Thanks, man."

"I'll let you know when I'm due to arrive."

"Okay. Crap. The cops are calling again. Gotta go." The call ended.

Rusty set the phone down and typed his password into the laptop. He searched for more information on his sister's death. There wasn't a whole lot of information, except that the suicide was suspicious and they were investigating Chris.

That certainly explained the complaints about the police.

He searched for flights to Florida, found a flight the next morning, and booked it. That would give him a chance to get some sleep before traveling. Or at least *try* to rest.

His body ached from the stress. Rusty went into the kitchen, drank a couple glasses of water, and then went to his bedroom and packed. It had been so long since he'd traveled, he wasn't even sure what was allowed on flights anymore. He pulled out his phone and did a quick search.

After he was finally packed, he fell into bed and stared at the ceiling.

How could Mandy be dead? His baby sister. He'd always meant to get back in touch with her. But with life… his own tragedy…

He'd pushed everyone else away. The truth was he'd wanted to avoid hurting anymore. But that had failed. He could barely breathe now. And he was sure he was in shock still.

It had been so many years since he'd seen Mandy, yet in a way, their last conversation felt recent. But that was back when they were both in their twenties. Or had she even reached twenty yet?

Tears blurred his vision. His face heated. Rusty blinked away the tears and they streamed down his face, pooling in his ears.

"Why, Mandy? You could have called me. I would have done anything for you. But I guess you didn't know that."

He'd barely survived losing his wife and children—he wasn't even over it. How could he cope with the added loss of his sister, with whom he'd never had the chance to make things right?

Well, the chances had been there. Years of chances. But he'd been so lost, wandering in his misery over his family that he couldn't bring himself to call Mandy.

And now it was too late.

Rusty rolled over and screamed into his pillow. Then he gave way to sobs so deep he hadn't felt them since the accident had taken Lani and the boys.

When he had nothing left in him, he rolled to his side and drifted into a dreamless sleep.

Two

~

RUSTY STEPPED OFF the airport shuttle van and stared at the house in front of him as the warm, summer sun warmed him after being chilled in the extra-cold air conditioning from the vehicle.

The home was just a typical, suburban split-level—brown, with a well-manicured lawn and trees, though the grass was a bit long. There was even a basketball hoop over the garage. A silver sedan and a white minivan sat in the driveway.

Mandy must have cleaned up for her family. Rusty would have never pictured her in a place like this, but then again, it had been over fifteen years since they'd seen each other.

The back of the airport shuttle squeaked as it opened. Rusty went over to where his luggage was stored and grabbed his suitcase from the driver.

"Thank you."

"And thank you for choosing the Super Shuttle Express." The man tipped his hat and left.

Rusty clutched the handle of his luggage and walked to the front door, stepping over a baseball. He tried to remember how old his niece and nephew were. The oldest might be thirteen.

What would they think of him? Was it true their mom had hardly spoken a negative thing about him?

Rusty reached for the doorbell, but stopped when he heard a commotion across the street. He backed up and glanced down a couple houses. A lady stood with her arms folded, staring at two other ladies storming off.

He went to the sidewalk. "Is everything okay?"

The lady turned to him and shook her head. "Never cross the Calloways."

Rusty tilted his head. "Who?"

She threw her arms in the air. "Be glad you don't know." She climbed into a car and sped off, peeling the tires.

"Okay…" Rusty went back to his sister's door.

Yelling sounded from inside. It sounded like his brother-in-law. Rusty recognized his voice from the phone. His stomach twisted in knots. Maybe this trip was a bad idea. He rang the doorbell, anyway.

"Coming," called Chris, sounding far less angry than a moment earlier.

The door opened, and a man with short, dark hair and dark eyes answered. He had a five o'clock shadow and dark circles underneath his deep brown eyes. "Rusty?"

He nodded and held out his hand.

Chris shook it. "Come on in. The police want me to come back down to the station. Do you mind staying with the kids?"

"That's why I'm here."

"You're a lifesaver. This last week has been a nightmare." Chris turned around and led Rusty up the stairs. He went left, and gestured toward a gray sectional couch with stuffing coming out of the armrests.

A girl, about thirteen, with hair as dark as his sat with her eyes closed, dancing in her seat to music only she could hear in the earbuds. A boy, about eleven, with light brown hair hanging over his ears had his full attention on the television. They both had the same dark bands under their eyes as their dad—the very ones Rusty was so familiar with, too.

"That's Kaylie. And that's Brady."

Neither glanced up.

"Kids!"

Kaylie pulled her earbuds out and Brady paused the show. They both turned to Chris, their eyes bloodshot.

"This is your Uncle Rusty. He's going to watch you guys while I'm out."

"I don't need a babysitter," Kaylie said.

"Me, neither," Brady said.

"I'm not here to babysit," Rusty assured them. "Just here in case you need something. Lunch, maybe?"

"Grilled cheese," Brady said and turned his show back on.

"I apologize for their manners." Chris turned to them. "Kids, be *nice*."

"Yeah, yeah." Kaylie stuck her earbuds back in and closed her eyes.

"Sorry to run," Chris said. "But make yourself at home. Thanks again."

"No problem." Rusty set his suitcase next to the couch on the brown shag carpet.

Chris hurried down the stairs, and neither kid seemed to notice. He stopped near the front door and his phone sounded. Chris's face clouded over as he glanced at the screen. He swore about a text.

"Is everything all right?" Rusty asked.

"What?" Chris looked at him, his face noticeably paler.

"Are you okay?"

"It's the CEO of my work. He's… I need to get the cops off my back so I can get back to work."

"Doesn't your boss understand you've lost your wife? You need time to recover and—"

"The only thing Travis Calloway cares about is the bottom line."

Calloway? Wasn't that the same name the neighbor had said outside?

Chris cracked his knuckles. "What I wouldn't give for just one drink."

"You don't want to do that. You've been clean for years, haven't you?"

His expression pinched. "Yes, I'm the one who helped Mandy get clean. I'm not *going* to drink. I just want one sometimes, you know? If my idiot boss and the cops would get a clue, I'd be fine."

Rusty leaned against the cracked banister. "Surely, your boss can understand the need to—"

Chris's phone rang. He swore and answered it. "I'm doing the best I can, Ricardo. The cops have it out for me. They won't leave me alone." He paused. "I can't tell the police to wait! You're going to have to tell Travis I'll work nights or something. My *wife* just died."

Rusty turned toward the kids and watched them, trying not to eavesdrop on Chris.

"Look, Ricardo, I can't afford to lose this job, but I can't tell the cops to take a hike, either. They want me down at the station now. The longer you keep me on the phone, the longer it's going to be until I can get back to work... You can't do that me! I have vacation days." Chris let loose a string of profanities and put his phone away.

Rusty turned back to him. "Can I help with anything?"

Chris stared at him, his face reddening. "I hate that pompous jerk." He picked up a potted flower and threw it against the wall. It shattered, sending soil in all directions. "No respect. None at all."

"Sounds like you should get going," Rusty said, keeping his tone steady. "How about I clean that up?"

"Speaking of cleaning." He rushed up the stairs, past Rusty. He glared at the kids. "Look at me!"

Both kids jumped and stared at him.

"Your rooms are pig pens! Clean them up. Now. If anything's out of place when I get back, there's going to be hell to pay. Do I make myself clear?"

They both nodded, not saying anything.

"And turn those devices off! You'd think they grew out of your butts. They're not attached. Clean those rooms now. I have enough to deal with without having to think about your stupid messes." He stormed past Rusty again, went down the stairs, and slammed the door.

Kaylie and Brady looked back and forth, and glanced nervously at Rusty. They seemed to be trying to get a feel for his reaction.

Rusty stepped forward. A floorboard creaked. "It seems like your dad's under some stress. Why don't you get to your rooms, and I'll take care of the mess by the door? Then I'll make some lunch. Sound good?"

They both got up and ran down the hall without a word. Rusty cleaned Chris's mess and thought about how to approach the kids about his blow up. Then he went into the kitchen. As he explored, trying to find what he needed, it was hard not to imagine Mandy in there. She had probably put everything where it was.

A lump formed in his throat. At least he could make a difference for his niece and nephew. They would never remember him as an uncle from their childhood, but perhaps he could be the one who helped them through the most difficult time in their young lives.

Before long, the sandwiches were done. He put them on plates and carried them out to the living room, where the kids now sat. Neither one seemed bothered by the earlier outburst. Both thanked him and scarfed down the food.

"Have you eaten today?" he asked, deciding to wait on asking them about their dad.

"Just cereal," Brady said, his mouth full of cheese.

"That's going to change. What's your favorite dinner?"

"Roast beef," Kaylie said.

"Hot dogs," Brady said at the same time.

"Ew." Kaylie shot him a glare. "Not for dinner."

"For any meal. Even breakfast."

Kaylie shook her head and begged Rusty with her eyes.

"Maybe we can have some for lunch tomorrow." Rusty winked at Brady and went back into the kitchen. They would have to go grocery shopping after lunch. The cupboards were close to empty. It would be good to get the kids out of the house, anyway.

He pulled some dried, brown flowers from a vase in the middle of the table. All the water had evaporated, leaving a residue on the glass. Small pieces of the flowers crumbled onto the table as he moved them. He got the mess cleaned up, made himself something to eat, and went back to the living room.

"Time to get groceries."

"Have fun," Brady said.

Rusty arched a brow. "You guys are coming with me."

Kaylie pulled both of her earbuds out. "Are you serious?"

"Of course. Things are starting to change color in there."

Brady laughed and Kaylie cracked a smile.

"Come on, it'll be good for you to get out. The sun will even give you some vitamin D."

Kaylie ran a hand through her hair. "But I haven't showered... in, like, days."

"Then get to it. That'll do you good, too."

She tilted her head.

"Or just go like that. I won't judge you."

Kaylie scrambled out of the chair and ran down the hall.

"What about you?" Rusty asked Brady.

He shrugged. "I can wear a beanie."

"Your call."

"Okay." Brady turned back to the TV.

Rusty went back into the kitchen and heard the shower start. He wasn't sure if Mandy ever learned to cook, but Rusty would see to it her family ate well while he was in town.

While the water still ran in the bathroom, he grabbed his suitcase and went down the hall, peeking in the rooms until he found one that looked like a guest room—generic bedding and not many decorations, save a framed picture of a field. He put the luggage on the bed and changed into a more casual shirt.

Rusty went over to open the blinds and noticed a lot of people out, walking. Everyone who passed, paused to stare at the house. Even the cars slowed. It was clear everyone knew what had happened. In fact, they probably knew more than Rusty did.

He went to the living room. "Where do your parents keep the car keys?"

Brady frowned. "Mom usually leaves them on their dresser."

He went down the hall and found the bedroom—and the keys.

When he passed the bathroom, he knocked. "Meet me out front."

"Okay," Kaylie called. A blow drier started.

Rusty turned off the TV. "Brush your hair and meet me outside."

Brady grumbled, but got off the couch.

"You'll thank me."

"Right."

Rusty went downstairs and out front. The minivan was gone, so that must have meant the sedan had been Mandy's. There was no button to remote-unlock it, so he quickly found the car key on the chain. He slid it in the keyhole, but it didn't want to turn. He jiggled it several different ways, used to dealing with all kinds of locks in his business.

"You want some help?" came a feminine voice.

He turned around to see a tall lady across the lawn next door. Over a bright yellow tank top, she wore a long, flowing black dress decorated with brown stitching. Several long, multi-colored necklaces swished as she walked across her lawn. It made her look part gypsy, part sorceress, but her friendly smile and bright eyes were at odds to her attire, completely welcoming him.

"I think I can get it," he replied. "I know a thing or two about locks. I run a towing business."

"There's a trick to this one. I always told Mandy she should just replace the entire car." She stopped just short of bumping into Rusty and smiled. She looked him over, seeming to like what she saw and pulled her layered long, black hair behind her shoulder. Her perfume smelled like the ocean. "I'm Laura Henley, and you are?"

Rusty tried to smile, but couldn't. He held out his hand, instead. "Nice to meet you, Laura Henley. I'm Rusty Caldwell. Mandy's brother."

"Oh…"

Was that an *oh, I've never heard of you* oh, or an *oh, the mystery brother I've heard so much about* oh?

She took his hand and shook it. "I can see the family resemblance. Here, let me show you how to unlock this beast."

Rusty stepped back and Laura pulled the key out just a little, jiggled it, and then slid it in the rest of the way while turning it. There was a click, indicating the door was finally unlocked.

Laura turned and smiled, brightening her entire face. "There you go. So, you helping to take care of the kids?"

He nodded, not sure what to make of the neighbor.

"I've seen a few people bringing them dinners, but that only goes so far, you know?" she asked.

"Right." His mind wandered back to all the uneaten meals brought to him after the accident that had taken his family.

"I would have brought food over, but Chris never liked me. It would have gone straight into the trash."

Rusty arched a brow.

Laura shrugged with an expression that showed she didn't care much for Chris, either.

Rusty leaned against the car. "So, why doesn't Chris like you?"

"Other than the fact that I encouraged Mandy to get out and have some fun? You know, do something for herself for a change."

"What do you mean?" he asked.

"He never wanted her out of his sight. And I always got the feeling he made her pay after she came home with me." She sighed.

Rusty's brows came together. "Pay? How?"

Laura glanced toward the house. She leaned closer to Rusty. "Sometimes I could hear the yelling from my house if we both had open windows. Then after that, I wouldn't hear from Mandy for a while." She frowned and locked Rusty's gaze. Tears shone in her eyes. "If I'd known he was this bad, I would have done something."

"You think Chris hurt her?" he asked.

"The cops haven't arrested him."

"That's not what I asked." Rusty studied her.

She stared at him. "I'd say it's a lot more likely than her killing herself."

Three

~

RUSTY TURNED OFF the movie, causing the room to go completely dark. He turned on the flashlight app on his phone and glanced over at the kids. They had both fallen asleep on the couch. Kaylie had curled up with a blanket, and Brady was using an armrest for a pillow. He considered letting them sleep there, but thought they would fare better in their own beds.

"Come on, guys. Let's get to bed."

Brady mumbled and Kaylie didn't respond. He went over and helped Brady up. "Time to get to bed."

"You're waking me up so I can go to sleep."

"That's right." Rusty patted his shoulders and guided him toward the hall. Kaylie walked by them, mumbling something.

Rusty's phone rang. It was their dad.

"I'd better get this. Don't forget to brush your teeth." He went over to the dining room and answered. "Chris, is everything okay?"

"No, it's not. They're detaining me for more questioning."

"More?" Rusty asked. "Is there a problem?"

"Yeah, but I don't have time to talk about it."

"Can I do anything for you?"

Chris sighed. "Can you take care of the kids?"

"Of course. They're getting ready for bed now."

"I can't thank you enough. Tell them I'll be back soon."

"Sure thing."

The call ended. Rusty slid the phone back into his pocket, trying to make sense of the whole situation. There was so little information online—he'd checked. The only thing he'd been able to find was that police had spent a lot of time questioning Chris down at the station. Far more than seemed normal spousal questioning.

He needed to look around and see if there were any answers in the house. But first, he needed to check on the kids.

Brady was brushing his teeth. He spit into the sink. "Where's Dad?"

"The police have a few more questions for him. He promises to be back soon."

"So, he's still there?" Brady rinsed his mouth with some blue liquid in a container with cartoon characters on the front.

"Unfortunately. But if you need anything, I'm staying here."

Brady spit into the sink. "Okay. And thanks for dinner. That was so good—like eating at a restaurant."

"Just wait until breakfast." Rusty winked at him, and Brady's tired eyes lit up. He went back out to the living room and cleaned up some popcorn that had spilled on the carpet and then took the bowls into the kitchen. He went into their rooms, finding them both asleep already.

He closed their doors and stood in the hall, trying to figure out where to start looking. The logical place was Mandy's bedroom. He was a little hesitant to poke around because of it also being Chris's room, but maybe he could find something that would prove his innocence.

Rusty brushed aside his reticence and headed for the room. It was small for a master bedroom. The faded paint appeared to have once been ocean blue, now peeled near the window and closet. The unmade queen-size bed took up most of the space. Some framed family pictures decorated the headboard. On the side nearest him, clothes were strewn across the floor along with pages from a newspaper.

He went over to the other side of the bed that had a nightstand full of hair products and makeup. A stuffed rabbit sat against a reading lamp, nearly falling over. Rusty's throat closed up. He'd won that for Mandy at the state fair when he was twelve. He picked it up and held it close. It smelled of her perfume—cinnamon and vanilla.

The hairs stood up on the back of Rusty's neck. He spun around, nearly dropping the stuffed animal. No one was there. It felt like someone was watching him, but the blinds were closed and the house was silent.

He glanced around for a camera, but didn't see anything. That, of course, didn't mean anything. He recalled their old nanny cams that rested in the eyeballs of teddy bears. They weren't visible unless you knew exactly where they were.

If Chris confronted him on being there, he would say the truth—he was trying to help. Plus, his brother-in-law *had* told him to make himself at home. Getting to know his estranged sister was just that.

Rusty returned the bunny and opened the top drawer of the nightstand. There were several romance books stashed in there. He picked up the stack, finding a variety of genres from horror to suspense. Another book sat beneath the others. It was different from the others. It looked like a journal.

Bingo. He set the novels down and picked up the diary.

Knock, knock. The front door.

Rusty's heart raced, feeling guilty for snooping. He shoved the books back and closed the drawer before putting the journal into the guest room. He slid it underneath the mattress and then hurried to the door.

From the window next to the door, he saw Laura. She waved at him.

Rusty opened the door.

"Hi," she said. "I noticed Chris's van is still gone, and wanted to check in on you."

"I just got the kids to bed."

Laura frowned, her pretty eyes widening. "Poor things. I can't even imagine what they're going through. How are they holding up?"

"About as well as can be expected." Rusty opened the door wider, and she came in. "I think they've been eating cereal all week, though."

"I have a feeling you put a stop to that." She took a deep breath. "Mmm. It smells so good in here. What did you order?"

"I made chicken marsala."

"A man who can cook?" She arched a brow. "Impressive."

"Plenty of men cook."

"Not the ones I know."

"Maybe you should teach them."

She twisted a strand of hair tightly around her finger. "Dad has other interests and you can't tell my ex-husband anything. Not that I'm the greatest cook."

"Oh. Do you want some food? I made plenty."

"I couldn't."

He shrugged and closed the door.

"Well, maybe I could. You talked me into it."

Laura glanced around, appearing curious. Had Chris forbidden her from coming inside? Rusty wanted to get back to Mandy's journal, but maybe he could learn something from her friend. He warmed her up a plate in the microwave and turned around. She held up a bottle of wine. "Want some?"

He shook his head. "I'm not much of a drinker."

"I can't think of a better time for it."

"How about some coffee? I make a mean organic creamer."

Laura tilted her head and gave him a once-over. "You're a man of many surprises." She returned the bottle to the wine rack. "If it's anything like the chicken smells, how can I turn that down?"

He set the plate on the table and prepared the coffee pot before gathering his ingredients for the creamer.

"This is heavenly. Have you ever been a chef?" she asked.

Rusty held in a snicker. "Hardly. I haven't always had an interest in cooking." He stirred milk in with the other creamer ingredients, poured the coffee into the mugs, and mixed in the creamer. He sat across from Laura and handed her one.

She took a sip and closed her eyes as though savoring it.

Rusty took a deep breath and thought about what to ask her. So many questions ran through his mind, it was hard to sort through them, much less pick where to start.

Laura opened her eyes and held his gaze. "That's the best coffee I've ever tasted."

The corners of his lips twitched. "What did I tell you?"

"You should seriously open a restaurant. I'd go—every day. I don't know why you bother with towing."

"It's a labor of love. I can't see myself cooking on a grand scale."

"Oh, I can. And you'd look great in a chef's hat, too."

Warmth crept into his cheeks. Sure, he was used to being hit on—but not usually by sober women. In most cases, he was trying to keep them out of their cars before they hurt themselves or someone else.

"Did Mandy ever learn to cook?"

"Not unless it came from a box. She liked to eat out."

"Sounds like her."

"Why did you two grow apart?" Laura took another bite of chicken.

"We had some differences of opinion. I always figured we'd have time to work them out." Rusty frowned. "I should have tried sooner."

She put her hand on his arm. "You couldn't have seen this coming. Heck, I talked to her every day, and I didn't."

"I can't believe she's gone. I don't want to think about her killing herself, but at the same time, I can't think about anyone hurting her, either. What do you think? Were you serious about Chris?"

They studied each other. Laura's eyebrows wrinkled and some hair fell into her eyes. She brushed it away. "Everyone has problems, and Mandy always seemed to have more than her fair share."

That certainly sounded like his sister.

Laura pulled some hair behind her ear and shrugged. "Trouble just seemed to follow her around, you know?"

"Like what?"

"Everything. Crazy stuff—like what you'd see on television. Not things that actually happen in the suburbs." Her eyebrows came together as she continued studying him. It felt like she was feeling out his reactions.

"Drugs?" Rusty asked.

Laura sat up straight. "No, nothing like that. She moved past all that long ago. Why do you ask that?"

Rusty looked into his half-full mug, not sure he wanted to talk about Mandy's past. It had been hard enough to live through it, watching his sister destroy her life one piece at a time. At least she had cleaned up.

"Rusty?"

He glanced up at her. "She struggled with it a bit in her younger years. It caused some… rifts… in our family." And by rifts, he meant ripping it apart. His parents had never been the same since cutting her out of their lives, but they'd had no other choice. "What was she like since you've known her?"

Laura took another sip of her coffee. "She always seemed worried about something. Looking over her shoulder a lot."

"For what?"

"She never really said."

"How close were the two of you?"

She shrugged. "We talked. When we could."

"Meaning?"

"Chris didn't really like her out of his sight. He didn't like me because I invited her out places. I don't know what he thought—that I was taking her out to bars to meet men?" Laura shook her head. "Mandy liked going out for dinner and talking. We'd discuss work, kids, whatever."

"And he didn't like that?"

"Nope. It got to the point where she stopped asking about hanging out anymore. She hated bringing it up with him, so she stopped."

"So, you haven't spent any time with her recently?" Rusty gathered the empty mugs and plate.

"Just talking in our yards. Leaning over the backyard fence to gossip about the neighbors. Or sneaking in discussions while working on the front yards."

"Hmm." Rusty put everything in the dishwasher and started it. "Did Chris still seem to hate you?"

"Hate is a bit strong. But he never liked me."

Rusty sat back down. "Why was Chris so distrustful of you? Or is it Mandy he didn't trust?"

A strange expression covered Laura's face for a moment, but then she smiled again. "Hard to say."

"What was that?"

"What?" Laura's eyes widened.

"The look on your face. Like you know something. All I want is to figure out what really happened."

"So, you don't think it was suicide, either?"

"I'm the last one to judge her, but if it wasn't, and I can help prove she didn't take her own life, at least that would be one last thing I can do for my sister." Tears stung his eyes and he blinked them away.

Laura rested her chin in her palm. "I do have one theory."

"What is it?" Rusty leaned over the table, staring into her dark, mysterious eyes.

She glanced from side to side and lowered her voice. "Mandy told me that she thought one of the kids isn't Chris's."

"Brady."

"How'd you know?"

"Just looking at him. He's a spitting image of Mandy at that age, except for his coloring. Neither she nor Chris have that light of complexion or hair."

Laura leaned back. "That's true. I wonder if she ever got the proof."

"What do you mean?"

"She was talking about DNA testing. Comparing hair samples from their brushes."

"Why wait until now?" Rusty asked.

"Well…" Laura played with her necklaces. "She thought she could make things work with Chris, and I guess they did for a while. But then last year, it was all she could talk about. To me, anyway. But then we stopped going out, and she didn't bring it up anymore."

"Do you know who the guy was?" Rusty twisted his hands together under the table.

Laura stared into his eyes. "Only the richest man in town."

Four

~

CONVERSATION WOKE KAYLIE. She checked her phone. It was the middle of the night. The male and female voices continued. Maybe Mom and Dad were arguing again.

She sat up. Mom? No, it couldn't be. She'd been carried away in a bag.

Tears filled her eyes as she listened. It wasn't her mom or her dad. No, it was Laura from next door. Who was the guy?

Kaylie wiped her tears and recognized the voice. It was Mom's brother. Rusty.

It was so weird that he showed up now. Never when Mom had been alive. At least he could cook. She was still full from all the food he'd made them.

She lay back down and closed her eyes. It still didn't seem real that her mom was gone. They'd been talking about getting mani-pedis. Both of them had been looking forward to some girl time.

Her mom hadn't killed herself. Kaylie didn't care what anyone said. Maybe it had been food poisoning or something. Or some weird disease nobody had ever heard of before. Something that there was no test for.

Or maybe her heart had just stopped working. Her health teacher had talked about the long-term damage drugs did to the body. Maybe a batch of something Mom took years earlier had finally caught up with her. It could have been anything. Just not suicide.

Kaylie had already been picked for one of the leading roles in the school play in the fall. Tryouts had been at the end of the year. With the eighth graders moving up to high school, Kaylie finally had a chance— and she'd actually gotten it. Her mom had been thrilled. She'd even bought a new phone so she could get better pictures.

Why would she do all that if she was just going to kill herself? She wouldn't. There was no way. Plus, she'd told both Kaylie and Brady plenty of times that she would never do anything to hurt them—and suicide would have been the worst kind of hurt. No. Not her mom. Plus, lately, she'd said it even more than usual. Probably three times the week before she'd died.

She wouldn't have said it that much if she hadn't meant it.

A lump formed in Kaylie's throat. Her lips shook and then a fresh, new wave of tears came, spilling on her face. She turned over and sobbed into her pillow.

Kaylie cried until no more tears would come. She sat up and tried to catch her breath. Would it always hurt this bad? Or could it get better? There was no way she could get through school feeling like this. Hopefully in a couple months, she would be functional.

She reached for her box of tissues. Empty. Again. She needed to grab a few boxes from the closet instead of just one.

After opening her door, she froze. The memory of her dad pacing the hall the night before Kaylie found out about her mom was so real, it was as though she was reliving it. She'd gotten up because she had forgotten her earbuds on the couch and wanted to watch videos on her phone.

But she couldn't even go into the hall because Dad had been pacing the length of it. She'd watched him for a few minutes, hoping he'd stop. But he hadn't. He kept muttering to himself. At first, Kaylie had thought he was on the phone, but he'd only been talking to himself.

She'd never seen him so upset. Well, not until the next morning.

Voices, heavy footsteps, and the hissing of dispatch radios had woken her. When she'd looked out of her room, she saw the gurney with the black bag strapped on heading toward their stairs.

Her dad stared at her, his hair sticking out in a hundred different directions and ordered her back into her room. She'd refused, coming out into the hall. "What's going on?"

"I said stay in your room."

"Where's Mom?"

"I told you—"

Brady's door opened and he came out. "What's going on?"

"Both of you! In your rooms—now!"

Brady ran back into his, slamming the door shut. Dad glared at Kaylie, his nostrils flaring until she went back into her room, too. She got on the floor and listened through the crack under the door. It was something she'd always done when her parents fought, but somehow this had felt worse.

The footsteps and conversation sounded down the stairs. Once she was sure no one was in the hall, Kaylie went out. She went into her brother's room. He was curled up in a ball on his bed, his face streaked with tears.

"Wh-what's going on?" he asked.

She sat down next to him and rubbed his back. "I don't know." She didn't dare talk about the bag. She'd seen enough TV to know what that meant, and she didn't want to scare him. Or was it that she didn't want to admit what she feared?

Brady leaned up against her, and she wrapped her arm around him.

"It's bad, isn't it?"

"I think so."

"Where's Mom?"

Kaylie's stomach twisted in knots. She opened her mouth to speak, but her stomach lurched.

"Where is she?"

Kaylie jumped up and ran to the bathroom just in time to yak. Her mom had been in that body bag. That was the only thing that made sense.

She threw up once more and then brushed her teeth before checking on Brady again.

"What's going on?"

"We better let Dad tell us. Come on."

His eyes widened. "I'm not going out there. Not when he's yelling at us."

Kaylie sighed. "Would you rather stay in here by yourself?"

"Yeah." He climbed under his covers. He could be such a baby sometimes.

"I don't want to go out there by myself. You know how he gets."

Brady's eyes shone with tears. "That's why I'm staying here."

"Fine." Kaylie spun around and went into the hall.

A clatter in the kitchen brought Kaylie back to the present. If Laura was there with Rusty, that meant her dad was still out. Still at the police station? He'd been there so much. She and Brady had stayed with some neighbors a couple times. At least with Rusty there, they could stay home. And eat more than dry cereal and crackers since the neighbors had quit bringing food.

Kaylie went out into the kitchen. Laura glanced up from a coffee mug, her eyes wide with surprise. Then she frowned—a look of pity Kaylie was already sick of seeing from everyone who talked to her and Brady.

"Are you okay, honey?" Laura came over and wrapped Kaylie in a hug.

What kind of a question was that? She'd probably never be okay again. Kaylie shrugged.

Laura stepped back, keeping her hands on Kaylie's arms. "If you or Brady ever need anything, just come and get me, okay? I'll do anything—day or night."

"Thanks." It was so awkward with people suddenly showing so much care and concern for their family.

"You should get some sleep, kiddo," Laura said.

"Okay."

Laura turned to Rusty. "If you need anything, let me know. I work from home as an independent consultant. I don't mind being disturbed."

"I'll be in touch about what we were talking about," he said.

If Kaylie wasn't so exhausted, both physically and emotionally, she'd have been curious. She went to the fridge and pulled the new OJ. Rusty had gotten her favorite kind—the one Dad always said was sickeningly sweet. She poured herself a glass while Rusty walked Laura to the door.

Kaylie actually liked her. Laura had always been really nice to her and Brady, but people had been coming and going ever since... the event. She liked that term. It was better than saying the death or the suicide or whatever. The event.

Rusty came back upstairs. "You okay?"

She finished off the glass and nodded. "Just thirsty, I guess."

"Did we wake you?"

Kaylie shrugged. She glanced around the messy kitchen. "Want some help?"

"Nah, I got it. You up for a midnight snack?"

"Like what?" She arched a brow.

"Don't look so scared," he teased her. "I bought everything needed for s'mores. I can whip some up in the oven real quick."

"Seriously?" Her mouth watered. She hadn't had those in years, and never from an oven. "That sounds really good."

"Of course. Grab the crackers from the cabinet." He turned the oven on. "So, what did you think I was going to suggest?"

Kaylie shrugged. "Dad would've said broccoli."

"With melted cheese, at least?"

"Nope. Just steamed." She pulled out the box of graham crackers.

"That would be the healthy choice, but we need comfort food."

Kaylie smiled and helped him make the s'mores. While they were cooking, Brady came out, looking disoriented.

"Do I smell chocolate?"

"S'mores," Kaylie said. "Uncle Rusty's idea."

Rusty startled, then smiled. She gave him a little nod. He was definitely cool enough to earn the title to his name.

"Nice." Brady sat next to her and rubbed his eyes. "Don't mind waking up to that."

The timer dinged. The chocolate sizzled just a bit as Rusty set them on the counter. "Who wants pop to go with that?"

Brady's eyes widened and he exchanged an approving glance with Kaylie. "Me."

"Thanks, Uncle Rusty." Kaylie got up and grabbed a liter of Mountain Dew.

"I was thinking something that *isn't* one hundred percent caffeine." Uncle Rusty smiled. "Since we're all going to bed after this. Maybe root beer?"

"Can't blame a girl for trying." Kaylie grabbed the bottle of root beer and got out their biggest glasses. With Uncle Rusty's back turned, she put vanilla ice cream in each glass before adding the soda.

"This is turning into quite the midnight snack." Uncle Rusty put a spoon in each glass, obviously approving Kaylie's idea.

They managed to have a fun time eating the sweets.

"What do you guys like to do for fun?" Uncle Rusty asked.

Brady had a mouthful of s'mores. He pointed to Kaylie.

She set her snack down and thought about it. Since Mom had died, fun hadn't been on her mind. "I really like to act."

"You've got the dramatic flair for it!" Brady laughed.

Kaylie rolled her eyes. "It's fun. I actually got a leading role in the school play."

"Good for you. I bet you'll do great. What about you?" Uncle Rusty turned to Brady.

He shrugged. "I like all kinds of stuff. Football, baseball, wrestling. It's hard to pick just one, you know?"

"I can understand that. May as well have fun and enjoy being a kid."

Kaylie smiled. It was actually nice to spend time with Uncle Rusty just talking about normal things. Kaylie was sure her mom would have been happy.

After the snacks were all gone, they continued talking for a little while. Then Brady announced he was too tired to stay up any longer.

"Brush your teeth again," Uncle Rusty said.

"Yeah, yeah."

He turned to Kaylie. "You should probably get back to sleep, too. It's almost one."

"I'm good." She helped him clean everything up and then they headed down the hall toward the bedrooms.

"How are you doing, really?" he asked.

"It sucks, but I'm glad you're here."

He put his hand on her shoulder. "I wish I'd come for a visit a long time ago."

Kaylie sighed. "Me, too. You should bring your kids next time. I can tell you're a good dad."

His expression clouded over. "We'll talk about them later. You should get some sleep."

She nodded and then stared at her parents' room. "I don't know if I'll ever be able to go back in there again."

Uncle Rusty frowned. "Is that where…?"

"Dad found her? Yep." A lump formed in her throat again. She cleared it. "It sucks."

"I know." He looked thoughtful and sad. "I definitely know."

She knew that look. "Did you lose your kids?"

He looked at her, his eyes wide. "You're very intuitive, aren't you?"

Kaylie shrugged. "What happened to them?"

"Car accident. Drunk driver."

"Oh, sh—crap. That does suck. Why do so many bad things happen in this family?"

"I wish I knew, but we gotta stick together. Right?"

"Yeah." Kaylie paused. "What were they like?"

He rubbed the top of her head. "I'll tell you what. We'll get some sleep and share stories later. I want to hear more about your mom because it's been so long since I saw her. You want to hear about your cousins. Sound good?"

Kaylie yawned. "Perfect."

Five

~

LAURA HENLEY RUBBED the flesh-toned cream under her eyes to hide the dark circles. She hadn't slept well since Mandy's death. She'd been crying most of the night and then powering through her work all day. It was exhausting.

At least Rusty had shown up. He, being Mandy's brother, would be just as interested in clearing Mandy's name as Laura was. Together, they could work through their grief by helping Mandy.

She checked her face in the mirror of the antique black vanity, added a bit more blush to her cheekbones, and then sprayed an extra spritz of her favorite summertime perfume. She turned to the right and left, checking herself out in the mirror. She looked pretty good—considering. She definitely wasn't her usual happy self. She still looked tired, but less so thanks to the makeup.

Her black camisole underneath the orange and brown crocheted tank went perfectly with her pecan-colored pendant and feather earrings. She ran her fingers through her black hair and fluffed it out just a smidgen. It helped to focus on the little details of life. To get her mind off her heart's ache.

Laura went into the spacious kitchen, her sandals tapping on the dark hardwood flooring. She grabbed an orange, peeled it, and sat at the table that matched the floor. She ate the orange, staring at the faux stone fireplace—who needed a blazing fire in Florida? But it was so pretty, she'd had to have it in her house. The mantle made a beautiful place to hang her pots and pans.

She threw away the peel, wandered into the living room, and took a deep breath. Usually, she could always relax in here, but since Mandy's death, not even her favorite rooms helped. She walked along the outer wall, brushing her hands against the dried flowers hanging from the ceiling. She stopped in front of her easel and stared at the mostly-done painting of multi-colored sunflowers exploding from a vase on a dark green table. It would get finished, eventually.

Laura turned around and stumbled over the black, white, and green throw rug. She fixed it and moved around some of the pillows and blankets on her evergreen couch. She straightened some magazines on the coffee table, but it was pointless. The house was getting messy and she needed to get next door.

It was a good thing Cindy was due to come clean. Was it that day or the next? It was hard to concentrate these days.

Her mind wandered back to Mandy. There was no way Mandy had committed suicide. Sure, like anyone, there had been things she hadn't been happy about. Things she wanted different in her life, but she wasn't depressed or anything like that. Mandy had been making strides to change her life for the better. Finding ways to get the happiness she wanted.

In fact, that was why Laura was about to leave to talk with Rusty. She had to tell him all the details about Mandy's plan to improve her life— plans that made two men look guilty for her 'suicide.' The controlling husband and the father of her youngest who didn't want to make waves by telling his new wife that he might have a son.

She left a note for Cindy, telling her she'd be next door, and then went outside, locking the door to her split level. Much to her relief, Chris's van was still gone. At least she wasn't the only one who questioned his involvement. But then again, she'd been completely open with the police. That had to have helped.

Laura noticed a pop can at the edge of her lawn on the sidewalk. She went over and picked it up.

A few women jogged by.

Laura waved. "Hello."

The group slowed, but didn't stop. The tallest, a redhead named Greer, curled her lip. "Nice makeup, Laura."

The other two giggled. They all stopped and stared at her.

Laura brought her hand to her face. "What are you talking about?

There's nothing wrong with the way I look."

"You look more like a raccoon than a person." Greer wrinkled her nose.

A brunette Laura didn't know rubbed her throat and grimaced. "Seriously. Where'd you get your makeup tips? The vet?"

Laura's mouth went dry and she clenched her jaw. She didn't want to dignify their comments with a response. Instead, she turned around and headed for her garage to deposit the litter.

"That's right," one of them called. "Run away like a scared little mouse."

"Don't all those bracelets weigh you down?" another called. They all laughed again.

Laura went around the house and leaned against the wall. Her entire body shook. She peeked around the corner to see them jogging away, whispering to each other.

A lump formed in her throat. Not only had she lost her friend, but now she had to face catty neighbors on her own. She took a deep breath and threw the bottle in the recycle canister.

The neighbors weren't worth the time it took to think about them. She needed to go speak with Rusty. Laura straightened her top and headed for Mandy's house. It was early, and the kids were probably still sleeping. Mandy used to complain about how late they slept, but they were at that age. Laura remembered days of sleeping past noon before she'd had to get her first job. Those kids needed sleep now more than ever. Poor Kaylie. She'd looked horrible the night before when she came out into the kitchen.

Rusty answered the door. Laura's breath caught. She wasn't one to be left without words often, but wow. He stood there, tall and leaning against the doorframe wearing a form-fitting V-neck. His mouth curved up—he could melt an iceberg with that grin. "Hi, Laura."

She took a moment to recover. "Good morning."

He stepped back, allowing her in. "The kids are still sleeping. Maybe we should talk downstairs."

"Sounds good." Laura followed him down, trying to think about how they would go about proving that Mandy hadn't committed suicide.

Once in the rec room, they walked around the pool table and sat on an old leather couch. Mandy had hated that thing, but Chris couldn't bear to part with it. He'd had it since college, and it showed.

"I should've asked if you wanted anything to eat or drink," Rusty said.

Laura shook her head. "I just ate."

He glanced to the side, looking thoughtful. "I've been looking through photo albums. It's nice to see she was smiling again. She'd lost it when I knew her—it was the drugs. It looks like she moved on from her problems, and clearly adored the kids." He paused and picked at a nail. "Tell me more about the guy she thought fathered Brady."

Laura leaned back against the soft couch. "Travis Calloway."

Rusty's head snapped up. He stared at her.

"You've heard of him?"

"He seems to be well-known around here."

"He's the rich and influential CEO of Clockworks, the company that keeps this town alive."

"Clockworks?" Rusty arched a brow.

"They make much more than clocks," Laura explained. "That was all they made when his grandfather started the business. Over time, they've moved into designing all kinds of things that tell time. They were one of the first companies to make pagers available to the general public."

Rusty looked lost in thought for a moment. "I'd forgotten all about pagers. Nearly everyone had one in high school."

"I know, right?" It had been middle school for her, but she didn't want to make him feel old.

"Now they make cell phones?" He asked.

Laura nodded. "They're on the cutting edge, pushing technology forward."

"If they're so influential, why haven't I heard of them?"

"The national companies pay for the rights to use Clockworks' designs. That's one reason Travis drives a different colored Maserati every day of the week."

His eyes widened. "Really?"

"I might be exaggerating, but the man has money and influence." Laura leaned forward. "If he didn't want Mandy bothering him about money, I'm sure he had ways to put a stop to it."

Rusty rubbed his temples. "How did Mandy meet him in the first place? Not to put anyone down, but I don't get the feeling she or Chris have much money or influence. Though I only spent about five minutes with Chris."

"Five minutes too many," Laura muttered. She cleared her throat. "Mandy and I were curious to see the infamous Calloway mansion, so we worked as servers for a couple of his parties until Chris got jealous."

"For good reason, it sounds like. If Travis did father Brady."

"You should see a picture of Travis." Laura pulled out her phone and searched online. She found an image where he had an especially strong resemblance to Brady and handed it to Rusty.

His eyes widened as he looked the picture over. "That's... that's... We need to find out if Mandy got those DNA results." He stared at the image a little longer and handed the phone back.

Laura's mouth curved down. "I'd say it's a good chance she got what she thought."

Rusty rubbed his chin and wrinkled his brows. "How would we speak with Travis?"

"Good luck. I've heard you have to go through twelve secretaries before reaching him, and each one is more hang-up-happy than the last."

"But Mandy knew how, right?"

"She said she had both his private cell phone number and a direct line to his office. He liked her for a while."

Rusty sat up straight. "What do you mean? Did he turn against her?"

"The man gets bored easily, and not just with cars—if you catch my drift. There have been a lot of whispers of many others he's seen private-ly."

"And you said he's married?" Rusty asked.

"Got married last summer. It was all anyone could talk about for months." Laura searched for images and found a plethora. "It was an exclusive event, and everyone who'd been there wanted to prove it, so there are more pictures online than the royal wedding."

She scrolled through them until she found a close-up of Angeline Calloway. The truly angelic blonde had a cascade of curls falling down her back, landing perfectly around the elegant strapless gown. Long diamond earrings poked out from her hair, nearly reaching her shoulders. But that wasn't even what drew the eye—it was her sweet smile and gorgeous blue eyes.

Laura handed Rusty the phone again. "Angeline Calloway."

He studied it. "I'm sure Travis wouldn't want her getting wind of an illegitimate child."

"Not at all. If the rumors are true, they have the picture-perfect life. And sweet Angeline as a stepmom isn't part of that image."

Rusty set the phone down and leaned back. "How do we look into this? Where would we even begin?"

"I think you're going to have to go through Mandy's stuff. If Chris hasn't destroyed any evidence, she had to have proof somewhere."

"Brady is a perfect mixture of Mandy and Travis. I noticed when I first arrived he looked different from everyone else, except Mandy."

"So, in other words, you're convinced without proof?"

He paused. "Yeah, but I do want to know what she found. Did she only prove that Chris isn't the father? Or did she find a way to prove Travis is the dad, too?"

"It wouldn't have been a hair sample." Laura picked up the phone and scrolled to a wedding picture that had Travis. Just like every other picture she'd ever seen of the man, his head was shaved bald. Rumor was that it made him feel powerful, but Laura always thought he had early-onset baldness. But purposeful or not, the man in the expensive suit was quite a catch. Rich, young, powerful, and gorgeous.

How many other Mandys were there? How many of the town's children were actually his? There were rumors, but nothing more.

Had there been any other strange deaths or suicides? None that she could recall, but that made sense. He could easily pay off anyone and not feel the financial hit. But if Mandy had wanted him to be involved...

Laura shuddered. Once, Mandy had mentioned it. Had she been serious? Might that be enough to get her killed?

"Do the Calloways have a lot of parties?" Rusty asked, interrupting Laura's thoughts.

"Huh?"

"Maybe we should apply to be servers. We could learn more about them."

She certainly wouldn't mind seeing Rusty in a suit. "Sure. I can call my old boss, Natalie. But don't expect to get chummy with the Calloways."

"I'm not. A lot can be learned just by listening. You'd be surprised some of the things I've found out in my business."

Laura chuckled. "I'm sure. People's lips get loose when they've had too much to drink."

"And I'm sure Mr. Calloway serves plenty of spirits to his guests."

She leaned against the armrest. "I like the way you think." Laura checked the time. "Tell you what. I've got some work to do, and when I finish that, Natalie should be in her office. I'll give her a call and see what I can manage. She always did like me, so if there's any availability, I'm sure we'll get in."

Footsteps sounded overhead.

"Sounds like that's my cue to check on the kids," Rusty said.

"And mine to get home. Can I get your number?"

Rusty told her, and she called his cell. It played a peppy tune. "Got it."

She added him to her contact list and rose. "Well, if the cops can't figure out what's going on, maybe we can help bring Mandy the justice she deserves."

"I certainly hope so." Rusty stood, also.

Tears stung her eyes. Suddenly, being in Mandy's house was too much.

Rusty wrapped his arms around her, engulfing her in a warm embrace. "I'm really glad she had a friend like you."

Laura blinked back the tears. "I just wish I could have done more. If I'd know what was going to happen, I would have done anything to prevent it. Anything."

He sniffed and stepped back, his eyes shining with tears. "From the sounds of it, she didn't know." He cleared his throat.

A tear spilled onto Laura's face. "I think she was trying to get money from Travis so she could move out of here. She wanted to be able to provide a nice place for the kids and not have to lean on Chris financially anymore."

Six

~

RUSTY DOUBLE-CHECKED THAT the kids were still on the couch, distracted. Brady was busy playing a video game, and Kaylie was texting while listening to music. He went to the hall and paused. Should he go through Chris and Mandy's bedroom or read the journal? He really wanted to know what his sister had written, but Chris was likely to be home soon.

He'd called earlier, saying he still hadn't been arrested for anything, but they were detaining him and would use up all their allowed time.

Rusty went into the master bedroom, once again feeling like he was being watched. If there was a hidden camera, maybe he could figure out where it was hiding later. With any luck, the footage would be in the device.

He went back to Mandy's nightstand and pulled the drawers out. He went through each book, shaking for any hidden scraps of paper. Maybe one had the direct number to Travis's private line. Then he wouldn't have to work as a server. The thought of giving people alcohol was enough to make his blood run cold. But if it was the only way to figure out what had really happened to his sister, he would do it.

There was nothing useful in the drawers. If Mandy was hiding anything, it was somewhere else. He put everything back as best as he could remember where it had been.

Rusty climbed onto his hands and knees, checking underneath the bed and nightstand. The only thing he found were some stray socks. He went over to the dresser and went through the drawers. Neither Chris nor Mandy had any hidden gems.

Time was drawing close. Chris would be home soon and the kids would want lunch even sooner. He went to the closet, checking pockets in shirts. Nothing other than a twenty in one of Chris's and a five in Mandy's.

If either of them had anything to hide, they weren't keeping it in the bedroom. All the more reason to dig into the diary. Rusty went back to the living room and found both Kaylie and Brady doing exactly what they'd been doing before. He grabbed a water bottle and drank it down. It was a hot summer day, and the air conditioning unit didn't work back in the bedrooms.

He wiped sweat from his brow, went back to the guest room, and lifted the mattress. The diary was just where he'd left it. He brought it out and sat on the bed, flipping through the pages. It was definitely Mandy's writing, although her penmanship had improved since he'd last seen it. When he got to the last page, he noticed a strange indent. He turned to the back cover and found a shiny, silver key with a round top taped to the journal.

Rusty's pulse raced. He took off the tape and examined the key. On the backside, 2497 was etched in clear, bold script. On the bottom of the key, 261. He rubbed off the sticky residue. The key was similar to the one he had for the bank lock box where he stored his grandfather's antique gun collection for safe keeping.

He took out his wallet and slid Mandy's key next to his golden one. That would probably come in handy soon enough. He balled up the adhesive and tossed it in the waste basket.

As he put his wallet back in his pocket, he peeked out the blinds. Chris's van was still gone. He sat back down and skimmed the first few entries. Nothing interesting, but maybe that was how Mandy wanted it. Appearances could be deceiving, and he wasn't about to be fooled.

The next few were equally unnoteworthy. Some neighborhood gossip. A few ladies in the PTA didn't like Mandy because her purse wasn't name brand. Brady hadn't made the football team. Kaylie wanted acting lessons.

He continued skimming until he reached nearly the middle. Then he noticed Travis Calloway's initials. He read over the entry slowly. It still wasn't much. Just that she'd seen him somewhere—Mandy hadn't even mentioned where.

Travis wasn't mentioned for a few more entries, but then it got interesting near the middle of one...

Now I'm glad I never got rid of his number. With the way Chris and I are fighting, I need to know I'll have the financial help of both of them if I'm going to leave. There's no way I can get a place on my own and take care of the kids, even if I manage to get a full time job.

TC didn't answer my call this afternoon, but that isn't surprising. He doesn't make a habit of answering unknown numbers, and he would have no reason to know the number of the throwaway phone I bought. But after I call a few times, giving at least a day or two in between calls, he'll answer.

I thought about leaving a message, but I'm not sure he'd call me back. When we parted ways last time, he'd made me promise a clean break and I've kept that until now. But now that I need help with Brady, he needs to step up. At least financially.

Rusty paused, taking it in. Mandy really was convinced that Travis was Brady's father. He couldn't deny the resemblance. His nephew certainly looked a lot more like the billionaire than Chris.

He pulled out his phone and did a quick search, looking at even more pictures than he'd seen earlier on Laura's phone. Rusty studied the tycoon from every angle, finding his nephew to be less of a spitting image of Mandy, and more of a perfect mix of his two parents.

Did Chris know about Travis? Or did he suspect there was a different father? Or even the possibility? If so, that definitely explained why the police had such an interest in Chris. But how would they know? Did they know Mandy was looking into all of this? Or had Chris done something to give them reason to suspect him of foul play?

There seemed to be more questions than answers. Rusty continued reading. The rest of the entry was more PTA drama and some stuff about the kids. The next few entries were like that, too. No mention of either Chris or Travis.

Brakes squealed outside. It sounded like someone had pulled into the driveway. Rusty stuffed the journal back under the mattress and peeked outside. The van was parked next to the sedan, and Chris was inside. He appeared to be gathering some things on the passenger seat.

Rusty went out to the living room to check on the kids. Kaylie was sprawled out, watching something on her phone and Brady was still engrossed in his game.

"Are you guys ready for lunch?"

Brady glanced at him. "Starved."

"Me, too," Kaylie said. "Thanks."

Rusty glanced back outside. Chris was across the street, checking the mail. Rusty's eyebrows came together as he studied his brother-in-law, trying to tell if he was acting guilty. It was too hard to tell from there. He'd have to gauge him after he came inside, and even then it might take a while to figure anything out.

In the meantime, Rusty would have to be the best uncle possible. That way, Chris would want him sticking around for a while. Rusty had no intention of going back home until this was resolved. Not only for Mandy, but also for the kids. He had to be one hundred percent convinced of Chris's innocence before he left town.

He went into the kitchen and warmed up leftovers from the night before. There would be plenty for all four of them. By the time Chris came in, Rusty had the table set and the house smelled like dinner all over again.

"You're just in time for some lunch," Rusty told Chris.

He yawned and set some envelopes on the banister. "You're a lifesaver once again. I'm starving."

"It'll be a few minutes." Rusty cracked open the oven to double check. "Feel free to get cleaned up. Do you need anything else?"

"A hard drink," Chris muttered, straightening his wrinkled shirt.

"How about coffee? I can make it strong."

Chris shook his head. "I'm going to bed after I eat."

"I can't say I blame you."

"Thanks for taking care of the meals." Chris headed down the hall.

Rusty peeked to make sure he didn't go into the guest room. He went into a home office Rusty hadn't looked into yet. Though, after reading the diary, he wished he had. Mandy had been contemplating leaving. Did Chris know? It was possible he didn't.

Given the nature of the focus of his job—towing drunks to keep them off the streets—Rusty knew that women usually lined up everything before breaking the news to their husbands. When they'd had enough alcohol to need a tow, they often spilled too much information to him.

For all Rusty knew, the only thing Chris was guilty of was being an argumentative and controlling husband with a short fuse. Travis could have easily been the one with all the reason to get rid of Mandy. He had a beautiful new wife. A reputation to uphold. Money to be lost. Maybe he was worried Mandy would have tried to claim a stake in his business.

Rusty went back into the kitchen and tossed a quick salad. He finished just as the timer beeped. Both kids hurried into the kitchen. Chris was a few steps behind.

"I've never seen them so eager to eat," Chris said as he sat.

"His food is so good, Dad," Brady said. "You should try it."

"I plan to. Kaylie, take those headphones out."

"Earbuds." She plucked them out and stuffed them into a pocket.

"Don't argue."

Rusty set the steaming chicken dish in the middle of the table. "You must be exhausted. Why are the police bothering you?"

Chris tilted his head down to his shoulder, causing a popping noise. "I don't want to talk about it in front of the kids."

"Understood." Rusty sat in between him and Kaylie.

"Dad, we're not babies," Kaylie said. "They don't think it was a suicide, right?"

Brady frowned and played with his food.

Chris closed his eyes and let out a long, slow breath.

"Your dad's right," Rusty said. "This isn't the time to discuss it."

"Thank you," Chris said. He took a bite of the chicken and his expression softened. "This is delicious."

"I told you," Brady said.

They ate in silence. Rusty studied Chris from the corner of his eyes. The man just seemed tired. The cops probably hadn't let him get a wink of sleep the entire time.

"Do you want me to take the kids out while you sleep?" Rusty asked.

"Would you?"

"Of course."

Chris dug into his pocket and pulled out a fifty. "They've been wanting to see some movie for a while."

Rusty didn't take the bill. "I can cover it."

"You've gone grocery shopping and have taken care of them for the last day. I insist."

"I don't mind. You guys are family."

"Just take it."

Rusty grabbed the money and slid it into his pants pocket, near his wallet.

Chris rose. "Thanks for the food. I'm going to fall asleep on my plate if I don't lie down."

"No problem. We'll clean up. Right kids?"

They grumbled, but Rusty couldn't help smiling. The longer he spent around them, the better it felt being around kids again. He'd shut himself off from all kids for so long, unable to avoid the pain. Perhaps he'd only added to it.

Chris told them to behave and then he left the room, rubbing his eyes.

"Let's get this stuff cleaned up and check the movie times."

"On it," Kaylie said. She slid her finger around the screen of her phone. "There's a showing in about forty-five minutes."

"Do we have time to make it?" Rusty asked. "Is the theater far away?"

"Maybe five minutes if you drive."

"Let's hurry." Rusty pulled out his phone and sent a quick text inviting Laura to join them. If they couldn't talk during the movie, they could always take the kids somewhere to blow off steam—an arcade, perhaps—and they could discuss what they'd learned then.

Seven

~

LAURA SAT AT a table by herself next to the concession stand at the theater, sipping an overpriced, watered-down soda as she watched the doors. Plenty of teenagers had come and gone, but so far, not Rusty with Mandy's kids. Maybe Chris had changed his mind about letting them go. That wouldn't have surprised her.

She dug her phone out of her handbag and sent Rusty a text.

Want me to save you guys seats in the theater?

Almost there. We're in line now.

I can get you something at the concessions.

We brought our own candy.

Living on the edge. I like that.

I never thought of it like that.

You're a real rebel.

She smiled as she slid her phone back in its place and walked over to the door. A couple more groups of kids came in, and then finally Rusty, Kaylie, and Brady. Laura's heart fluttered. Rusty was just as gorgeous as before. She adjusted her crocheted tank and walked over with her best smile.

He returned the grin and the kids both said hi.

"Are you guys ready?" she asked.

Kaylie's face lit up, but then clouded over.

"What's wrong?" Laura asked, concern washing over her.

She didn't answer, but stared at something behind Laura. Turning around slowly, Laura saw a group of kids about Kaylie's age, pointing and whispering.

"What's their problem?" Laura asked.

Kaylie stood taller and narrowed her eyes. "They've never liked me, and now they have more reason not to."

"Why?"

"Think about it."

"Because of your mom?" Laura asked, anger churning in her stomach. Kaylie nodded.

"Want me to talk to them for you?" Laura clenched her fists.

"No." Kaylie's eyes widened. "Don't."

"You've got to stand up to those types, or they'll just continue to—"

"It's fine," Kaylie said. "I don't care. Let's just see the movie." She grabbed her brother's arm and pulled him toward the theaters.

Anger continued to burn toward the group of kids. It was rude enough to pick on someone in normal circumstances, but to up the game after their parent died was unacceptable.

"Are you all right?" Rusty asked, giving her a concerned glance.

"I can't believe those kids."

"Then they'll grow up and be even worse. Although, I've noticed things like that have a way of catching up with people."

"They'd better watch out, if that's the case. If Karma doesn't get them, I will."

They found the right theater and Rusty turned to the kids. "Do you guys want us to sit with you?"

"Yeah," Brady said. "Wait. You mean you'd let us sit by ourselves?"

"If you want to. I'm sure you'll stay in your seats, right?"

Brady's eyes lit up. "Awesome."

Kaylie glanced over the crowd. "Let's sit in the back."

"But I wanna sit up close by the screen."

"It's huge. You'll see it from back there."

They stared each other down, and then Laura exchanged a glance with Rusty.

"Fine," Brady said. "I guess it's cool enough that we can sit by ourselves. Thanks, Uncle Rusty."

"Sure." Rusty nodded. "Just find us at the end."

"You bet." The two of them scrambled up to the top corner and pulled out candy.

"You sure have a way with them." Laura smiled. "Sure you've never spent time with them before?"

"I wish I had. No, all I do is imagine how I'd feel in their shoes. It's not hard. I've experienced a deep loss myself." He looked deep in thought for a moment. "Do you want to sit near the back? I'd like to sit where I can see them."

"Sure." Laura wanted to ask him who he'd lost, but he hadn't offered anything, so she'd wait until he was ready.

They settled in a couple rows in front of the kids, but on the other end of the row. Brady and Kaylie were busy eating candy, and didn't seem to notice them.

"Did you talk to your old boss?" Rusty asked.

"Thanks for reminding me." Laura pulled out her phone and looked at the calendar. "Natalie said Travis has two parties this week, and she's short-staffed for both. People on vacation, college kids being away for the summer, and all that jazz."

"When are they?" Rusty asked.

"One's tonight, so that doesn't give us much time. The other one is two nights from now."

"On Friday?" Rusty asked, pulling out his phone.

Laura nodded. "They're both in the evening. Tonight's starts at seven, and the other one at eight."

"If Chris is going to be home, I'll go tonight."

"On such short notice?" Laura asked.

"Do you think it's a bad idea?"

"Not at all."

Rusty leaned closer to her, practically speaking in her ear. "I want to meet the man who might have had reason to kill my sister."

Chills ran down her back as his breath grazed her skin. "You mean the other man."

He leaned back in his chair and nodded.

"Did you learn anything new?"

Rusty shrugged. "You know what I'd like to see?"

She arched a brow. "What?"

"Mandy's cell phone. I think that would say a lot about how they were doing."

"She wasn't very fond of Chris, I can tell you that."

Rusty was quiet for a moment. "I found a journal."

Laura's eyes widened. Now *that* would say something. "What did it say?"

"I haven't gotten far yet, but she and Chris were arguing a lot."

"Like I said. Anything else?"

"She wanted to contact Travis, but hadn't gotten a hold of him yet. I still have more to read."

They discussed the diary until the movie started, making it impossible to hold a conversation. Laura's mind spun. Had Mandy talked with Travis? Had he agreed to give her some money to keep her quiet... and what if she'd told Chris she was leaving?

Or had Travis freaked out and done something to her? Or threatened her, making her feel trapped, leading to an actual suicide? Or actually killed her?

Then there was another huge question. If either of them were actually able to talk to Travis, would they learn anything useful? It wasn't like he was going to openly admit anything. Not at a party, with so many people within earshot. But at least it would be a start.

Maybe Rusty could say something about losing his beloved sister and see if a flicker of guilt passed over Travis's face. Or perhaps sadness over the loss of someone he'd known.

Before long, the movie ended, and Laura had hardly paid any attention to any of it. She turned back to check on the kids. They seemed happier than before. Hopefully, Kaylie had forgotten about the group of kids from earlier. The last thing she needed now was to worry about a bunch of selfish brats.

"They didn't budge the whole time," Rusty said.

"I'm glad they're able to get out and just do normal teen stuff."

He nodded. "They need that."

"I haven't heard anything about a funeral. Is anyone planning anything?"

"The police haven't released her body." Rusty frowned.

"Is that really necessary?" Laura asked. "Viewings seem so… morbid."

"It's a final chance to say goodbye." Sadness covered his face again.

"Who did you lose?" Laura placed a hand on his well-defined arm.

He looked to the side and took a deep breath. "My wife and kids."

Laura's mouth fell open. She struggled to find words. "I'm so sorry. I shouldn't have asked."

"It's okay." He turned back to her. "It was a long time ago. My boys were three and five. They would have been about Brady and Kaylie's age—each a year younger."

A lump formed in Laura's throat. "I can't even imagine. And now Mandy…"

"And now my sister." Rusty nodded, his eyes shining.

He blinked several times and focused on something behind her. "Did you guys enjoy the movie?"

Brady and Kaylie both spoke at once, talking excitedly. Laura couldn't focus, though. She studied Rusty, suddenly understanding why he was single. And why she'd been so drawn to him. She always seemed to especially like the ones who were emotionally unavailable. The look on his face when he spoke about his family made it clear he hadn't moved on.

They made their way outside. The bright summer light seemed especially cruel after being in the freezing cold, pitch black theater. Laura couldn't stop thinking about everything Rusty had gone through. Sure, she'd experienced her own losses, but nothing like that. Even with Mandy's death, it was nothing like losing *family*.

Laura had been overwhelmed with grief since Mandy's death, but she had to keep herself together or she'd start losing clients. She and Mandy hadn't been close recently—because of Chris—and that fact brought about a strange mix of emotions after her death.

One thing she knew. She was glad Rusty had shown up. With their focus on finding the truth, it gave her grief a purpose. Together, maybe they could clear Mandy's name. With the stigma of suicide, a lot of people wouldn't even attend her memorial service. It was probably a good thing nothing was planned yet.

Rusty's voice broke through her thoughts.

"What?" Laura asked. "I'm sorry."

"I'll text you and let you know about tonight. When do you need to know by?"

"Whenever. She said we could just show up since she needs all the help she can get."

"I won't wait that long. Thanks for joining us. I had fun."

Laura forced a smile. "Me, too. Thanks for the invite." She waved and headed for her car at the other end of the lot, deep in thought.

Did she have anything that would point toward Chris's or Travis's guilt? She and Mandy had often texted and emailed, especially when Chris was on one of his rampages. From what Mandy had said, when he was in bad mood, he yelled constantly. The kids would hide out in their rooms while Mandy did her best to avoid him, but she would often take the verbal beatings so the kids didn't have to.

Laura tried to think of anything incriminating Mandy might have said in any of them—something that would prove Chris had motive. Nothing came to mind. She'd have to read over everything to see if anything came up. Between those, the diary, and talking to Travis, maybe they could come up with the truth and clear her friend's reputation. Not to mention Kaylie's and Brady's, and before they had to return to school. That would be even better if those kids in the theater were any indication of what the kids would have to deal with.

When she pulled into her driveway, she scrolled through her texting conversation with Mandy. It didn't go back as far as she'd hoped since she'd recently bought the latest and greatest phone. They hadn't texted a lot over the last several months.

Laura's stomach twisted in knots. She should have tried harder to fight for their friendship, and not allow Mandy to push her away so easily.

She'd probably needed a friend more than ever.

Could that have been a sign that Mandy had actually committed suicide? Backing away from friends? Laura hadn't seen her talking with anyone else, either. She'd assumed her friend had been busy contacting Travis and planning her divorce. She'd been so eager to get away from Chris.

Laura glanced over at the house next door. "I'm sorry, Mandy. Whatever happened, I should have been there for you."

She put her phone back in her purse and went inside. She would go through her emails with a fine-toothed comb. If the answer was there, she would find it and make sure the right person was put away.

She hadn't been there for Mandy when she'd needed her, but she would do her best to make up for that now. Her kids deserved that—not to think that their mom had taken her own life. Laura could imagine the lasting psychological scars that would leave.

"I won't let that happen," Laura whispered to Mandy. "I know you wouldn't have wanted that. We'll fix this the best we can."

Eight

~

TRAVIS CALLOWAY PICKED up a glass of champagne as he walked by the server and took a sip, looking around his ballroom. Another perfect party full of beautiful people. What more could he ask for? He'd just landed a ground-breaking deal with a major international company. It would bring in millions, easily. Probably more.

A bigger company from New York City had been vying against him for the deal. Travis had thought for sure they would get it—everyone knew who they were. But it hadn't deterred him. He just pulled in his best people and hired a few more for good measure. Regardless of brand name recognition, he had the better products. Hands down. And they'd proved it.

It wouldn't be long before his family business was world renowned. And this one might actually be the project that would make it happen.

A hand landed on Travis's shoulder. He spun around to see Wes Kirkpatrick, his executive assistant CEO grinning at him.

"Well done, friend." Wes beamed.

"It was a team effort." Travis slapped him on the back. "Couldn't have done it without you."

"That's why I put in the long hours. Pretty sure the wife hates me."

Travis laughed. "But she loves the money."

Both men glanced over at Camille and Angeline, their two beautiful wives, sitting together, laughing.

"True," Wes said. "I promised her a newer BMW. She's already bored with this year's model."

"I should probably get a gift for Angeline, as well." Travis brought his finger to his chin. "I was thinking about a diamond watch, but if you're getting Camille a car…"

"What about that house in Hawaii you were talking about?" Wes asked.

Travis sipped his champagne. "Oh, the bungalow on the beach. I'd almost forgotten about that. Good thinking, Wes. Maybe that'll be enough to get her to stop bringing up babies for a while."

Wes shook his head. "You guys are still newlyweds."

"Tell me about it. She whines that I'm never home, but that's why she has friends."

"Not to mention everything you've bought her. She's living the dream every woman wants."

Travis studied his wife from across the hall. She leaned across the table to whisper something in Camille's ear, pulling her already-tight black dress tighter. His breath caught. She was just as gorgeous as the first time he'd laid eyes on her—maybe more so. He'd give that woman anything she wanted.

Except more of his time, and that would mean sacrificing his work. The one thing he couldn't afford.

Wes patted Travis on the back. "I'll catch you later, Trav. I need to speak with Maggie from accounting."

Travis nodded and walked over to Angeline. Camille nudged her, and Angeline looked up, her eyes brightening. Her baby-blues shone almost as bright as the long diamond earrings framing her face.

"Are you going to join us?" The hope in her voice was undeniable.

He pulled a wisp of blonde hair behind her ear. "And let everyone see me sitting with the most beautiful woman in the room? Of course."

Angeline scooted over into the next chair and Travis sat in hers.

"What are you ladies discussing?"

They exchanged mischievous grins and laughed.

"You wouldn't understand," Camille said. She played with the emerald pendant on her necklace. "Girl talk."

Travis leaned back and set his glass on the table. "I'm sure I wouldn't."

Angeline ran her fingers over his just-shaved head. "You know, most men can't pull of this look. But you…" She stared hungrily into his eyes.

He ran his hands through the length of her hair and pressed his lips against hers. They were soft and sweet as always. He trailed kisses to her ear and whispered, "Tonight I'll make it home before you fall asleep. I promise."

She shivered, leaned back, and took his hand, squeezing it. "I can't wait." The look on her face showed she meant it wholeheartedly.

The CEO of Masterson International entered the party.

Travis scrambled to his feet, taking his attention from Angeline. "But first, I need to make the guest of honor feel at home."

"See you soon." Angeline winked and wrinkled her adorable, button nose.

Travis glanced back at her and let his gaze linger as he gave her another once-over. Before they'd married, he would sneak off with her during parties. Suddenly, he wanted to do that again. But he couldn't leave Marcus hanging. Not when this business deal could change everything.

He blew Angeline a kiss and spun around.

"I told you that tight, strapless dress would do it," Camille said. She'd always been too loud for her own good. But he couldn't complain. He was glad she'd talked his wife into wearing it.

Travis cleared his throat and brought his mind back to business. Marcus was only in town for the night before flying out to Europe in the morning.

"Welcome." Travis smiled widely. "I'm glad to have you in my home. Do you need anything?"

"Something to eat. I just got done with an online conference that went entirely too long."

"I know how that goes. I'll find Wes, and we'll join you. Have a seat anywhere you'd like."

"Much appreciated." Marcus headed for the bar.

Travis turned, scanning the ballroom for Wes. He was near the bar already, talking with some investors. Travis took a step, and a tall waiter stepped in front of him. He held out a tray of champagne glasses.

"Another drink, sir?" The man stared at Travis as though he knew him.

Travis's brows came together as he studied the server. He was tall and slim, and his hair was dark brown, but with auburn hues where the light hit it. His short, trimmed beard had more red. The man looked more like he belonged as a guest than staff.

"No thank you," Travis said. "Have we met before?"

"You took some champagne from me a few minutes ago."

"Before that. You seem familiar." There was something about him that made Travis feel like he should know him.

The server shook his head. "Sorry. I've never been out this way before. I just arrived in town."

"Okay." Maybe he just reminded Travis of someone else. He saw so many people every day, so that had to be it. Travis went over to Wes and greeted the investors with a wide smile, but deep down, he couldn't shake the feeling that he should know the server.

They made their way back over to Marcus and had spirits and snacks. Before long, the music grew louder and people started dancing. He noticed Angeline glancing his way. At least she'd finally learned to leave him alone when he was with business colleagues.

Marcus rose from his stool. "Time to find someone to dance with. Nice talking with you gentlemen." He turned to Travis. "You really know how to throw a party."

Travis laughed. "I try."

"And you succeed." Marcus gave him a firm, solid handshake and joined a group of ladies.

Wes turned to Travis. "Looks like we'll have to dance with our wives tonight."

Travis eyed Angeline in that dress. He was looking forward to not just dancing with her, but showing her a good time later, as well. "That we will."

They crossed the dance floor, and after they'd only made it a few steps, Angeline met his gaze. Her entire face lit up and she rose from her chair, whispering to Camille.

When he reached Angeline, he held out his arm. "May I have this dance?"

Angeline grinned, showing off her perfectly straight, bright white teeth. She looped her arm through his. "Of course."

He led her to the dance floor, and they glided around it flawlessly with ease. A slow song came on, and he pulled her closer, feeling each curve pressed against him. "You look especially beautiful this evening."

"I was hoping you'd like it."

Travis stared into her eyes. "I do. Very much."

"I'm glad you decided to have dancing this time."

"How could I not when you look like this?" He ran his fingers through her hair. The truth was that Marcus had mentioned his love of dancing, but Angeline didn't need to know that.

She tilted her head. "You set that up just now?"

He laughed. "You got me. It sounded good though, didn't it?"

Angeline leaned her head against his. "It's just nice to have some time with you."

Travis braced himself, ready for a guilt trip, but it didn't come. "I'm glad, also. Now that the deal with Marcus is sealed, I should have more time." At least until the next one comes along.

Her silence indicated that she knew what he was thinking.

The songs went on for about an hour, and for the first time in a while, he and Angeline truly enjoyed the time together. She didn't complain about a single thing. Almost like they were dating again, and it was nice. Maybe they were turning a new leaf.

After the last song ended, he took her hand and gazed into her eyes. "That was really fun."

Her eyes sparkled. "It really was. I haven't had that much fun in a long time."

Travis pulled her close and brushed his lips across hers. "And there's more to come. I'll find our best bottle of wine and meet you in our room."

Angeline's smile widened. "And I'll have the staff prepare some melted chocolate and fruit."

He squeezed her hand. "Sounds perfect. I'll be up soon."

She pressed her mouth over his and walked away, her wavy blonde hair bouncing against her tanned bare shoulders.

Travis watched until she was out of sight. Then he turned to find Wes. They needed to confirm some details about a meeting in the morning.

The server from earlier stepped in front of him. "Champagne?"

"Are you sure I don't know you?" Travis asked.

The server smiled. It was one would make women line up in droves. And it made Travis jealous.

"I just have one of those faces." The server shrugged.

Travis scratched his chin. He made it a point to remember names and faces, and it was starting to bother him that he couldn't figure out why the man was so familiar. "What's your name?"

"Rusty Caldwell." He balanced the tray and held out his hand.

Travis shook it. Rusty had a confident grip. And Travis would remember a name like Rusty. It was one he rarely heard. And his last name wasn't familiar, either. "You must just look like someone I know."

"Probably. Though you might know my sister. She used to serve at your parties from what I've been told."

"Really?" Travis grabbed a glass of champagne. Maybe that explained why he look familiar. If his sister was as good-looking as him, Travis had probably made a point to remember *her*. "What's your sister's name?" He took a sip of the drink.

"Mandy Oates."

Travis spit out the champagne and choked. He cleared his throat and stared at Rusty. "Mandy? You're Mandy's brother?"

Rusty wiped his face and nodded. "I'm in town helping her family, actually."

"Give them my condolences." Travis set the glass down and continued clearing his throat. His entire body shook.

"I will. So, you remember her?"

Travis adjusted his tie, which all of a sudden felt constricting. "Of course. She worked here for some time. Mandy was one of the hardest workers I've had. Why are you here?" He stood taller and held his head high, doing his best to exude his typical confidence.

Rusty set the tray down on a table. "I hadn't seen her in so long, I'm trying to get a feel of what I missed. Her friend said she'd worked here, and that you were short-staffed, so I thought I'd help out."

Travis kept a straight face, hiding his surprise. How strange that he would take the job while mourning his sister's death.

The head of the wait staff, Natalie Armstrong, came up to them. "Is everything all right, sir?"

"Yes, thank you," Travis said, turning to her. "I was just thanking Rusty for his exceptional service. Have a wonderful night, you two."

Travis hurried away from them, careful to keep his composure. His hands still shook. He hadn't expected to hear Mandy's name again, much less that night. He'd planned on leaving her family a donation at her funeral.

What if she'd told someone about her claims about her son? Had she told Rusty? Was he there to collect for his late sister and his nephew?

"Are you okay?" asked Wes, seemingly appearing from nowhere.

Travis took a deep breath and readjusted his tie. "Of course. Is everything ready for the meeting tomorrow morning?"

Wes arched a brow.

"I'm fine." Or at least he would be once he figured out a way to take care of Rusty. Travis scanned the room, and his gaze landed on the person he needed. "Excuse me," he said to Wes.

"Sure." Wes curled his lip down, showing Travis he didn't believe everything was okay.

Travis picked up a glass of wine from a server and walked over to Kevin Baldridge. "Hello. Congratulations on the recent job change. I take it your stress levels are down?"

Kevin flinched. "Oh? You heard about that? I haven't gone public yet."

Travis nodded and sipped his wine. "You know me. Ears everywhere." Kevin had left his job as police captain to become a private investigator.

The investigator shifted his weight. "Another great party, Travis. Always appreciate the invite."

"And I appreciate your skills." Travis sat next to Kevin and scooted close enough to make sure Kevin would be uncomfortable. "So, I need a favor."

Kevin squirmed. "Travis, your last favor nearly cost me my marriage."

"Robyn forgave you. I need you to look into Mandy Oates's brother. Dig up everything you can."

"My new boss is watching me like a hawk. Thinks I'm undercover to take him down. I'll need a reason. Something."

Travis scooted closer and narrowed his eyes. "Here's a reason. If you don't, something will happen that Robyn *won't* forgive."

Kevin's face paled. "What?"

"You don't want to know." Travis rose, nearly knocking over his chair. "I expect to hear back from you by the end of the day tomorrow. And use your influence to make sure the police department has no reason to suspect me of anything."

"You got it."

Travis leaned back and sipped his wine. He would never allow Angeline to hear Mandy's paternity theory. Ever.

Nine

~

RUSTY CLOSED THE door as quietly as he could behind him. The house was both silent and dark. He went upstairs, finding the living room empty. Light snores sounded down the hall.

He sighed in relief. Not only was he in no mood for conversation, but he was glad Chris and the kids were sleeping. The party had gone well past midnight, and he was exhausted. Between dealing with Mandy's passing, taking care of the kids, and jet lag, he'd reached his limits. It was his turn for some sleep, too.

It was too late to even try to process Travis's reaction to him being Mandy's brother. Laura had been excited to hear about it—she'd thought for sure that was proof of his guilt. Rusty wasn't so easily convinced.

Maybe he didn't know about fathering Brady. He was eleven, which meant that Travis and Mandy had been together twelve years earlier. And Mandy's diary indicated that he hadn't even talked with her since then.

They may have had a quick fling, and if Mandy wanted to work things out with Chris, she wouldn't have even told Travis about the pregnancy. If she had, he probably would have been supporting her financially since day one, but it didn't sound like it.

Rusty grabbed his toothbrush and went into the bathroom. He tried to process everything as he brushed, but his eyelids were too heavy and his thoughts too jumbled. If only he was awake enough to read a few more journal entries.

He made his way back to the guest room and fell asleep as soon as his head hit the pillow. His dreams were full of champagne splattering against his face and reading diary entries.

When he woke up, bright summer light shone on his face through the blinds. Sounds of video games came from the living room and he could smell a mixture of bacon and coffee. Burnt coffee—like it had been spilled on a burner and caked on.

He rubbed his eyes and stretched. It was the best sleep he'd had since hearing about Mandy. His cell phone showed it was after nine.

Rusty's stomach growled. He hadn't eaten since before the party, but he really wanted to read some more from the diary. Once he got up, he would be busy with the kids and Chris—someone else Rusty wanted to speak with.

His stomach rumbled again, but he decided to ignore it. He got up, grabbed the journal, and flipped to where he'd left off. Again, most of it was normal stuff. If he hadn't known anything about Travis, he would have given up long before, but the little snippet he'd found before gave him hope that there was more like that in there.

A pang of guilt stung him for reading Mandy's diary. But this wasn't like when they were kids. This was *for* her.

He skimmed, looking for mentions of either Travis or Chris. Mostly, it was the kids and their activities. If the journal was any indication, Mandy had been a good mom. It sounded like she'd kicked her demons.

Rusty's stomach twisted with guilt. He closed the journal and sighed, facing the ugly truth. He'd been a coward. Scared that he would be rejected on top of all the other heartache in his life. But spending time in this house—with her kids and even Mandy, through the journal and photos—it was obvious that she'd cleaned up and they would have probably gotten along. Perhaps even as well as they once had, before drugs.

Why hadn't *she* reached out? Told their parents she had changed? Or had she, and they just dug their heels into the ground, refusing to forgive? Their dad was one to keep his word no matter what it cost him. He'd told her if she didn't clean her life up, he would never talk to her again.

Rusty's guilt turned to anger. As a parent, he couldn't understand how his father could act like that. Granted, Rusty would give just about anything to see his boys again, but even so, he couldn't imagine cutting them out of his life on purpose even if they had grown up and screwed up. He couldn't even picture doing that to his niece and nephew.

He thought of Brady and Kaylie. It was the kids who were important, and they needed a strong support system. Chris was too stressed to provide that for them. They needed not only Rusty, but their grandparents, too.

Rusty picked up his phone and found his parents' number. He was ready to give his dad an earful—he had no idea what he was missing out on. Or what he was making his grandkids miss. Kids needed a relationship with their grandparents. Rusty couldn't imagine his childhood without his.

A headache was forming near his eyes. Sure, yelling at his dad would feel good. It would alleviate some of his anger, but it wouldn't accomplish anything. Nothing could break through his dad's stubbornness. Not even Mandy's death. Why would telling him how great his grandchildren were?

Or would it? Rusty traced the shape of his phone. His pulse picked up speed. He really needed to do this, both for the kids and his parents. Mostly, the kids. They were both missing out, and all because of his dad's foolish pride.

Rusty pushed aside his own feelings for Brady's and Kaylie's sake. He made the call and waited as it rang. He took a deep breath, preparing himself for the confrontation.

"Two calls in one week?" his dad asked, answering the call.

"I'm here at Mandy's place. I've been spending a lot of time with your grandchildren."

There was a brief pause. "Have you, now?"

"They're really great kids. Smart, fun."

Silence.

"Don't you want to get to know them?"

"I need to get going. Is there something you need from me?"

"Not me, them. Dad, they need their grandparents. Now more than ever."

"What are we supposed to do about that?"

"How about be their grandparents?" Rusty snapped. "Come by and comfort them. Maybe bring them a present. Tell them how much you've always wanted to meet them."

"Mandy made her choices."

"It's not their fault! And haven't you learned anything from Mandy's death? Now you'll never have a chance to restore that relationship. At least you can reach out to her kids. Our family has been through enough."

"I'll talk it over with your mother. Will that make you happy?"

"It's not about making me happy, Dad. It's about those kids. They need you."

"Like I said, I'll speak with your mother."

"I suppose that's all I can ask. Talk to you later."

The call ended. Rusty shook his head. He needed some food, some coffee, and a strong painkiller. He returned the journal to its place and stuck his phone in his suitcase.

In the kitchen, he found Chris sipping from a mug and reading something on a tablet. Rusty went into the living room and said good morning to the kids and then grabbed a piece of bacon.

"Is it okay if I have some?" he asked.

Chris glanced up. His eyes were bloodshot and the skin around them was puffy. "Sure. I made plenty. You bought enough for an army."

"Can't have too much bacon." Rusty piled some on a plate and put some bread in the toaster. "What are you reading?"

"Just the news." Chris frowned. "Somehow, word got out about me being down at the station, and now they're speculating why. Whatever happened to innocent until proven guilty? Can't they just leave me alone to grieve? I haven't even had any time to do that." His eyes shone.

There was a time Rusty had been uncomfortable with tears, especially from another man, but after all his years towing people home, he'd become a counselor so to speak. He knew people usually just needed a listening ear, and sometimes a shoulder to lean on.

He buttered his toast and prepared his coffee before sitting down. "Do you want me to take the kids out again today? Give you some time?"

Chris sighed and rubbed his temples. "I don't know what I want anymore. Well, except to have Mandy back. Things weren't perfect, but they weren't horrible, either. You know how marriage is, right?"

Rusty nodded. "I was married."

"Didn't work out?"

"I lost my wife, also."

"Oh. I'm sorry. Did you already tell me? My memory is shot these days." His face clouded over. "What happened?"

"A drunk took out my entire family."

Chris stared at him for a moment. He swore. "I had no idea."

Rusty sipped some coffee. "It was a long time ago." And thinking about it now, with Mandy's passing, the wounds felt more raw than healed. He cleared his throat. "What does the paper say?"

"It's always the husband. How many times have you heard that one?"

"Too many." Rusty considered his words. He wanted to seem sympathetic, but at the same time, he needed to find out what he could. "It's pretty convenient."

"Exactly." Chris put his face in his palms. "Sure, our marriage isn't— wasn't—perfect. Whose is? Doesn't mean I killed her. I loved her. Just ask the kids."

Rusty's throat tightened. "You don't think the police are going to question them, do you?"

Chris looked up. "They'd better not, but I guess they're next if the cops don't believe me."

"Why do you think they won't leave you alone?"

"She had some drug in her system. I'd never even heard of it—how could I have slipped it to her, you know? More importantly, why? The most important thing to me is my family."

Rusty finished off his toast. "Do you think she'd gotten back into heroin? Or drinking again?"

Chris pulled on his hair. "I didn't see any signs. You'd think I would have, right? I was the one who helped her clean up. The only person who believed in her."

Ouch. That was a personal jab. Rusty pretended not to notice. "How did it get into her system, then? I mean, how do you think?"

"That's what the police have been asking me. How the hell would I know?" Chris slammed his fist on the table.

Rusty sat taller. "Not making accusations. I just want to find out what happened—like you do. What was going on in her life right before she died?"

Chris grumbled. "You think the cops haven't been asking me that?

Over and over."

"What was she doing the day before? Was she acting depressed? Did she—?"

"I didn't do anything! It could have been one of those PTA moms for all I know."

"You think one of them slipped her something?"

"Or sold it to her. She was always complaining they didn't like her because she didn't have enough nice stuff. Used car. Generic purse. Drugstore makeup. How the eff would those women know that, anyway? I think they just had it out for her. I told Mandy to find better friends, but she preferred ones who had more money. Like that ho next door."

"Laura?"

Chris groaned. "Worst of the bunch. Lives in that big house by herself, has a maid and everything. Added onto it a couple years ago. It's fifty percent bigger than any other house in the neighborhood. She's just a showoff."

Rusty nodded. His brother-in-law's hatred toward Laura made sense. She made him feel emasculated. And if Mandy had been as good friends with her as it seemed, that would have likely only added salt to the wound.

"What was Mandy like as a kid?" Chris asked.

The question surprised Rusty. He thought back to their childhood. "She cared about her family and friends, and she always had an eye for the finer things in life. Mandy was a lot of fun back then."

Chris picked up his mug and sipped. "She didn't talk about her childhood much. Maybe once in a while when the kids did something to remind her. I never saw any pictures or anything."

"Makes sense. Mom and Dad have hung onto all of that."

"Even though they cut her off?" Chris scowled.

"Those are the days they like to remember. We had a lot of fun back then."

"There had to be problems, especially with parents who are willing to kick a child out of their lives. I can't imagine anything bad enough to make me do that to mine."

Even if one of them weren't his? Rusty kept quiet about that. "She was pretty messed up by the drugs. They—"

"I know. I was the one who helped her out of it."

"They thought it would be a shock of reality that could help her turn her life around," Rusty continued. "I disagree with a lot of things my parents do, but that was one time I didn't. She was really destructive, and it ruined relationships. Mandy got really cruel."

Chris laughed bitterly. "Believe me. I know that, too. I was there when she was getting clean. It wasn't easy. But when you love someone, you don't give up on them." He stared Rusty in the eyes.

"Not everyone is equipped to deal with that, either. I had my own rehab to deal with after I lost my family. When Mandy was on drugs, I had no way of understanding what it was like. It wasn't until I turned to alcohol myself."

"What was your excuse after?" Chris leaned over the table. "For not reaching out to her?"

"I had my own demons to work through, but I'm here now. And a relationship is a two-way street. She cleaned up years ago, but I never once heard from her."

"Why do you think that was?" Chris narrowed his eyes.

"Couldn't say. I never got the chance to know her in recent years."

"Maybe you should have tried."

Rusty took a deep breath. "Obviously, but I can't go back in time and change anything now."

"Nope, and you'll have to live with that, won't you?" Chris stared Rusty down.

Rusty stared at him for a moment before rising from the chair. "I'm here to help. If you need anything, let me know."

He put his dishes away, went into the guest room to gather his clothes, and took a shower. It was challenging not to let Chris get to him. Rusty reminded himself how painful it was to lose a wife. He was sure he hadn't been himself during the process. That had been when he'd turned to alcohol and pot himself.

When he returned to the guest room, he locked the door and checked under the mattress for the journal. It wasn't there. Blood drained from his head and the room seemed to shrink. He'd put it back there. Hadn't he?

Rusty rifled through his luggage, not finding it. He dumped it out and went through each item, one by one. It was just the stuff he'd packed. He folded it all and returned everything, his mind spinning.

Had Chris taken it? Did he have cameras all over the house? The only room Rusty had felt like someone might have been watching him had been the master bedroom. That might have been enough to cause Chris to go through the room. He would have seen Rusty going through the stuff and leaving with the journal.

He pulled out his wallet and checked for the key he'd found. It was still there. Maybe it was time to look into that. He and Chris both needed some breathing room. Or maybe the house just wasn't big enough for the two men.

Ten

~

LAURA CLIPPED A dead rose from the bush and added it to the yard waste pile. A door closed nearby and she glanced up to see Rusty walking down Mandy's driveway. Tears stung her eyes. She needed to stop thinking of it as Mandy's. Laura blinked away the tears and waved to Rusty.

"Hey, neighbor."

Rusty glanced over and gave a little wave. He walked over, and as he neared, Laura noticed the frown on his face.

"Are you okay?"

"I'm starting to see what you mean about Chris."

"Uh, oh. Do I want to know?"

Rusty leaned against a maple tree. "I'm trying to chalk it up to the grieving process, but he's not making it easy."

"He doesn't make anything easy." Laura jammed the clippers into the dirt. "If you need somewhere to stay, I have plenty of spare rooms."

"Thanks, but I'd like to keep an eye on the kids. If that means putting up with their dad, then I'll deal."

Laura nodded and brought her hand up over her eyes to block the sun. "It's already getting hot out here. Want to come in for some iced tea?"

"That sounds great."

She slid off her gloves and threw them next to the clippers. "Come on in. Let's talk about Travis. That'll get your mind off what's-his-name."

"There's not much more to tell."

Laura opened the front door and let Rusty in. "I want to hear about him spitting champagne on you again."

"It wasn't nearly as glamorous as it sounds."

She smiled and dusted dirt from her knees and came inside. "Kitchen's this way." She led him up the stairs of the sprawling split level and washed her hands before grabbing the freshly made iced tea.

Thank goodness for Cindy, who was much more than just a one-woman housecleaning service. Without her, the house would have been a mess.

She and Rusty sat quietly sipping the tea. He appeared as lost in thought as she was.

"What set Chris off this morning?"

Rusty groaned. "The fact that I deserve the award for the worst brother of the year."

"Oh, don't let him get to you. Mandy never reached out to you, either. She didn't hold a grudge against you, though. I could tell by the way she talked about you."

He set his glass down and stared at it. "That's good news, at least. I just wish I would have tried to contact her. If I'd have known..."

"You didn't." Laura reached over and put her hand on his arm. "There was no way you could have. None of us could have. You know what?"

"What?"

"I'll bet she was planning on getting in touch once she got her own place. She was pretty excited about getting out on her own. I think she felt like she'd always lived under someone's thumb. From what I gather, your dad isn't much different from Chris."

Rusty glanced up, looking deep in thought. "I can't deny there are similarities. Some of them came shining through this morning."

Laura's phone buzzed in her pocket. She pulled it out and saw a text from a blocked number.

Rusty had his phone out, too.

They exchanged a curious glance. Laura opened the text and gasped.

You need to mind your own business. Now. Or there will be consequences. Serious ones. Undoable.

She looked at Rusty. "Did you...?"

They showed each other their phones. Rusty had the same message from a blocked number.

"Do you think it's from Chris?" Rusty asked.

"I was thinking Travis."

"Chris took Mandy's journal from my guest room."

Laura's stomach dropped to the floor. "What?"

"It's gone, and before I had the chance to read all of it. I was hoping to finish it today."

"I'll bet it had incriminating evidence."

"We won't know now. He'll hide it somewhere I'll never find it—I'm sure of it."

"Me, too." Laura leaned back in her chair. "I wonder if there are any more diaries lying around."

"Maybe, but I'll bet he's searching for them now."

"At least we're going back to Travis's party tomorrow night. It'll give us a chance to see if we can find anything out."

"You think he's going to fess up to knowing about Brady? Or being behind Mandy's death?" Rusty wrinkled his forehead.

"No, but maybe we can find something out."

"We should take this to the police."

"Why?" Laura asked.

"They already suspect Chris. They wouldn't have held him for a full day otherwise. And they let him go, so obviously, they couldn't find anything. If we tell them about Travis, they'll—"

"What? Confront the wealthiest and most powerful man in town?" Laura shook her head. "That won't happen. Not without evidence."

"The resemblance between him and Brady is undeniable."

"You don't understand the influence of the Calloways. They built this place. We weren't even on the map until Clockworks came around. They employ at least a quarter of the adult population. Clockworks employees get discounts and benefits everywhere. Did you notice the signs around town?"

Rusty shook his head.

"Look around next time you go out. You won't be able to miss them. We'll have to think of something else."

He opened his mouth like he was going to say something, but closed it.

"What? Do you know something?" Laura twisted a strand of hair around her finger. It was a nervous habit she'd had since she was a child.

Rusty brought out his wallet and pulled out a shiny, silver key.

"What's that?" Laura eyed it. It seemed familiar, but she couldn't figure out why. It was too small to go to a house or a car. A safe, maybe?

"It was taped to Mandy's journal. At least I had the sense to remove it."

"Let me see that."

He handed it to her, and Laura studied it.

"Do you know what it goes to?" she asked.

"No, but it's similar to my own bank lock box key."

"That's it!" Laura looked at the key again. "I have one to the First Security bank downtown. It looks just like this one."

"Sounds like we need to take a trip over there."

"Yeah, we do. Do you think he'll go through your stuff?"

Rusty shrugged. "I don't have anything to hide. Or anything worth stealing—at least that I brought."

"Maybe we should head down to the bank before he finds the key."

"Even if he knows it's missing from the diary, he wouldn't know where to look."

"Your wallet isn't exactly a tough guess."

"And he wouldn't likely know the difference between my key and Mandy's. He'd be stupid to risk taking mine."

Laura held up her phone. "Someone's already pissed that we're looking into her death."

He leaned back. "I have a feeling we haven't seen pissed yet. You want to head over to the bank?"

She pushed the button on her phone to turn on the screen. They would probably get there a little before it opened, but they could sit near the fountain and talk. And Laura rather enjoyed their conversations—she wasn't sure if it was because he also grieved for Mandy or because there was something about him that reminded Laura of her. "Let's go. We can take my car."

They got into her car and Rusty pushed the passenger seat back, reached into a pocket, and slid on some sunglasses. He was obviously comfortable letting her drive. Laura liked that. So many men were too insecure and had to be in the driver's seat—not that Laura was one to hand over the keys to her car.

No. Guys like that could take a hike as far as she was concerned.

She slid on her own sunglasses and started the car. A top twenty song played on the radio.

"Hope that's okay."

Rusty's foot tapped in time with the music. "Perfect."

They listened to music on the way downtown. Rusty hadn't struck Laura as the type who would know the most popular songs, but he sang along with each one. He actually sounded good, too. Unlike most guys she'd known who just thought they did.

She turned into the bank's nearly-empty parking lot and pulled into a spot near the door.

He tapped his fingers along with the new song that played.

"Do you listen to a lot of radio for your job?" she asked. "Seems like you would, spending a lot of time in the tow truck."

"It comes with the territory. If someone is being especially obnoxious, then I crank it up. How do you like your job?"

Laura shrugged. "Consulting is what it is. But I love the flexibility and being able to work from home."

"Nice."

"It looks like we're a bit early. We can hang out in here or we can wander outside. There's a fountain and some benches out front."

He slid his sunglasses to the top of his head. "I wouldn't mind stretching my legs."

"You and me both. I haven't gotten nearly enough exercise since... all of this."

"The two of you were pretty close?" Rusty unzipped his hoodie and set it on the middle console.

Laura's breath caught. The light blue t-shirt clung to his muscular frame.

He turned to her, his brows raised. He'd asked her something. Crap.

What, though?

"You and Mandy were close?" he asked.

Guilt flooded Laura. They were there to clear Mandy's name and here she was getting distracted by Rusty's physique. She didn't want to have feelings for him—or anyone. After her dad left her mom high and dry, Laura had always had a bad taste in her mouth about marriage. Her ex-husband and the few serious boyfriends she'd had hadn't helped matters, either.

Laura would never forget when her last boyfriend had raised a fist at her. That had been enough for her to write off men forever. She'd sent him packing and had started gardening. It brought a lot more purpose to her life than relationships ever had.

She remembered Rusty's question. "Yeah, we were close. I suppose she was my best friend."

"Suppose?"

Laura let out a long, slow breath. "We both would have liked to have hung out more."

"But Chris..."

"Exactly."

A smiling family stared at her from the bank's window—a decal advertising a CD promotion. Laura focused on the little girl with pigtails. Anything to get her mind off losing Mandy and the growing feelings for Rusty. She didn't need any kind of relationship. It only brought pain, and she certainly didn't need any more of that in her life.

"Let's see the fountain." She scrambled out of the car and kept her attention on the family on the window. They were the perfect distraction.

Rusty closed his door and Laura locked the car with her remote. She hurried around the building. The tall, three-tiered fountain came into view. Water shot from the top, overflowing into the lower levels. Little birds chased each other around it, darting in and out of the top part only long enough to shake off after a quick dip.

Another great distraction. Rusty stood next to Laura, but she kept her focus on the birds.

"That's a good reminder," he said.

Laura kept herself from turning to him. "What is?"

"Those guys. They're just playing without a care in the world. Nature provides gentle admonitions, don't you think?"

She arched a brow. He was almost too much. "I hadn't thought about it that way, but you're right."

He leaned against a bench, still watching. She stayed in place.

Something dark caught her attention. A couple crows flew down to the fountain, scaring away the little birds. They scattered in all directions. A crow cawed, and then they took off, too.

"What's *that* a sign of?" she asked and turned to him, keeping her focus on his eyes.

Rusty's lips curved down. "A reminder to watch our backs."

Eleven

~

USTY HELD HIS breath as he walked into the bank. Would whatever was in the lock box give him any more clues to what had happened to Mandy? A little pang of guilt stung at him. What if the box was hers and Chris's? But no, it couldn't have been. If that had been the case, it wouldn't have been taped to the back of her diary.

She wanted it to be kept from her husband. And it was a good thing Rusty had found it before he had.

They stood in front of the row of tellers. All three were busy turning on their computers and otherwise organizing their workspaces.

"Are you ready?" Laura asked.

He held his head high. "We have to be. For Mandy and those kids."

"What do you think is in there?"

"You'd have a better idea than I would."

She turned to him, her piercing blue eyes pleading. "The Mandy you knew, what would she have had in there?"

Rusty frowned. Drugs. Contact info. But she'd left that life behind—at least that was how it sounded from what everyone else had said. Even the family pictures indicated as much.

"I can help you," called the teller in the middle.

Rusty sighed in relief. They walked up and the middle-aged teller smiled, her eyes looking tired.

"What can I do for you?" she asked, glancing between Laura and Rusty. Her tag read Nancy.

He pulled out his wallet and set the key on the counter. "We need to open a box, Nancy."

"I'll need to see identification." She stood taller.

Rusty groaned. He knew it wouldn't be that easy. When he'd first rented his own box, he'd been assured of the safety—that someone who found the key, if lost, couldn't just walk in and take his contents.

"The box belongs to Mandy Oates," Laura said, her voice and demeanor exuding authority.

"And I assume neither of you are she."

Laura leaned over the counter and tapped the key. "No, because she's deceased. Surely, you've heard about her. Accused of taking her own life."

Nancy's face softened. "Are either of your names on the documentation?"

Laura leaned even closer. "We're not entirely sure, but what we do know is that the contents of the box could clear a young mother's name."

"Let me pull up the information and see what I can do." Nancy turned to her computer and began typing. "Is Mandy short for Amanda?"

"Miranda," Rusty corrected.

Nancy typed some more. "And Oates, with an 'e'?"

"Yes," Laura said.

More typing. "These boxes can be very difficult to get into without the proper documentation. There's a lot of red tape, and a court order may be necessary."

Rusty's stomach twisted in knots. Chris would have more rights than anyone, being her husband. And it was possible that his name was on the account, anyway. They might have to go through him to get in, and there was no way he would let them see the contents.

Nancy glanced at them. "Russell and Lani Caldwell?"

Hearing his wife's name was like a punch in the gut. But he recovered quickly. Mandy had done some homework and granted him access to the box. He cleared his throat. "I'm Russell."

"Identification, please."

Rusty's hand shook as he pulled his driver's license from his wallet. He handed it to Nancy, who studied it and then typed into her computer again.

Laura nudged him. "Look at that, Russell."

Heat crept into Rusty's cheeks. He'd always hated his given name. That was something he and his sister had in common. They'd both chosen nicknames early on, and insisted on them.

Nancy handed him back the card and key. "Follow me."

She walked to the far end of the counter and opened a door for them. After it closed behind them, Rusty and Laura followed her down a hall and to a large, steel door. Nancy typed in a code on a panel next to it. A click sounded, and she turned the large knob slowly before finally opening the door.

Rusty's heart pounded. Whatever was in there, Mandy had wanted him to see it. Had she thought he was the only one she could trust? Had she hoped to one day reconcile with him? His heart warmed, but at the same time, more guilt stung.

Nancy put a key in a box on the left wall. She turned to Rusty, clearly waiting for the other key.

He took a deep breath and slid Mandy's key in next to the bank's. They both turned the keys and the little rectangular door opened. Nancy removed hers and Rusty took Mandy's, sliding it back into his wallet.

Nancy brought the box out and put it on a table in the middle of the room. "I'll be out there. Just let me know when you're done."

Rusty stared at the box. An unmarked manila envelope sat on top.

"Thank you," Laura said and stood next to Rusty. They stared in silence for a minute. "Are you ready?"

"I hope so." As much as he wanted to rip open the envelope, he was equally hesitant.

"Take your time."

He nodded a thanks, not taking his focus from the box. It was now or never. They hadn't come to stare.

Rusty took another deep breath and reached for the envelope. It shook in his hands. He was about to open it when he noticed something shiny in the box. Jewelry.

"Those are gorgeous," Laura whispered.

He sat down the pouch and stared at the watch, diamond earrings, and emerald necklace.

"Why do you suppose those are here?" Laura asked. "Did Travis give those to her?"

Rusty shook his head and picked up the necklace. "These belong to my parents. They came up missing when she was into drugs. We all assumed she sold them."

Mandy had been furious at them for disowning her. They all thought it had been payback. These had been her parents' favorite pieces. Dad never removed the watch except to bathe, workout, and swim.

Why had she held onto them, if not to sell them? To have something to stay close to them despite being apart?

His mind reeled. Maybe on some level, she'd understood why they'd drawn the line in the sand—that it was from a place of caring. At least initially.

"What's this one?" Laura asked, picking up something from the corner of the box. Rusty couldn't see it from his angle. She held up a delicate gold chain with a small cross. "This one doesn't look too valuable."

"Can I see that?" Rusty asked.

Laura dropped it into his palm. As he studied it, the room seemed to spin around him. He thought he'd lost it years earlier. Never once had he connected it to Mandy. She'd been out of his life over a year before he realized it was missing. It had been a gift from his grandparents when he was young. He'd stopped wearing it around the time he became a teenager and had become too cool for just about everything he'd had as a kid.

Rusty unhooked it and slid it around his neck. It barely fit now.

"That was yours?" Laura asked.

"A long time ago."

"I can tell. She took all these from you guys?"

He nodded and rubbed the tiny cross between his fingers. It had seemed so much bigger before.

"What do you want to do with this stuff?" Laura asked. "Should we make copies of the papers or take them with us?"

"They might be safer here. Without Chris's name on the account, he can't get in. You heard Nancy."

Laura leaned against the table. "She also said someone could open it with a court order."

Rusty rubbed his temples. "It seems like with everything else going on, this would be the last thing on his priority list. As far as we know, he doesn't even know about it."

"What if she wrote about it in the journal?"

His stomach squeezed.

"You didn't finish it, right?"

Rusty shook his head and then picked up the envelope again. He undid the clasp and peeked inside. There was about an inch and a half of papers sitting in there. He slid them out a little ways and ran his thumb over the edge, fanning them out.

"It's going to take a while to read through all of those," Laura said.

And Rusty had nowhere safe to keep them. Even if Chris did calm down, Rusty didn't want to bring them into the house. Not even if he purchased a locking briefcase. Not even if he purchased a safe.

The only thing that would provide protection would be if he rented his own lock box. One without Mandy's name on it. He didn't know the laws for this state, but he couldn't risk Chris gaining access because he had been Mandy's husband.

Would that be wise? Could Chris find a way to get into that since Mandy had put Rusty's name on her box? It was unlikely, but probably not out of the question. Plus there was the issue that Rusty wasn't a resident.

Maybe he would be better off purchasing a locking briefcase and renting a car to keep it in. If he continued using Mandy's sedan, it would be too easy for Chris to search. Technically, he was the owner, even if it was in Mandy's name.

Of course, he needed to find out what the papers said first. If there was anything worth hiding.

"We'd better make ourselves comfortable," Rusty said.

"You want to go over them here?" Laura asked, her eyes widening.

"Do you have a better idea?"

She glanced around, letting her gaze linger at the various cameras around the room.

"Really?"

"Anywhere else would be better. Put the box back empty. She wanted you to have the stuff or she wouldn't have put your name on it."

"I suppose you're right." He didn't have much room, but he managed to get the jewelry in his jeans pockets. The envelope would have to be carried out. "Do you mind taking me to a car rental place, too?"

"Sure. I'll get Nancy," Laura said and left the room.

Rusty double-checked the empty box before putting it back into place.

Laura came back with their teller.

"Did you need anything, sir?" Nancy asked.

Now he was a sir? "No, ma'am."

They locked the box, and then he and Laura made their way back to her car.

"Where to?" he asked.

"I don't know about you, but I'm hungry. Want to go over these at a restaurant?"

Rusty checked the time, surprised to see how close it was to lunchtime. "Sure. I should call and see if the kids know how to heat up the leftovers. I don't know if Chris would even think to feed them. They were eating cereal all day before I arrived."

"They're probably having breakfast now. Lunch is the furthest thing from their minds."

He chuckled. "You're probably right."

"We can bring them some food if you want." Laura pulled out of the spot. "Do you prefer Mexican or burgers?"

"Whichever you like."

"Mexican it is." She turned left. "I have a hankering for some greasy chips and salsa."

Rusty chuckled. "Sounds good."

Before long, they were seated in a solitary booth. Traditional mariachi music played from nearby speakers.

Laura sipped from a pink margarita. "Where's the server? We need more salsa."

Rusty's gaze lingered on the drink. He knew the dark path a simple drink would send him down, but with everything going on, the sweet taste and even better feel of it gliding down sounded so good. He forced his eyes to move to a brightly-colored painting of a parrot behind Laura.

The waiter came by and dropped off another dish of salsa. "Are you ready to order, *muchachos*?"

Laura ordered fajitas and Rusty got a sampler. The more he had to focus on, the less he would be distracted by the drink across the table. Usually, he was fine. He was around the stuff all the time since he spent so much time in bars before driving home drunks. Seeing people plastered was a great reminder of what he wanted to avoid. But watching Laura sip in moderation, chatting naturally, and appearing to relax...

He grabbed a salty chip and scooped a pile of salsa and bit hard enough to crack a tooth. If he had any tequila, the relaxation would only last a short time. Then he would spiral down a path he never wanted to go again.

"Did you hear me?" Laura asked.

Rusty took a deep breath and turned his focus to her. "Sorry."

"When do you want to see what's in there? I want to know if she got proof that Travis is the father."

He glanced at the envelope next to him. "I suppose now is as good a time as any." He picked it up, straightened out the brad, and opened it. Was he holding proof of his sister's murder? Life-changing news for his nephew?

It was almost too much. Almost. Rusty slid out the stack of papers and thumbed the top edge, feathering out the papers. There was a wide variety of documents. Some appeared official while others were handwritten notes.

Near the back was one that looked something he'd receive from a doctor's office. He pulled it out and studied it.

"What is it?" Laura asked.

"Some kind of test results." He scanned the paper and stopped at Chris Oates. His pulse quickened. "It's a paternity test."

"What does it say?" She leaned over the table.

"It's confusing." Most of it didn't make sense to him. Rows of information he didn't know what to do with. He turned to the next page, and near the middle was his answer.

Negative.

Rusty's mouth went dry. He scanned everything again.

"What?" Laura exclaimed.

"It looks like Chris isn't Brady's father."

"She was right," Laura whispered. "Can I see?"

Rusty handed her the two pages and flipped through the rest. There were no other paternity results. No proof as to whether or not Travis was the father.

"Anything about Calloway?" Laura asked.

Rusty shook his head.

"Good thing we're serving at his party again."

He arched a brow. "He's not going to own up to it if we ask."

Laura handed him back the papers. "No, but we can find a way to get some DNA from him."

Rusty's stomach dropped. "How are we going to do that?"

Twelve

~

KAYLIE STRETCHED ACROSS the couch and nudged Brady with her foot. He ignored her, engrossed in his game. She did it again.

"Stop." Brady didn't look away from the screen.

"No."

He paused the game, turned, and glared at her. "What's your problem?"

"I want to ask Dad what happened with Uncle Rusty."

Brady flinched. "What do you mean?"

Kaylie rolled her eyes. "You're so dense sometimes."

"I have to focus when I play this one."

"Yeah, well, they had a fight and Uncle Rusty left without saying anything to us."

"A fight? Like, they were hitting each other?"

Kaylie shook her head. "I don't know why I try sometimes. They were *arguing*, okay? I think about Mom."

"Dad's always mad about something. I'm sure they're fine." Brady turned back to the game.

"You're coming with me." She sat up and grabbed his arm.

"Hey." He yanked it away. "You're annoying."

"And you're selfish. Come on."

Brady scowled, but he set the controller down. "What are you going to say?"

"Just going to ask him what's going on with Uncle Rusty."

"And you need me why?" he asked.

"Ugh. Just come on. One day you'll understand."

"Stop trying to sound like Mom."

She glared at him. "I'm not. Stop being a baby." Kaylie got up and went out onto the deck before her brother could complain anymore.

Dad glanced over at her, a guilty expression covering his face. He stepped in front of three or four empty beer bottles by his feet. If he was trying to hide them, he was doing a crappy job. "What's going on, guys?"

"Where's Uncle Rusty?" Kaylie asked.

He shrugged. "Out."

"Where?" Kaylie stepped closer.

"He's a grown man. He doesn't have to check in with me."

"Why were you guys fighting?"

Dad leaned against the railing. "We were just discussing Mom."

"Sounded like you were fighting to me."

He tipped his chin. "Don't worry about it, kiddo. It's adult stuff."

"Give me a break. You didn't kick him out, did you?"

His eyes narrowed. "What? Of course not."

"Good." Kaylie held his gaze. "I like having him here."

"Don't get too attached. Can't guarantee how long he'll stay. He doesn't have a great track record."

"What does that mean?" Kaylie stepped forward.

"Exactly what I said. Where's he been all your lives? Where was he when Mom needed him?"

"Where were *you* when she needed you?" Kaylie snapped, anger festering in her gut.

Dad's eyebrows came together and he leaned forward. "What did you just say?"

"Uh, oh," Brady whispered behind her.

Kaylie didn't care about making him mad. He deserved it. "You heard me. She killed herself, and where were you? Did you even know anything was wrong?"

He raised a fist and aimed it at her.

"Dad!" Brady shrieked, his voice raising an octave.

He lowered his fist, but his mouth formed a straight line and turned white. "Watch it, Kaylie."

"Or what?"

His brows furrowed and he got in her face. Their noses nearly touched. "Just watch yourself. We're all under stress—I get that. We all want to be able to give Mom a proper funeral and say goodbye. But we can't, and that makes things worse. We can't turn on each other, do you understand?"

Kaylie swallowed and nodded.

"The cops have their own theories, and the last thing I want is for you kids to get involved with that. It's the last thing you guys need to worry about. Let me deal with it, but give me space to do that. Trust that I'm doing the best I can."

"Okay," she whispered.

"Things weren't always easy, but I loved your mom. I love you kids. My family means more to me than my life itself."

Kaylie stepped back. "Sorry."

"I hope—"

His phone rang. He swore and pulled it out. "I've got to take this. Can you see what we have for lunch? We can talk after this call."

Kaylie nodded and moved out of his way.

"Hello?" he snapped into the phone. "Why are you calling me? I told you not to call on this line…" His voice trailed off as he walked farther into the house.

Brady and Kaylie exchanged curious expressions.

"What's that all about?" Brady asked.

"No idea. Want to find out?"

"You're supposed to make lunch."

Kaylie flipped her hair behind her shoulder. "Have I ever told you what a baby you are?"

"Have I ever told you to shut up?"

They stared each other down for a moment before Kaylie walked past him and went inside. She followed her dad's voice down the hall to his bedroom. He sounded upset at whoever had called.

"See?" Brady said. "Like I said, always mad. We'll be lucky if Uncle Rusty stays while Dad's here."

"Shush. I want to hear what he's saying." She tiptoed closer to the door, but even so, could only make out some words.

"Can you hear anything?" Brady asked.

"Quiet." Kaylie moved closer and pressed her ear to the door, careful not to step in front of it. Just in case he could see the shadow of feet underneath.

"Look, don't threaten me," Dad said. "You need to stop calling me. The cops are already looking into me... *No*, I haven't told them anything about that. I swear, I'm going to block your number."

"What's he saying?" Brady whispered.

"Shut up," Kaylie whispered.

"He's saying 'shut up'?"

Kaylie shoved him.

"I don't know what to tell you," Dad continued. "But if this blackmailing doesn't stop, you're the one who's going to have to watch your back. You know what I'm capable of... That's right."

Kaylie's mouth dropped. Someone was blackmailing Dad? Who? About what?

"What?" Brady cried.

Something hit the other side of the wall next to Kaylie, and Dad shouted a bunch of profanities. She jumped and stared at Brady. His eyes were as wide as dinner plates. Glass shattered inside the room.

"I think we better make lunch," Brady whispered.

"Good idea."

They hurried down the hall. Kaylie ran into Brady. "Hurry up."

"I *am*."

Her heart nearly pounded out of her chest by the time they reached the kitchen. She couldn't even think straight, but she needed to find something to make for everyone.

"What about last night's leftovers?" Brady asked.

Kaylie turned to him. "What?"

"For lunch. We can warm them up."

"Right. Sure. Whatever." She couldn't even remember what they'd eaten, but at least it would be easy. And Uncle Rusty was a great cook. Kaylie went into the fridge and found the platter. She was shaking and nearly dropped it.

Brady caught it.

"Thanks."

"See? I'm not completely useless." He put it on the counter and removed the plastic wrap.

Guilt stung at her. "You're not useless."

"Not completely. Hand me the plates."

She did and then grabbed a green and red plastic spatula with snowflakes painted on the handle. It had been Mom's favorite.

Brady grabbed it, but Kaylie yanked it away. She picked out a black one and handed it to him. "Use this one instead."

"Whatever." He piled food onto the plates and shoved the first one into the microwave. "How long? Like five minutes?"

"If you want to burn it to a crisp. Try ninety seconds."

"Okay." He slammed the door shut and pushed the buttons.

"Wait. You have to put a paper towel over it."

"Why?"

"Because if it splatters, Dad's going to freak."

Color drained from his face. "Oh, yeah." He was obviously remembering the time Dad had screamed at Mom over something splattering onto the microwave walls. She and both kids had ended up in tears.

Kaylie ripped two paper towels from the roll and handed them to Brady. He covered the food carefully while Kaylie finished piling food onto the plates.

The microwave beeped. Brady took the plate and set it on the table. Kaylie put the next one in the microwave, careful to cover it, and started it.

Footsteps sounded down the hall. She and Brady exchanged a worried expression. He hurried over to the counter and wiped up some spilled food that had fallen while they'd scooped it onto plates.

Dad came in. His face was red.

"You can have that one." Brady gestured to the plate on the table.

"Want something to drink?" Kaylie asked. Usually, after Dad threw a fit, it was Mom who stepped in and tried to appease him. Now it was their job. Mostly hers, as the oldest. Unfortunately.

He rubbed his temples and sat at his spot. "Yeah, sure."

Kaylie went to the fridge and saw some beers in the back. She decided on an organic lemonade. It was good for a hot day. She poured some for each of them and handed Dad his first.

"Sorry about the mess in here," she said. "We were just about to clean it. Right, Brady?"

"Yeah, but we thought you were probably hungry."

Chris rubbed his eyes. "Sorry for yelling at you two about your rooms in front of Rusty. You know I'm the worst offender. I was upset at my boss and used the mess as an excuse to blow up. I shouldn't have."

"No problem," Brady said.

"Yeah, we get it." Kaylie forced a smile. "We should have kept them cleaner, anyway."

"I know Mom usually does most of the cleaning. I guess we all have to chip in more."

"I don't mind," Kaylie said.

"Me, neither," Brady added. "Just tell us what we need to do."

"We'll start with the kitchen." Kaylie got up. "In fact, I'll just do that now."

"Sit down and eat," Dad ordered.

She slid into the seat and slouched.

The microwaved beeped. Brady pulled out the last plate from the microwave and they all ate in silence at their usual spots at the table. Mom's seemed especially empty. It was hard to believe she would never sit there again—or anywhere. The finality of her death started to sink in.

The numbness of shock had worn off.

Kaylie blinked back tears and forced the food in her mouth, staring at her plate. She didn't want to talk to anyone except Mom, and that would never again happen. If she was buried, Kaylie could pretend to talk to her at her grave, but she was old enough to know it was nothing more than make-believe.

Her tears fought to come to the surface. She didn't want to give Dad a reason to yell at her. When he was in a bad mood, any sign of weakness was reason enough to unleash his temper.

"I miss Uncle Rusty," Brady said.

Kaylie flinched and prepared herself. Why couldn't her brother think before speaking? He was old enough to have learned by now. Don't ever do anything to upset Dad when he was in a mood.

"I'm sure he'll be back," Dad said.

She looked up in surprise. The calm before the storm? There was no sign of the earlier anger on his face. His skin was no longer red and his features relaxed. Sad, even. Probably tired. Neither of them were likely getting any more sleep than she was.

"When?" Brady asked.

"No idea." Dad picked up his glass and drank the entire lemonade in one gulp. "We might have to figure out dinner tonight."

Brady's face fell.

"Don't worry," Kaylie said. "There's plenty of food in there. We'll figure something out."

"I wish Mom was here." Tears streamed down his face.

That was all it took for Kaylie's floodgates to open. "Me, too."

She braced herself. When Mom was out and one of the kids said they wished she was home, he would often fly into a rage saying something along the lines of him not being good enough.

Instead tears shone in his eyes. Dad nodded in agreement.

Kaylie got up and hugged Brady. To her surprise, Dad rose and wrapped his arms around both of them.

Thirteen

~

TRAVIS HELD UP his champagne glass and tapped it against all the others at the table. The deal with Marcus was set in stone and had gone through without a hitch. Usually, something went wrong, but maybe his luck was changing. How nice would it be if everything started going through just as smoothly?

The music over the speakers grew a little louder and a few couples entered the dance floor.

Wes turned to him. "The first deposit came in today."

Travis arched a brow. "Really? How do you know?"

"Maggie from accounting." Wes smiled and sipped from his drink.

"You've been talking with her a lot lately."

Wes shrugged. "I wouldn't say a lot." His gaze lingered behind Travis.

Travis turned around and saw Camille with Angeline at their typical table. This time, a couple other women had joined them. Travis wished that Angeline was wearing the dress from other night again. Not that she didn't look fantastic in the red one she wore, but that other one…

He turned back to Wes. "Does Camille know?"

"Nothing for her to know. I've just been keeping close tabs on the bank accounts. That's all."

"Okay."

"I know I've made mistakes in the past," Wes said, "but Camille and I are working on things. And besides, Maggie has no interest in me."

Travis snorted. "Right."

"I'm serious."

"She batting for the other team?" Travis asked and sipped some more champagne, holding the sweet liquid in his mouth for a moment to savor it.

Wes shook his head. "Married. Kids."

"So?" Travis asked. Wes had nearly as many women falling at his feet as Travis did. They were the two wealthiest men in the county—maybe the entire state. He hadn't checked in a while.

"Seriously. I just want to make sure there isn't another mistake in accounting. Not after what happened in the spring."

Travis set his glass on the table. "We took care of Amy. There won't be a financial loss like that again. Ever."

"Right," Wes agreed. "I headed up the intense training we forced the rest of the department to undergo, remember? I just want to keep a close eye on things. So far, everything's as it should be. As long as they know I could stop by at any moment, no one will dare try to steal from Clockworks again."

"Good man." Travis pushed his chair back. "Time to mingle. Everyone wants a piece of me." He sighed as though it was such a huge burden, but both men knew how much he loved the attention.

"I'll catch up with you." Wes turned back to the other men at the table and laughed at a coarse joke.

Travis rose and finished off his champagne. A nail snagged on his pants. He pulled out his clippers, snipped it off, and tossed it onto his dinner plate.

He glanced around the room. Angeline was still chatting with the ladies at her table, and she actually seemed to be enjoying herself. He hadn't once seen her glance his way, begging for attention with her sultry eyes.

A couple women came up to him, giggling about something. He smiled and joined the conversation, barely paying attention. It kind of bothered him that Angeline was ignoring him. He'd always wished she would give him space at these parties, but now that she was, it irritated him.

Could she be right? No matter what she did, he wasn't happy with her?

Travis shook his head, and with it, the thoughts. He was in the company of beautiful women who were obviously glad to have his attention.

There was no reason to worry about Angeline. She adored him. It was a good thing she was distracted with friends. He finally had some space.

He laughed with the group for a little while longer before making his way to another group. An intern—a young guy who looked like he was trying to grow facial hair—held up his smartphone. "Can I get a picture with you?"

"Uh, sure." It didn't happen often, but occasionally Travis received celebrity treatment. He leaned close to the kid and smiled while the guy snapped the selfie.

They made small talk for a few minutes before Travis excused himself. He made his way through the room, interacting with as many as possible. Still, Angeline paid him no attention.

Travis scanned the room and noticed a beautiful redhead standing by a window alone, sipping a wine glass and watching the dance floor. She wore a long, low cut backless burgundy gown. Maybe she could get his mind off being annoyed with his wife.

He made his way over to her. She glanced up, her eyes widening with surprise. "Mr. Calloway?"

"Travis." He extended his hand.

She switched the wine glass into her other hand and shook with a firm grip. "Rita. To what do I owe this pleasure?"

"Well, Rita, I couldn't help wondering what such a beautiful woman was doing here all by herself."

Rita smiled and held his gaze. A wisp of golden copper hair rested near her eye, seemingly unnoticed. "I just like to take everything in before throwing myself into a situation."

Travis grabbed a wine glass from a server as he passed by. "Oh? Is this your first time attending one of my parties?"

She nodded, blinking her long lashes slowly. "It lives up to the reputation."

He leaned against the wall. "What's the word on the street about them?"

"Gorgeous decorations. Lavish food and drinks. Great music. Beautiful people." Rita gave him a once-over, nodding in obvious approval.

"Glad to hear it." Travis sipped some wine and glanced around the room. Her description was accurate, and perhaps even a little underdone. "What would help you to feel more comfortable?"

She twirled a strand of hair around her finger. "I'm happy right now."

Travis smiled and glanced back over at Angeline. He nearly choked on the wine. She was laughing with Rusty. What was he doing back? Aside from joking with Travis's wife.

"Excuse me," Travis said to Rita.

"I'll be waiting right here."

Eyes narrowing, Travis made his way across the ballroom to Angeline. How dare he speak with her? What if he was asking her about Mandy? She would know nothing because Mandy had long been out of Travis's life by the time Angeline and him had met.

Travis picked up his pace. His heart raced. He had half a mind to punch that lowlife across the face. That would shut him up, and hopefully send the message to others to leave Angeline alone.

He took a deep breath as he approached them. As much as he wanted to knock Rusty's lights out, he couldn't do that. Not at the party. The last thing he needed was any negative press. And journalists always found their way into his parties. Their write ups were quick to share the gossip the following day.

Travis and Wes had gone as far as to hire someone whose sole job was to keep tabs on the media and put out any potential flames before they had the chance to engulf anything.

"Hello, Angeline," Travis said. He fought to keep his voice even.

She smiled. Her light hair framed her face like an angel. "Hi, Travis. I want you to meet—"

"Rusty. We've met." Travis gritted his teeth and glared at the squeaky-clean jerk. All Kevin had been able to find on him was some time spent in rehab after losing his family. Not even a parking ticket in the last five years. Now his sister was dead. His only likely motivation was that he was desperate and alone.

Travis needed to see to it he was fired. All connections to Mandy needed to be kept as far away from the Calloways as possible.

Angeline wrinkled her forehead. "No, I mean my friends from college. This is Sierra and Elle."

Travis nodded toward the two woman, not paying them any attention. "Pleasure." He turned to Rusty. "You can leave now."

"Rude much?" Angeline arched a brow.

Rusty smiled at her. "No, he's right. I should serve the other guests."

Travis glared at him and waited for him to get lost.

"Can I take your empty glass?" Rusty glanced at Travis's nearly-empty wine glass.

Anything to get rid of Mandy's brother. Travis finished off the last bit of wine and handed it to him. Rusty put it near the edge of the tray and wandered off.

"What's gotten into you?" Angeline asked.

"Nothing." Travis continued watching Rusty. He stopped and spoke with Laura, Mandy's friend. Travis scanned the room for Natalie Armstrong. One word from him, and she'd let those two go and never return. He couldn't find her, so he turned back to Angeline and her friends. "Nice to meet you ladies. If you need anything, it's yours."

"Thank you," said the one with layered black hair.

Travis would have to get her name again later. He took Angeline's hand and kissed it. Then he made his way through the crowd, looking for Natalie. She had to be in the back, handling the behind-the-scenes stuff that Travis never had to worry about. He'd find her later. There was no way anyone with any connection to Mandy and her dangerous claims would be allowed back to his place.

He stopped and made small talk with a few people before finding his way back to Rita. Now she was sipping a martini. She lowered the glass and smiled at him.

"You're back."

"Said I would be. Still haven't joined anyone?" He cringed at his stupid question. Of course she hadn't. She was still standing off by herself. He'd let that loser get the best of him.

Rita shook her head, showing no signs of irritation. "I like to watch people, actually."

"Really? You wouldn't rather be in the action?"

The corners of her mouth twitched. "Sometimes, of course. Your wait staff is taking exceptional care of me, though."

"Glad to hear it." Travis glanced around the room. With Rusty and Laura out of sight, everything was perfect. "What brings you here?"

Rita finished off the martini. "I'm a journalist."

"Oh? Are you here to learn more about the big deal we just signed?"

She shook her head. "I work for a fashion magazine. Actually, I'm here for the party itself."

Travis relaxed. "In that case, I'm glad you're so happy with it. Do you have any suggestions?"

Rita smiled. "Do you really want to know?"

"Absolutely. I haven't gotten to where I am by ignoring the advice of experts in their field."

"In that case, you might want to take notes."

He pulled out his phone and opened the notes app. "Shoot."

"For starters, the music is so six months ago. You really need something more up to date."

"Interesting." He started a new note and started it off with new music. "Anything else?"

"Do you want to hear about the decor?"

"You know it. Shall we sit?"

They made their way to the nearest empty table—there were a growing number of choices now that more people had begun dancing. Despite the music choices. He chuckled.

"Something funny?" Rita arched a brow. Her eyes sparkled as though amused.

Travis shook his head. "Let's hear about the decor."

She leaned back in her chair and spoke about color schemes. Apparently, Travis was half a year behind on that, too.

"I'm sensing a theme," he said as he added more to his note.

Rita shrugged. "I'm sure most people wouldn't even notice."

He stared into her eyes. "But you do. And you're telling me. Why?"

Travis wasn't an idiot. He knew that nothing came free, and that included information like this.

She smiled and took some caviar from a passing server. "I like making friends in high places."

He returned the grin. So, she would want a favor later. Perhaps an inside scoop on something in the future. Maybe she thought their new deal would be fashionable. "Do you have any other tips?"

"The tables need flowers. Fresh ones."

"You think so?" Travis got ready to add more to his list.

The two of them talked and laughed for nearly an hour, giving Travis the opportunity to forget about his worries. Only until he glanced over at Angeline's table and saw Rusty handing out glasses of wine.

Fury burned in his gut. He rose, pushing the chair back farther than he'd meant. "Excuse me for a moment."

"Is everything all right?" Rita asked.

Travis continued watching Rusty. The loser laughed with the women about something.

When Travis was through with him, the man would never work in this town again.

"Travis?" Rita asked.

"I'll be right back." He picked up his phone and stuffed it in a pocket.

"Okay…" Rita sounded worried.

Travis marched over to Rusty, his body tensing with every movement. That jerk really had nerve. Travis had made himself more than clear earlier. And no one crossed Travis Calloway. No one.

"What are you doing?" Travis demanded, glaring at Rusty.

"Travis." Angeline's cheeks were red.

He stepped closer to Rusty. "I thought I told you to stay away."

"It was me," said Elle—or was it Sierra? "I requested he return to our table."

Anger churned in Travis's already twisting stomach. He glared at Rusty, his nostrils flaring. "I appreciate you trying to keep the guests pleased, but I am your boss. When I say to do something—you do it! Do you understand?"

"People are staring," Angeline whispered.

"Let them," Travis seethed.

Angeline pressed her face into her palms.

"You're right," Rusty said. "I'm sorry. Wine?"

That was the final straw. "No, I don't want wine!" Travis raised his arm and struck the tray. It flung several feet away. Glasses and alcohol flew through the air. As the chalices hit the ground, they shattered, sending glass shards in all directions along with the liquid.

"Travis!" Angeline exclaimed.

"Shut up."

She gasped, gave her friends a horrified look, and ran off.

Travis had no time to deal with her. He turned to Rusty. "After you've cleaned your mess, never return! If you're ever seen on any of my properties ever again, you will be placed under arrest." He lowered his voice and stepped close enough that only Rusty could hear him. "No one messes with me and gets away with it."

He went back over to Rita and sat next to her.

"Can I put that in an article?" she asked. "That was crazy. Nobody's going to believe it."

"In a fashion magazine?"

"I also have a gossip column on a popular blog."

"Perfect." Travis didn't take his attention from Rusty as Rita rambled on excitedly. Once the two fired servers finally left, he turned back to the pretty redhead. "I have some really juicy news for you. It can be exclusive."

Her eyes widened. "Really?"

"Keep my name out of this part, okay?"

"You've got it." Rita pulled out a tablet and slid her finger around the screen. "Tell me everything." She nodded, appearing more eager with each passing moment.

"I ran a thorough background check on Mandy's brother." Travis leaned back in his chair and cracked a knuckle. "You won't believe what I found."

Her fingers flew across the screen as she texted in every word Travis spoke. "Tell me everything."

"It appears his nephew might also be his son."

Fourteen

RUSTY SAT UP, twisted in the sheets, and gasped for air. His heart felt like it would jump through his chest. Sweat stung his eyes. He wiped them with his hands and then used a blanket for his forehead. He was drenched.

The nightmares had stopped long ago, but it appeared they were back. It took him a moment to realize he was in the guest room of Mandy's house rather than in his own bedroom.

He picked up his phone from the nightstand. Just after four. It was too early to get up, but there was no way he would fall back to sleep. There would be no use even trying. Using the flashlight on his phone, he grabbed some clothes, went into the bathroom, and started the shower.

As the water warmed, he tried pushing away the images of his dream—nightmare—from his mind. It was the same as every other one. Trying unsuccessfully to prevent his family from getting into the car that fateful evening. The events in every dream were different, but the result was the same. He never got to them in time.

Rusty took deep breaths, trying to soothe his frayed nerves. He was shaking worse than usual.

Was Mandy's death going to send him into a new spiral of depression? He already had enough guilt in his life. Enough that it was suffocating. He had nearly lost his house, but he'd learned to deal with the depression and guilt between his meetings and the treatment center.

Would adding the guilt of having not reached out to his sister finally be what crushed him? Could helping to find her killer relieve some of that?

The water finally warmed over his hand. He climbed in and let it stream over him. The water burned, but he didn't care. He needed the pain. It would help him focus. Rusty closed his eyes and gritted his teeth. Then after a minute, when he could no longer take it, he turned it cold.

Icy water ran down, shocking his system. Again, he let it rain over him until he could no longer take it. Then he put the water at a comfortable level and took a deep breath. It was nice to have a couple minutes not to have to think about all the pain and loss in his life. But it never lasted long enough.

And it definitely didn't bring anyone back. Nothing would. The gaping hole of pain in his life would only grow. It had just gone from three people to four. His parents—as aggravating as they could be—weren't getting any younger. His father's lifelong negativity would likely do him in early. And then there was his mom, living with the constant stress of her husband's domineering attitudes.

The water cooled, indicating it would run cold soon. Rusty quickly soaped up and rinsed while he still had time. Nervous energy buzzed through him. Maybe he would feel better after a run. He'd seen a trail not too far away.

After getting dressed, he grabbed his key and went outside. The air was surprisingly chilly considering how hot the days were. He shivered as he locked the top bolt. The sun was already starting to rise. Shades of pink colored the horizon.

Rusty jogged to the sidewalk and headed for the park where he'd seen the trail. Birds chirped in the distance. The air smelled of fresh-cut grass and too-sweet flowers. He picked up his pace and made his way to the park. There was the trail, down near the small lake. It led into some woods.

Perfect. With any luck, he wouldn't run into anyone. He just wanted to be alone with his thoughts. Actually, no. He wanted to forget them. Just burn off his energy.

Rusty ran into the woods and focused on the scenery. Had Mandy spent any time on the same trail?

Stop.

He focused on the light peeking through the branches. It made some interesting patterns. Each was different as he blazed through. He came out of the woods—already?—and to the end of the lake, as well. Some ducks wandered around near the trail. Two big ones followed by five little fuzzy ones.

The trail continued alongside the road. Rusty felt like he'd barely begun, so he decided to keep going until he tired. With as late as they'd gotten home—despite his being kicked out of the party by Travis Calloway—he was sure Laura would sleep in. They would have plenty of time before submitting the DNA they'd managed to get from Travis.

Rusty had wiped the wine glass with a clean swab and placed it in a plastic bag. Laura had found a nail clipping on his dinner plate. Between the two samples, they had to have gotten enough for one to be viable.

If not, they would be stuck. Travis had ordered Natalie to fire both him and Laura—in front of everyone at the party. It had taken every ounce of Rusty's self-control not to lose his cool. Sure, he was used to people being rude and saying stupid things. He worked with drunks. It didn't usually get much worse than the crap coming out of their mouths.

But public humiliation was another beast altogether. It didn't matter that no one in town knew who he was. Scratch that. Now everyone knew. Laura warned him that word would travel fast and that they would want to lay low for a few days. She'd even suggested waiting to take the samples to the lab.

No way. Rusty wasn't going to let a bunch of busybodies get in the way of finding out if Travis had actual motivation for killing Mandy. If he was Brady's father, that would be enough evidence to take to the police. And after last night, they would need solid evidence. Otherwise, it would appear they were being vengeful for having been fired.

He pushed his speed, feeling his muscles burn. It was a good thing he'd thought to pack his running shoes, or his feet would ache. It had already been too long since he'd gotten out for a good run. He'd likely be sore the next day. Not that it mattered. He felt better out on the trail than he had in a long time. At least since he'd found out about Mandy, and that felt strangely like a long time ago.

A couple ladies headed his way, also jogging. One turned to the other and they whispered, staring at Rusty. It had to be his imagination. Surely, people weren't talking about the party already.

He gave a slight nod and smiled. Neither returned the gesture. Maybe it wasn't his imagination, after all.

The sky continued to brighten, and after a few more blocks, he came to another couple joggers. They were less subtle. The blonde nudged the brunette and they both stared.

The brunette wrinkled her nose. "Sicko."

"How do you live with yourself?" asked the blonde.

Rusty stared straight ahead and focused on the path in front of him. He hadn't imagined *that*. The trail winded along with the quiet two-lane road. Maybe next time, he would have to bring his earbuds and listen to some music from his phone to provide more distraction.

He managed another four blocks before passing a runner. She glared at him, her eyes narrowed, and made a point to stay as close to the far edge of the path as possible.

Chills ran down his back from the look on her face—like he was some kind of predator. Rusty slowed his pace and turned around. It was time to head back to the house. He'd far rather deal with Chris than any of this. At least his brother-in-law didn't think he was a criminal.

The runner in front of him turned around. "Are you following me, perv?"

His eyes nearly popped out of his head. He stared directly into her eyes. "What makes you say that?"

She flipped her bangs out of her eyes. "You're Mandy Oates's brother, right?"

"What does that have to do with anything?" he demanded.

"Get out of my way." She shoved past him, muttering under her breath.

"I am not a pervert," Rusty insisted. "What did you hear, and from whom?"

She spun around and glared at him. "Don't you read the local blogs? Leave me alone before I call the cops. You're disgusting." She jogged away.

Rusty ran his hands through his hair and started shaking. His stomach heaved.

Travis had to be behind this. He'd warned Rusty that no one got away with messing with Travis. He really had some nerve. It was clear he didn't care about destroying someone's reputation to save his own. Just how far would he take it?

He waited until she was out of sight. Next time, he would hop into his rental car and go to the next town over for some exercise. But how far did Travis Calloway's influence reach?

He slowed his pace and kept his gaze near the ground every time he passed other joggers. He tried to ignore the stares and whispers from the corner of his eyes.

Once Rusty got back to the neighborhood, the people out made a point to cross the road rather than go near him. Cars slowed as they drove past him. He couldn't get inside the house fast enough. It was still quiet. He went to the guest room, grabbed a new set of clothes, and took another shower.

As he scrubbed, he imagined washing away all the stares, but mostly the accusation of being a pervert. He was only trying to clear his sister's name. The sooner he could get the samples to the lab, the better.

After getting dressed the second time that morning, he stepped out into the hall and nearly crashed into Chris.

"Sorry," Rusty said.

"It's fine," Chris grumbled. He wore slacks and a button up shirt, and had the start of a beard and bags under his eyes.

"Are you okay?"

"Have to get back to work. Bills aren't going to pay themselves."

"Do you want me to pay rent while I'm here?"

Chris gave him a double-take. "What? No. You're doing plenty. Thanks for getting the groceries and helping with the kids. I don't know what I'm going to do when they start school."

"Let's just take this one step at a time. I'm sure I can help you figure something out. Don't they take the bus?"

He shook his head. "Too close to the schools."

"Then they can walk."

"Too far. It's just over a mile."

Rusty gave him a double-take. "Then why can't they take the bus?"

"Budget cuts. Red tape. Idiots running the system. Look, I gotta get going."

"Sure. Sorry. I'll take care of things around here." Rusty would put up with being treated as an outcast as long as he had to in order to help out the kids. Hopefully whatever rumors were floating around weren't enough to damage the kids' reputations by being seen with him.

"Thanks." Chris hurried past Rusty. The front door slammed and then a car started out front.

Rusty threw his clothes into the guest room and checked on the kids. Both were still sound asleep, and probably would be for some time. Would Laura be up? He was anxious to get their collected samples to the lab, and she was the one who knew where it was. They could probably even get back before the kids woke.

He was tempted to get online and see what the accusations were, but part of him really didn't want to know. It didn't matter, anyway. The lies were just distractions to keep him from doing what he needed to— clearing Mandy's name. And Travis was looking guiltier by the minute.

Rusty went into the kitchen and put out some breakfast in case the kids got up while he was out. Then he went next door and knocked softly. Just in case she had decided to sleep in. If his mind would have left him alone, he would have gladly done the same. He was glad the kids were able to get some rest.

The top locked clicked and the door opened. Laura stood there wearing a red flowing dress under a black shawl. Her hair was wet and she wore no makeup. She had a real natural beauty, and for some reason, it took him by surprise.

"Are you okay?" she asked.

"Just tired," he fibbed. They needed to stay focused. "Are you up for a quick trip to the lab? I was hoping to leave and come back before the kids wake."

"Yeah, sure. Just let me finish getting ready real quick. Want some coffee? I have some brewing."

"That sounds perfect."

He followed her up the stairs of the spacious split-level. Laura waved toward the kitchen. "Everything's in there. I'll be out in a couple minutes." She hurried down the hall and then he heard a hair drier.

Rusty grabbed a mug and poured himself some coffee. After the morning he was having, black was what he needed. He took a sip. It was especially strong. Even better.

He had a feeling he would need that to get him through whatever was coming the rest of the day.

Fifteen

~

"**S**URE YOU DON'T want me to drive?" Rusty asked.

Laura shook her head and locked her door. "We'll just take mine. It isn't a problem. Let's just hurry. I've got to get some work done today."

"Am I interrupting you? I can just take them down myself."

"It's fine. I want to go, and besides the route is a little tricky."

Rusty held the envelope close to him. "Let's go then, driver."

They walked down the driveway. Laura remotely unlocked the door. Just as Rusty pulled on the handle of the passenger side door, a car slowed in front of the yard and blared a horn.

"Classy." Laura shook her fist at them, her bracelets jingling together.

"Are people always like that?" Rusty asked once they were in the car.

Laura grumbled and started the engine. "Small town. Some people are idiots and like to show it off."

"You think it's because of the party?"

She pulled into the road. "I know it is."

"I went for a run earlier and received similar treatment."

Laura stared at him. "Did you get any sleep?"

"Not much."

"Put on a movie for the kids later and take a nap."

Rusty yawned. "Not a bad idea."

"And don't worry about the local jerks. They'll forget about us in a couple days. Something more interesting will come along."

They made small talk as Laura drove through town, and then down a bunch of winding side roads. Rusty tried to memorize the route. It was worse than a maze, but he managed. Finally, she pulled into a parking lot in front of a large building with at least ten floors.

"Seems an odd place for such a building," he noted. "Right in the middle of a neighborhood."

"Yeah, but it's the only place to send lab work around here. I worked as an office manager for a pediatrician clinic for a while."

Rusty checked the time. A quarter to ten. "Are they open yet?"

"Nine to five."

He held the envelope and got out of the car. The sun was already getting hot. He followed her to one of three doors along the main floor of the building. They went to the elevator and Laura pressed floor three.

Rusty's heart picked up speed. If Travis had so much influence, what would happen if he found out these results? Did he have enough power to have them destroyed? Would he create new rumors?

He turned to Laura. "Maybe we shouldn't mention who the samples belong to."

"We definitely won't."

"But what about when the results come in?"

She stared into his eyes. "We won't say who they belong to. We just need to prove paternity. The who isn't important to them. They're just running tests. It's one of many."

"But what if they have his DNA on file? They could—"

"You worry too much."

Did he? He couldn't ignore the stares, the blaring horn, or being called a pervert. None of that was in his head.

The elevator opened, and he followed Laura down a hallway nearly as confusing as the roads leading to the building. Finally, she stopped in front a door in the far back of the building.

His mind spun with images of what could be behind the door. A dark room full of mysterious people conducting odd experiments. A chemistry lab, not unlike the one he'd used in high school. A room with bright lights shining from all sides. Cops ready to arrest him for pissing off the most influential man in the town.

"Stop," he muttered to himself.

Laura turned to him. "What?"

He shook his head. "Nothing."

Laura opened the door, and they walked into what looked like a doctor's office waiting room. White walls, soft lights, semi-cheerful paintings, and piles of magazines. It was neat and tidy, and smelled of bleach and other cleaners.

Rusty chastised himself for allowing his mind to run wild. Maybe Laura was right and he needed a good nap. The problem was that he wasn't sure he'd sleep soundly until he found out the truth about Mandy. He owed her that much.

She went up to the counter and greeted the receptionist by name. "Hi, Lisa. We've got a paternity test. Think you can run this for us real quick?"

Lisa pushed her wire-rimmed glasses up her nose, shot Rusty a glare, and muttered something.

"It's not for him," Laura said.

"Right. You're Mandy's brother?" Lisa asked.

Rusty nodded.

"Paternity test, you said?" Lisa asked and typed.

"Yes," Laura replied. "We need this back as soon as possible."

Lisa continued to type away on her computer, while staring at the screen. "It's going to be at least a couple days."

"What?" Laura exclaimed. "But the paperwork says it only takes a few hours to run."

"It does." Lisa turned to her. "This isn't high priority. It goes to the back of the queue. And right now, that means a couple days." She narrowed her eyes.

Laura set her purse on the counter and opened it up. "What's it going to cost to move it up?"

"I don't work like that anymore." Lisa glanced around. "I follow the order as directed by the rulebook."

"Oh, come on. Don't give me that."

"Sorry. I can't move it up for you. I'll call you as soon as they start the tests. I promise."

Laura sighed dramatically. "Okay, but if you get the chance to move it up, please do."

"I wouldn't hold your breath. Like I said, I'll call you."

"Whatever." Laura spun around and gave Rusty a defeated look.

"Let's go."

Rusty and Laura left without a word. Laura nearly punched the arrow button on the elevator pad.

"Easy there."

"I can't believe her. Lisa has always pulled strings for me. For a lot of good people."

"Sounds like that's put her job on the line."

"Or maybe it's personal. Did you see the way she was looking at me?"

Rusty shrugged. All he'd noticed was the judging look she'd shot him when Laura had said paternity test. She'd probably read the papers and blogs, and knew all about whatever rumors Travis had spread. It made him want to get online and look.

The elevator opened and Laura grumbled under her breath as she pressed the button for the main floor. Once they arrived, Rusty had to hurry to keep up with her. In the car, she drove so fast, he clutched the armrest for dear life.

"Waiting a couple days isn't the worst thing in the world," Rusty said.

She glared at him. "That's not the point. And maybe it is the worst thing. It just gives Travis more time to cover his tracks—and he knows we're onto him."

"Maybe he doesn't know we know about Brady. I doubt he would have let us walk out with his DNA, you know?"

"Oh, I'd say he definitely knows we know. He just doesn't realize we swabbed his saliva or found a nail clipping. Let's just hope it's enough."

"Even if he is the father, that doesn't mean he hurt her," Rusty said. "If Chris found out, he could have done something really stupid. Especially given that he's already prone to a temper. This gives us some more time to figure out his motives. He's angry, but I don't get a killer vibe from him."

"You just haven't had enough time with him." She turned a corner, nearly giving Rusty whiplash. Maybe next time, he would insist on driving. Even if it made him look like a sexist.

He turned up the music and they rode in silence the rest of the way. When they arrived in her driveway, she cut the engine and tapped her fingers on the steering wheel.

"Are you going to be able to work?" Rusty asked.

"Yeah. You want to meet later? Dinner?"

"Sure. If Chris is back, I'll probably be eager to get away, anyhow. I'm not his favorite person."

"Nobody is. Well, if he's not back, bring the kids. It'll probably do them some good to get out of the house."

Rusty nodded, but couldn't help thinking that with the way the townspeople were acting, they were all better off staying inside. Unless he took them somewhere farther away. Like across the country.

"See you about six?" Laura asked.

"Sounds good."

They got out of the car and parted ways. Laura muttered a goodbye and Rusty waved, watching her walk up to her door and hurry inside. In a way, it was a relief that she was so furious. It gave him permission not to be. And that was a good thing since he really needed to be in a good mind frame for the kids.

He unlocked the trunk of his rental car and slid the envelope into his new locking briefcase. He flipped through the contents, making sure everything was in its place. Everything looked as it should.

Inside, he heard the shower running. Kaylie's door was open and the room empty. Brady was still sound asleep. Oh, to be young again. He went to the kitchen and got out eggs and bacon.

By the time he was done, both kids were at the table. Brady was rubbing his eyes and his hair stuck out in all directions. Kaylie had her wet hair in a ponytail and she had on a bright pink tank top with too-short shorts. Or was that the style? He wished he could ask Mandy or Lani what they thought. All Rusty knew was that he didn't like the idea of Kaylie wearing those out in public. Boys would definitely stare.

He kept the conversation light and away from Mandy while they ate. They helped him clean up.

"You guys mind if I take a nap?" he asked. "I didn't sleep much last night."

Kaylie shrugged. "I don't care. I think I'm going to rearrange my room."

Rusty arched a brow. "Really? Why?"

Brady elbowed his sister. "She does that, like, every other week."

"Not that much. Shut up."

"Be nice, you guys. We're all on the same team."

"Tell him that." Kaylie spun around and left the room.

Brady rolled his eyes. "No, tell *her*."

Rusty ruffled Brady's already-messy hair. "You guys remind me of your mom and me when we were younger."

He tilted his head. "Really?"

"Very much so." Rusty started to smile, remembering back to his days bickering playfully with Mandy.

"What was Mom like as a kid?"

He thought back. "She loved to play video games like you."

"Yeah?" Brady's face lit up.

"And she was competitive, too. Always challenging me to play against her—but only when she was sure I'd lose."

Brady laughed. "Sounds familiar. I think that's why Kaylie won't play with me anymore."

"Maybe you should let her win once in a while." Rusty winked. "She might actually want to play with you again."

"You think so?"

Rusty nodded. "I know so. Anyway, I'm going to get some rest. Shout if you need anything."

"Okay." Brady went into the living room and Rusty double-checked that everything was off in the kitchen. Then he yawned and headed back to the bedroom. He slid off his shoes and froze.

His stuff had been moved around. The luggage sat on the floor next to the wall. He had definitely left his suitcase on the end of the bed and had left some stuff on the nightstand, most of which was moved around.

Rusty unzipped the bags, and sure enough his clothes and toiletries were all messed up—and not just from having been moved. He pulled the clothes out and folded them before they wrinkled. Then he rearranged the things on the nightstand before lying down.

Had he gone back into his room after seeing Chris? He didn't think he had. He'd just thrown his clothes in without looking. Rusty closed the door and found them in a pile right where he'd left them.

That meant Chris had gone in there while he'd been in the shower. Chills ran down Rusty's back. Was it payback for going through Chris and Mandy's room? He was sure there had to have been a camera in there. How else would Chris have known to look for Mandy's diary? And why else would he have felt watched when he was in there?

Maybe Rusty would be better off checking into a hotel and just helping out with the kids during the day. It might be best for everyone.

Sixteen

~

LAURA PUSHED THE chair back and rose. She stretched, unable to focus on her work anymore. Not that her concentration had been great earlier. As always, since Mandy's death, work just didn't seem important. Obviously, she needed to pay her bills. And she couldn't go back to being someone else's employee.

She saved her spreadsheet and headed downstairs. Yoga or the exercise bike? The bike made more sense with all her nervous energy—she was still pissed at Lisa for not helping. How many times had Laura helped her out in the past?

Laura hiked up her dress, too angry to bother changing into workout clothes. She got on the exercise machine and took out all her anger on the pedals. She chewed out Lisa under her breath until she felt a little better. Her mind wandered back to Mandy... again. She mulled over everything since her death.

She and Rusty had made progress, but it wasn't enough. They needed to solve this for Mandy. She deserved as much. Someone was guilty and so far was getting away with it.

Laura peddled faster and faster. Maybe she needed to find something to motivate Lisa to push them up in the queue. The DNA evidence of Travis Calloway fathering Brady would be huge. The police department couldn't ignore that.

Even if they tried, she wouldn't let them. Chances were, though, that they would take a closer look at Chris first. The husband is always the first suspect, and they'd already spent plenty of time questioning him. If they came up empty with him, then they'd look at Travis. He obviously didn't want pretty Angeline knowing about this.

She'd already wasted more than enough time. There was so much more to get done before her date with Rusty. No, it was just dinner. Or was it? She'd see if he tried to pay the bill. If so, it was a date.

Her pulse quickened at the thought. As much as she didn't want to be attracted to him, she found herself growing more and more fond of him. Not only was he someone to talk to—the one person who understood how she felt about Mandy—but he was sweet and funny, too.

And that was the scariest thing she could think of. No, he wasn't like her dad, ex-husband, or any of her ex-boyfriends, but she couldn't take the risk. People always changed once they were in a relationship. She didn't want to see Rusty's bad side. Things were perfect the way they were.

Laura went upstairs and took a long, hot shower. She just kept her mind on work, and today that meant spreadsheets and numbers. That was the perfect distraction from both Mandy and Rusty.

While she was working, she kept glancing at the time. It was really dragging. Usually, even when working this part of the business, she found time flying faster than the consulting. But nothing had been normal since Rusty showed up. It was better than getting depressed over Mandy. Now she and Rusty were actually able to do something useful.

If it turned out that Travis was guilty, and they pointed the police in the right direction, they would be able to do something right for Mandy—clear her name. Travis was probably the last person on their minds. They likely had no idea that Mandy's path had ever crossed his, much less that Brady was a result of that path.

Focus.

Laura closed her eyes and rubbed her temples. If she didn't get these numbers crunched, she would have to stay up all night to get it done. And she needed some sleep. Even when she did get some, it was so restless these days. Hopefully once Mandy's name was cleared and those kids had the knowledge that their mom hadn't killed herself, she could get some real rest.

But Mandy would still be dead. And they would have to deal with their mom being murdered. Was that really any better? Especially if it was their dad? Her chest tightened. No matter the outcome, she was still dead.

Mandy was gone.

Laura had moved here to get away from heartache and pain. Apparently that was just part of life. There was no escaping it.

A sharp pain stabbed her lower abdomen. Then it radiated out, making the rest of her body ache.

She grasped her abdomen. "Not now."

When she was stressed and her monthly cycle came around, she tended to have horribly painful cramps. Bad enough that she'd passed out from them. Luckily, she knew what to do, and the pain had just started. She might have time to take care of this and still make her dinner date.

Laura scrambled out of the chair and hurried to the kitchen, still clutching her middle. The pain was intensifying already. She turned on the tea kettle, opened the cabinet with her teas and reached for the back, knocking several boxes and bags onto the counter. She found the one she needed.

Raspberry leaf tea. She shook it. Half a box. Good.

She pulled it open, took out two packets and opened them, sticking them in a dark green mug. The water seemed to be taking forever.

Pain radiated outward in all directions. White dots appeared in her vision and she felt light-headed. This was going to be a bad one. As much as she hated medicine, she was going to have to take some.

She ran to the bathroom, cursing mother nature the whole way, and found some ibuprofen. It was likely expired with as rarely as she took it, but it would still work. She grabbed two and swallowed.

The tea kettle sang, alerting her that the water was ready. Laura brought the bottle of painkillers with her and poured the steaming water into her mug. Hopefully she could wait the fifteen minutes it would take for the raspberry leaf bags to steep.

Pain squeezed her middle. She massaged the area. Mother nature was a wicked, cruel witch. Laura took deep breaths.

She checked the time. Ten more minutes. Would she make it? She continued to pace while taking deep breaths. She could do this. Not could. Would. Cramps weren't going to keep her from settling Mandy's score.

Hot pain squeezed her back like giant, boiling fingers.

Laura found a rice bag and stuck it in the microwave.

Another five minutes for the tea. She considered drinking it anyway. It would be mostly ready. She could always make more. Except that hitting the early pains with the full strength concoction was the only thing that would help. The medicine was just to take the edge off.

More white dots danced before her eyes. Laura took a deep breath and glanced at the clock. It switched over to the time she had been waiting for. She let go of her middle and ran to her mug. In one swift motion, she took the bags out and began drinking. She had to ignore the burning sensation. Her mouth would heal. She couldn't afford to spend the next two days in bed, likely puking from the pain.

The mug was empty before she knew it. The microwave beeped. She grabbed the rice bag and headed for the couch. She reclined, spreading the rice bag over her lower abdomen. There wasn't much else to do except wait for the pain to go away.

And take care of the impending flow. She groaned, closing her eyes. Her body ached too much to move. She would take care of that soon enough. She closed her eyes and waited.

From the kitchen, her phone notified her of a text. She rubbed her eyes, feeling groggy.

Had she fallen asleep? The rice bag was cool and aside from some body aches, she wasn't in pain anymore.

Laura sat up and set the bag next to her. The light-headedness had gone away, too. Her work wasn't going to do itself, but at least she felt better. She got up and checked her message. It was from Rusty.

Running a little behind. Mind if we meet a half an hour late?
No problem. See you then.

At least that saved her from coming up with an excuse for needing some extra time. She turned the tea kettle back on and got a new mug ready for some tea.

Laura went into the bathroom and took care of business. She looked in the mirror. Dark circles sat under her eyes. She pulled out all the necessary makeup and concealers and got to work. By the time the kettle sang to her, she looked normal. Maybe even better than normal. Rusty would never know how much pain she'd been in earlier.

She poured water over the tea bags and headed back to the bathroom to fix her kinked hair. She hadn't meant to sleep on it.

Laura ran water over her hands and raked it through her tresses. It didn't help, so she pulled it up into a loose bun. She preferred it down, but this would do.

The doorbell rang.

She swore under her breath. Had it been a half hour already?

"Coming," she called and ran into the kitchen. She swallowed the tea as quickly as possible, not bothering to take the bags out. Then she took another couple painkillers for good measure and grabbed her purse. It was time for a dinner date, and she wasn't about to let him know she felt like a zombie that had gone through a wood chipper.

Laura hurried down to the door, opened it, and forced a smile.

Rusty returned her smile, looking as tired as she felt. "You look really nice."

"So do you. Did you get any rest?"

"Some. You? You seem a bit tired."

So much for covering it up. "I am, but I'll be okay."

"And you're okay with me driving?"

"I'd appreciate it." She turned around and locked the door. "Where are we going?"

"What's good around here?" He led the way to his rental next door and held the passenger door for her. She climbed in and he closed it for her before going around and getting in.

"Do you like Dim Sum?" Laura asked.

"Can't say I've even heard of it." He started the car.

"If you like Chinese, you'll love it."

"All right. Let's give that a try. Where to?"

Laura gave him directions.

"Looks like a popular place," Rusty said. People milled about outside and the parking lot was full.

"We can go somewhere else," Laura said.

He shook his head. "I have to see what this is all about now." He drove around the lot three times until they came to someone pulling out.

They made their way around the crowd and into the busy restaurant.

"Welcome," greeted a beautiful twenty-something Cantonese girl with a big smile. "Can I get your name, please?"

"Rusty."

She scribbled a note on a pad of paper. "It'll be about a half an hour."

"Thank you."

"Do you want to wait in here or go outside?" Rusty asked.

Laura glanced around. People were staring at them. Some were even so bold as to point and whisper. It took her a moment to realize it was because of what had happened at the Calloway party. "Let's get outside for some air."

He nodded and led her outside. A couple standing near the door glared at them.

"If it's going to be a half hour," Laura said, "maybe we should go next door. There's a lovely candle shop."

"Sounds good." He held the door open for her and they entered the sweet-smelling store. It held a mixture of citrus and floral scents.

Laura breathed in deeply, holding onto the aromas.

"Much more peaceful in here," Rusty noted.

"I take it you noticed the stares."

"How could I not?" he asked.

"People are jerks, but like I said before, they'll find something else to gawk over soon enough."

"Let's hope so. I'm not one who enjoys the spotlight."

"Oh?"

"I'm just a simple guy who enjoys quiet walks in the woods. That's a perfect day in my book. Stopping at a lake to watch the wildlife." He glanced up, looking lost in thought.

Laura's heart nearly leaped into her throat. Was he perfect? It was sure starting to seem more and more that way.

"Can I help you with anything?" asked a lady with long, curly red hair and small, round glasses. She held a box of red and purple candles.

"We're just looking. Thanks." Laura smiled.

"Let me know if you need anything." The lady disappeared down an aisle.

Rusty turned to her. "Are you into candles?"

"Oh, I love them. I have several in every room."

The door opened and a group of four ladies walked in. A tall blonde stopped when she saw them. She turned to her friends. "That's them."

Anger burned in Laura's chest. "If you've got something to say, why don't you say it to our faces?"

Rusty put a hand on her arm. "Laura, don't."

She narrowed her eyes at the blonde but spoke to him. "No. I'm sick of people whispering."

The blonde started to walk away.

"Hey," Laura said. "Don't gossip about us and then ignore us. Grow a set and say it to our faces."

"Fine." She stood even taller and glared at Laura and then Rusty. "You two should just leave town. Nobody wants you guys here."

Laura stepped closer. "We deserve to be here every bit as much as anyone else. Try having some compassion, would you? He just lost his sister, and I lost a close friend."

One of the ladies behind the blonde gave her an apologetic glance.

"Mandy Oates?" asked an auburn-haired girl behind Blondie. "That piece of trailer trash? The suburban wanna-be. She—"

"How dare you?" Laura balled her fists. "Shut up. You don't even know her."

Rusty grabbed Laura's arm and pulled her out of the candle shop.

"What'd you do that for?" Laura exclaimed. "They can't talk like that about Mandy."

"And fighting isn't going to solve a thing. What are we going to do? Fight everyone in town?"

"If we have to, but once people hear not to mess with us—"

"Like you said, people will move on and forget about Travis kicking us out of his party soon enough."

Seventeen

RUSTY BIT INTO the white, puffy pastry-like thing. He expected sweet fruit inside, but instead it was a savory meat. It was the latest plate on their table. Every few minutes, carts with small plates would come by and they would pick one or two.

"Do you like?" Laura asked. She had just finished one off.

"I think so. It's different."

She sipped her rose wine. "I love the variety. And no matter how many times you come here, there's always something new to try."

"That I believe." He glanced around the table at all the plates. There were several he hadn't even tried yet.

A woman in a traditional red Cantonese dress stopped at their table and held a glass of champagne. She turned to Rusty. "Are you sure you don't want something to drink with that?"

He held up his glass of grape juice. "This is all I need."

She raised the bottle. "But this tastes so good with that." She looked down to the rice and vegetable dish on his plate.

"Maybe later."

"Okay, then." She walked off.

"Now you've done it," Laura said.

"What do you mean?" Rusty asked.

"You told her later. I guarantee she'll be back."

"We'll see." He sipped on his juice. Part of him wanted to accept the drink. More than part of him, if he was being honest with himself. He didn't want to admit to her that he was a recovering alcoholic—and that scared him. It meant he cared about what she thought. That he was dangerously close to opening himself up to another person again.

Laura stopped a young man pushing a cart. She pointed to something near the middle. "We'll take that."

Rusty slid a hand down to his lap and felt his sobriety coin in his pocket. He traced the shape over his jeans and remembered the struggles he'd endured to earn the chip. He didn't want to start over. Go back to day one. He'd come so far. Years without a drink. He hadn't even craved one in such a long time. It had become easy.

Now, not so much. In fact, he might be wise to find a local meeting to keep his focus.

The lady in red returned. She smiled sweetly and held the champagne bottle up.

Rusty pressed his palm against the coin and shook his head. She held it higher, smiling wider. He shook his head and picked up his fork. Something pink was now on his plate. Laura must have slipped it there.

"You'll love that. I could eat those all day long, but they rarely prepare them."

He cut it and took a bite. Whatever it was, the sweetness melted in his mouth.

"Good, huh?" Laura asked.

Rusty nodded, his mouth too full of food to respond. He finished it off and took a bite of his rice.

A group of teen girls walked by, giggling. They stared as they walked by Rusty and Laura.

Laura rolled her eyes. "I feel like I'm back in junior high."

"Maybe next time, we should eat somewhere else—far away."

"I'm sold."

The champagne lady walked by again and smiled at Rusty. His gaze lingered on the bottle. He almost said yes, but shook his head no. He would stay strong. He had to.

His gaze lingered to Laura. Her face was pinched, like she was in pain. "Are you okay?"

"Yeah… headache. I think I need to take something."

"I'm sorry. Do you want to go back home after this?" Going anywhere else public was sounding less and less appealing, anyway.

Laura shook her head. "I'm glad to be out with you, and I'll be fine.

It's just one of those things." She dug into her purse, opened a tiny pill bottle, and dropped one into her palm.

Someone bumped into their table. Two women walked by, whispering to each other.

"Do you see them?" asked one. "Losers."

"What do you expect? They're associated with the Oates family."

Rusty glared at them, but kept his mouth shut. It wasn't worth it. He glanced back at Laura, who was drinking the last of her water. Hopefully she'd been too busy with her painkiller to notice the loudmouths.

How could Mandy have lived in this place? If people could talk so badly about her after her death, how rude had they been when she was alive? It almost made the suicide theory seem believable. Who would want to live in a community where people were so rude and condescending?

His chest tightened as he thought about what she'd gone through—without being able to talk with her parents or brother. Guilt hit him, this time like a punch to the gut.

The lady in red came by. She held up a different bottle. "White wine this time. Goes well with your rice."

Rusty nodded.

"You'll have some?"

"Please."

"A wine man. One of good taste."

Laura's eyes widened. "I thought you didn't drink."

He took a deep breath and put his palms on the table. "Tonight I do."

The server set a wine glass in front of him and filled it about three-quarters full. "Enjoy."

Rusty flicked a nod. "I will."

She walked away, smiling.

"It's just one drink," Rusty muttered under his breath. "Not a big deal. It won't even give me a buzz."

He picked up the glass and stared at the almost-clear drink. His pulse picked up speed and mixture of emotions ran through him—guilt, excitement, and the desire to escape the pain. He raised the glass. "To Mandy."

Laura raised hers and arched a brow. "To Mandy."

They clinked the glasses and Rusty brought his to his mouth. The smell tickled his nose and made his mouth water. He had a moment of doubt. Did he really want to do this? Break his sobriety?

He glanced around the room. Two couples sat kitty-corner from them, laughing loudly. One of the guys turned and glared at Rusty. The group burst into louder laughter.

Rusty filled his mouth with the sweet wine. It had a citrusy, slightly-floral taste. He closed his eyes for a moment and focused on the taste and the sensations of the alcohol. His heart raced, wanting more.

He swallowed it and took another large sip. It would take more than a couple sips to relax someone his size. He took another sip and then another. Before he knew it, the glass was empty. His heart sank.

That had gone too fast.

The server returned. "More white wine? You seemed to enjoy it."

Rusty opened his mouth to speak.

"Maybe you should try one of these." Laura held up a plate of spring rolls. "You know, since you don't usually drink."

He glanced back and forth between the two women. The server held up the bottle higher. Laura gave him a knowing look.

Rusty picked up the glass and held it toward the server. "Maybe just one more."

Laura stopped a guy with a cart and asked for a plate with something that looked like dumplings.

The server poured Rusty more wine and headed to a different table.

"Try these," Laura said. "They're very filling."

He sipped the wine. "I'm fine. It's just two glasses. Not even enough to give me a buzz." He leaned back against the chair, feeling himself relax.

She put one on his plate. Then a spring roll. "Eat up."

Rusty set the glass down and picked up his fork and bit into a dumpling. It didn't taste anything like a dumpling—it was extremely sweet, like a dessert.

"Good, huh?" she asked.

He nodded and took another bite. "Are we going to be able to eat all of this?" There were so many half-full plates covering the table.

She shrugged. "If not, leftovers are always delicious."

"Of course." He picked up the spring roll and took a bite. At least that tasted as it should. His stomach started to protest all the food, so he returned it to his plate and sipped the wine. It had never tasted better.

The lady in red came by again. "More?"

"Actually," Laura said, "we'll take the check now."

"Oh? Are you sure?" She turned to Rusty.

"We are," Laura replied.

The server stared at him, waiting for an answer.

Rusty moved the glass. The little bit of wine swirled around. It was barely two sips.

"We have someplace to be," Laura said. "Can we get the check?"

"Sir?" asked the server.

He nodded. It was time to stop. He was only going to have one glass, but now he'd had two already. And then he needed to stay away from the stuff after this.

Laura smiled at him. "Do you want to split the leftovers?"

"You can take them. There's plenty of food at Mandy's."

"I won't be able to eat all this before it goes bad."

He shrugged. "Maybe the kids will want some."

"Perfect." She stopped a guy with a cart and asked for some to-go boxes.

While they were divvying up the leftovers, the wine lady came by with the check. Rusty slid her a credit card without looking at the bill. She returned just as Laura was scooping the last of the food into a little white box.

Rusty signed the slip and handed it to the lady.

Laura looked up. "I can help with that."

He shook his head. "I've got it."

She gave him a funny look, but then a slow smile spread across her face. She was really gorgeous. "You didn't have to."

"I know. I wanted to."

Her smile widened even more. Rusty couldn't help admiring it. Her. She was a beautiful person, inside and out. Not only was she being a friend to him, but she'd been one to Mandy.

"Do you just get used to it?" he asked, gazing into her eyes.

"What's that?" She held his gaze.

"People."

"Come again?" Her eyes softened, appearing inquisitive.

"The rudeness around here."

"Ah, that." She rested her chin against her palm. "I suppose I'm used to it. But then again, I've never been one who fit in very well to begin with."

"Haven't you? All the girls jealous of you?"

Pink crept into her cheeks and her stunning smile widened again. "Hardly."

"I can't see one reason anyone would have a problem with you. You're smart, sophisticated, and dazzling."

She laughed. "I've never had anyone describe me like that. Must be the wine talking."

"All me. And why wouldn't anyone think that?"

Laura tapped the table. "I've always dressed a little eccentric. Growing up, kids would accuse me of being a witch."

"Eccentric? No, you have your own style, that's all."

She glanced around. "Though I've toned it down quite a bit, it doesn't stop rude comments and stares."

"Let me guess. You grew up around here, with all these *fine* people." He swept his hands, gesturing around the room.

"Actually, no. I'm a move-in. People are just people."

"Stupid, you mean."

Her eyes sparkled. "Maybe."

Rusty rose and walked around the table. He helped her out of her chair. "What do you say we get this food into a fridge?"

She let her palm linger on his. "Sounds like a plan."

They gathered the boxes and managed to get to the car without even one person giving them a sideways glance. Rusty put the food in the trunk and then held open the passenger door for her.

"You okay to drive?"

"After two glasses of wine? On a full stomach. Definitely."

"Just checking."

"I wouldn't put your safety on the line." And the last thing he wanted to do was be another drunk driver and risk killing someone else's family. He climbed into the driver's seat and started the car. "Where to?"

"Somewhere without a lot of people."

"I couldn't agree more. Unfortunately, I don't know of a lot places around here. I'd suggest the beach, but that's bound to be packed."

"There's a park just outside of town. It's usually pretty empty, and it has a nice view of the lake."

"Perfect." He put the car in reverse and brushed his arm against hers. Their gazes met and Laura flashed him her beautiful smile. He returned the grin and then pulled out of the spot. "Tell me where to go."

Eighteen

~

"**W**ANT TO SIT?" Rusty asked as they neared a set of benches. He and Laura had walked around the empty park on the high hill several times, stopping near the edge each time they passed it. It overlooked the lake he'd jogged by that morning. The people looked like ants, and after the way he and Laura had been treated, an immature part of him imagined stepping on them. And liked it.

"Sure. Front row seats to the sunset."

"Is it really that late?" He pulled out his phone and checked the time. Sure enough, it was.

They sat, and he was close enough to put his arm around her. He hesitated, not wanting to ruin the good thing they had going. What if she got offended? Not only that, but he hadn't been involved with anyone romantically since Lani. Guilt kicked him in the stomach. Or was it the wine from earlier?

Surely, Lani would have understood. It had been years since her death. She wouldn't have wanted him living a solitary, lonely life for his remaining decades. Lani would have wanted him to move on—it had been his choice to keep everyone at a distance.

"It's beautiful," Laura said.

Rusty brought his attention to the sky. Pink and orange hues were beginning to crowd out the blue. "It really is." And he was with a gorgeous woman with whom he'd just spent the last couple hours exchanging memories of Mandy. They'd laughed, shed a couple tears, and she had given him her stunning smile a few times.

He didn't give himself another moment to talk himself out of putting his arm around her. If she didn't want him to, he would simply apologize.

He stretched his arm, awkward like a middle school boy who'd never kissed a girl before.

Laura scooted closer to him and leaned her head against his shoulder. Rusty's pulse pounded in his ears, but he managed to relax. It was good to be away from everything and everyone else. And the human contact... it felt good. When was the last time someone had been in his arm?

The sky changed colors before their eyes.

"This is nice," Laura said.

Did she mean the sight or being with Rusty? He cleared his throat. "It really is."

"I love the colors. I've tried getting a picture of the night sky so many times, but it never comes out as magnificent as the real thing."

He played with a bit of hair resting on her shoulder. "I think that's the way nature intended. We weren't meant to quite capture it with photos. It's not just how it looks, but the entire experience."

"Hmm. I think you might be right."

Before long, darkness took over most of the sky and stars shone brightly overhead.

Laura shivered. He squeezed her bare shoulder. "We should have brought something to keep you warm."

She nestled closer to him. "I did."

Rusty's cheeks warmed. He really did feel like a gawky kid—he was so out of practice. Plus, part of him felt like he was being untrue to Lani.

He'd always blamed himself for the accident. If only he'd been there, he might have been able to prevent it.

And deep down, if he was honest with himself, he knew he wasn't really to blame. It was just easier to torture himself emotionally if he took it on.

He thought back to the first time he kissed Lani. He'd been so confident, surprising her and sweeping her off her feet—literally. He'd scooped her up and kissed her. Rusty had known he would marry her, and the way she looked at him, he had been certain she felt the same way.

What would she think of him and Laura? Lani had been one of those people who always found the good in others. And with him alone now, she would want him happy. Right?

"Mandy would have liked this," Laura said, bringing him back to the present.

"She would have. When we would go camping as a family, she'd always drag me out to a clearing to watch the stars come out. We would make up stories about each star representing something."

"Like people's dreams?" Laura asked.

"How'd you know?"

"That's what she told me."

A lump formed in Rusty's throat. He could easily spend years wallowing in regret over Mandy, too. It was a pattern he knew well. He could beat himself up like a pro.

They sat in silence for a while, and Rusty focused on the scenery, trying to push the accusatory thoughts from his mind. Even if he had done things differently, there was no guarantee that anything would have turned out any better for his sister or his wife and kids.

"I'm glad Mandy had you for a friend," he said.

Laura looked at him. "Thanks. I wish I would have pushed harder for our friendship after she backed away, though. Maybe I could have done something, you know?"

He nodded. "Trust me, I do."

They stared into each other's eyes. The nearly-full moon reflected in her pupils. She leaned a little closer to him, holding onto his gaze with more intensity.

Rusty's heart thundered, nearly bursting out of his chest. She inched closer.

He backed up. "You're shivering." She wasn't. "We should get going." They really should.

"I'm happy here."

So was he, and that was a big problem. Wine circulated through his system. They were both vulnerable because of Mandy's passing. If ever there was a time for mistakes, this was it. He couldn't risk ruining the friendship they'd begun. He needed to think with his head. Not his heart, not his pain, not anything else.

Rusty tried to get up, but Laura leaned against him, making it impossible. He took a deep breath. Maybe it wasn't such a bad thing to stay a little longer. The view was pleasant, and the company even more so. It was nice to relax after such a stressful day… and that was the last thing he wanted to think about was why the whole town thought he was a pervert.

Actually, the last thing he wanted to think about was Laura finding out why. Whatever the story was, it was obviously something disturbing. He couldn't get some of the glares from his mind.

"Are you okay?" Laura asked.

"No, I'm not. We're so focused on Mandy's death. The jerk neighbors. I want to remember the good times, you know?"

Laura rested her palm on top of Rusty's hand. "Me, too. She was so funny. I'll never forget the time she was convinced it was St. Patrick's Day. She and the kids came out of the house wearing green from head to toe. She wouldn't admit to being wrong, so she said it was a dry run, and proudly went to work that day wearing all green."

Rusty chuckled. "That sounds like her. Never liked to admit to being wrong. That's how I ended up with several board games dumped on my lap over the years."

Laura laughed. "I can just see her doing that. You know, whenever I was having a bad day, I could always count on her to cheer me up. She had a stockpile of jokes and funny stories."

"She sure did." Rusty yawned. "I should get you back home. We both need our sleep. Those lab results might be ready tomorrow. Maybe Lisa changed her mind and decided to help you out, after all."

Laura didn't appear convinced. "Maybe. I have some work to get done, too."

He rose and held out his hand. She slid her hand on his and he helped her up. Neither released their hold. Rusty wrapped his fingers around her slender, soft hand. As they walked back to the car, she stepped closer to him, their bare arms touching.

Rusty wasn't sure what to make of his growing feelings. One thing he knew—he didn't want to take advantage of her. They both had raw emotions, and with the world against them thanks to Travis Calloway, it only made sense for them to move toward each other.

The only fair and right thing to do was to wait until everything had calmed down. Then they would know whether or not they had something they both wanted to pursue.

He remotely unlocked the car and opened Laura's door. The smell of Dim Sum escaped. Both coughed and stepped back.

Laura stepped away. "We should have refrigerated that."

Rusty opened all four doors to air out the car. "I forgot it was in there. We'd better throw it out after sitting in the hot car."

She went to the trunk. "There's a garbage can over there."

They unloaded the food into the trash.

"Now do you want me to help pay for the meal?" she teased.

He shook his head. "I can take you out for lunch tomorrow to make up for not being able to warm that up."

"You mean I can take *you* out."

"I'm a gentleman. I can't let you pay."

"And I'm strong twenty-first century woman. I insist on paying my share." She gave him a playful shove.

Rusty chuckled. "We'll see."

He helped her into the car and then unrolled all the windows once it was on.

"Sorry about the car." Laura coughed.

"It'll be fine. Besides, it's not mine, remember?"

"I hope you can get the stench out before you return it. I'd hate for them to charge you."

"I'm not worried about it." He pulled out of the parking lot and headed for their neighborhood. They talked about the sunset off and on until he pulled up to the sidewalk in between the two houses.

Laura unbuckled and turned to him. "I had a really great time."

"Me, too. It was good to get my mind off everything for a while."

"The company wasn't so bad, either." Laura took his hand and squeezed.

Rusty found himself squeezing back. "No, it definitely wasn't." He stared into her eyes for a few moments before clearing his throat. "I should get inside. See how everyone's faring in there. Chris wasn't in a good mood when I left."

She rolled her eyes. "Why doesn't that surprise me?"

"I feel bad for those kids."

Laura frowned. "Yeah, me, too. Tell them I said hi and that they can stop by anytime. That goes for you, as well."

"I'll keep that in mind." He got out and opened the door for her.

"Do you want me to get some air fresheners or something? I'm sure I have something to neutralize the odor."

"Nah. I can just leave the windows open."

Her eyes widened. "This is a safe neighborhood, but not that safe. You'd be asking for someone to break in."

"Really?" he asked, surprised. "Guess I don't think much about that living where I do. Nobody disturbs anything, ever."

"You live in the middle of the woods?"

"Something like that. Let me walk you to the door."

A slow smile spread across her face. "So chivalrous."

He arched a brow. "Do you find that odd?"

"Actually, I do. But I like it." She looped her arm through his and they walked up the driveway. After she unlocked the door, she turned to him and leaned close.

Rusty's heart leaped into his throat. He was about to back away when she gave him a quick peck on the cheek. "Thanks for restoring my faith in humanity."

His mouth gaped.

"No, really, you have. Between the way people act around here and some other things in my life... I really had given up on people. But now I have hope."

He rested his palm on her arm. "I'm really sorry anyone has mistreated you. You don't deserve it."

She held his gaze. "Tell me you're for real."

Rusty's pulse pounded in his ears. "I am."

Laura gave him a kiss on the other cheek and went inside. "Goodnight, Rusty." The door closed.

"Goodnight," he whispered. He stared at the door for a moment, regaining his bearings. She seemed as vulnerable as he felt.

He turned around and meandered back to the car. It still reeked of overheated food. He might have to take Laura up on her offer for air fresheners the next day. In the meantime, he needed to get his briefcase out of the trunk before it and all the paperwork ended up smelling like old Dim Sum.

He got it out and locked the car. Inside, Kaylie and Brady were watching a movie.

"Hi, Uncle Rusty." Brady threw some popcorn into the air and caught about half of it in his mouth.

"Nice." Kaylie threw a handful at him. She turned to Rusty. "Hi. Dad's already asleep. He said we could stay up."

"Mind if I join you?"

"Sure." She scooted over to give him some room.

He set the briefcase next to the couch and sat between the kids.

"Popcorn?" Brady held his bowl in front of Rusty.

Rusty had seen some kernels fall from his nephew's mouth into the bowl. He hesitated, but didn't want to offend the kid. "Thanks." He grabbed a handful and stuck them in his mouth. "What's this movie?"

Kaylie paused it, and they both explained the plot, speaking over each other.

Rusty laughed. "I think I get it."

She started the movie again and they all watched together, laughing and teasing each other. If he didn't know better, he would have never guessed they were all dealing with such high levels of grief. He was glad he had flown out. It was something they'd all needed—Laura included.

The movie ended. Rusty stood and stretched.

"Wanna watch another?" Brady widened his eyes, begging.

"Oh, leave him alone," Kaylie said. "Don't give him your puppy eyes."

Brady stuck his tongue out at her. "We're having fun."

"Indeed we are," Rusty agreed. "But I didn't get much sleep last night—or much of a nap. I'd better hit the hay before I end up falling asleep on the couch and drooling all over one of you."

"Ew." Kaylie wrinkled her nose.

Brady giggled.

"'Night, kids. Make sure you get some sleep."

"We will." Kaylie smiled.

"Speak for yourself." Brady shoved her.

It was good to see them acting like typical siblings. Not overtired, mourning kids who needed a break.

He picked up the briefcase and went to the bedroom. Although the briefcase was locked, he still didn't feel good about having it in the house. Not after the diary went missing. He set it on the bed and then pulled the dresser in front of the door. No one would be able to sneak in now.

Rusty pulled back the covers and fell asleep as his head hit the pillow.

Sounds of glass shattering woke him.

Nineteen

RUSTY JUMPED OUT of bed and ran to the window. A car alarm wailed. His rental car was partially blocked from view by a maple tree. But he could see broken glass shining from the ground next to it. His heart sank and his pulse raced.

The alarm continued to shriek, undoubtedly waking everyone within earshot. He spun around and ran for the door. He stubbed his toe on the dresser. Right. He'd moved it to protect the briefcase.

Holding in a curse, he shook his foot to work out the sting. Then he pushed the dresser back into place.

The briefcase. He double-checked the lock and then slid it under his luggage, hoping no one would find it and try to open it. At least it didn't smell like rank Chinese food anymore.

His car alarm continued to scream. Where had he put the keys?

Rusty checked the nightstand. Not there. He wouldn't have been so stupid as to leave them out. But where had he put them? He checked his pocket and felt them.

Relief rushed through him. He pulled out the key chain. The sobriety chip fell to the ground.

A fresh wave of guilt washed through him. He wouldn't need that anymore. Once he got home, he would have to start over, and it would take a long time to get back to where he had been.

Footsteps sounded in the hall, followed by Chris grumbling about the idiot who needed to turn off his blasted car alarm.

Rusty went over to the window, aimed the key chain toward the car, and clicked the button. The noise stopped. He spun around and hurried outside. The front door was already open. Chris stood on the steps, looking out. Rusty passed him, the rocky cement digging into his bare soles, and he ran down to his car, stopping in the grass.

From his angle, it looked like all the windows had been smashed. The doors were dented up. He moved closer and the overhead streetlight flickered on. Broken glass shone all over the sidewalk. Each window except the back one was smashed.

Hushed conversation sounded not far away. Neighbors stood together, whispering. He wanted to scream at them.

"Oh my gosh," came Laura's voice from the shadows. "Are you okay?" She appeared at his side.

"I am, but the car's not."

She stopped next to him and gasped. "Who did this?"

He glanced around at the whispering neighbors. "Could've been anyone. Think someone's sending a message?"

Laura's eyes widened. "Have you called the police?"

Chris swore behind them and a door slammed.

"Someone's tired of seeing the police," Laura said.

Rusty tried to pull himself out of the shock. "I haven't called them. My phone's inside."

She handed him hers.

"Thanks." He called 9-1-1, reported the vandalism, and handed her the phone. "They're on their way."

Laura put it in her bathrobe pocket. "Do you need anything?"

"Other than for people to leave me alone? Or a full night's sleep?"

"Exactly." She frowned.

"I can't think of anything."

"The car's insured, isn't it?"

"Yes, I paid for extra coverage."

"Good." She stepped closer and examined the mess. "I just can't believe anyone would do this."

"Maybe I should have left the windows open after all." He tried to smile at his weak attempt at a joke.

"Not funny."

Sirens sounded in the distance.

Rusty felt a headache coming on. He rubbed his temples.

"It'll be okay." She put a hand on his arm.

"Will it?" he snapped. "Sorry. I know none of this is your fault."

"And I know how stressed you are."

The sirens grew louder, and red and blue lights lit up the street. A police cruiser pulled into the driveway.

"This is going to be fun," he muttered.

"I'll stay here with you if you want," Laura said.

He nodded and then turned to the officers. They introduced themselves, and then one looked around the car while the other took Rusty's statement.

"You didn't see anyone?" he asked.

"Nothing. The noise woke me, but by the time I got to the window, whoever did this was gone. But maybe someone else saw something." He gestured around at all the gawkers.

The officer waved his partner over. "We'll have to talk to the neighbors. Someone might have seen something, or maybe a home security managed to get something. A perpetrator running away, or maybe even in the act."

"Thank you," Rusty said.

He handed Rusty a card. "If you think of anything else, call us. Be sure to call your insurance tomorrow."

"Will do." He turned to the mess. "Guess I'd better clean it up."

"I've got a broom in my garage," Laura said. "I'll grab it."

"And I better get my shoes before I get more than a stubbed toe." Rusty spun around and headed for the house. He stepped on a sharp rock in the middle of the yard. It dug into his flesh and broke the skin. He bit his tongue, not wanting to say anything unbecoming within Laura's earshot.

Limping, he made his way through the yard, up the steps, and into the house.

"Are you okay, Uncle Rusty?" asked Brady. Both kids stood at the top of the stairs.

"It's all going to be fine. You guys go back to bed."

"Someone broke into your car?" Kaylie asked.

"Yeah, but they're gone now. Everything's fine."

Neither appeared convinced.

"I'm serious. Get some sleep."

Kaylie grumbled, but turned around. She grabbed Brady's arm and pulled him down the hall. Rusty made his way to the bathroom and cleaned his foot. The wound didn't look nearly as bad as it felt. His stubbed toe, on the other hand, was swollen and throbbing.

He went into his room and slid on socks and shoes. By the time he got outside, Laura was already sweeping.

"You don't have to do that."

"Sure I do. It's not like anyone is offering to help." She glared at a cluster of neighbors barely twenty feet away. None of them responded.

Rusty reached for the broom. "Let me do that."

She shook her head. "Take care of the car. I'm sure there are shards inside. Who knows what other damage?"

He shrugged, too tired to argue, and then stuck his hand inside and found the switch to unlock the doors. Glass fell around his feet as he opened the door.

"Wonderful." He reached in and swept his hands across the seat, careful not to cut himself as he guided more shattered glass outside. The bottom of his foot throbbed, reminding him of the rock that had cut him. He didn't want to add his hand to the list of injuries, so he opened the glove compartment and pulled out some papers. He used those to get the rest of the glass from the seats.

By the time he and Laura were done with the mess, most of the neighbors had disappeared.

"If you want, I can help you vacuum tomorrow." Laura leaned against the broom.

"You certainly don't have to."

She chuckled. "I know. That's why I'm offering."

Rusty yawned. "I'm going to call the rental agency in the morning. They might take care of that."

"Yeah, but you don't want to risk sitting on a shard. We should at least vacuum the front seats before we return it."

"We?"

"Someone has to drive you back." She smiled.

"Unless I rent another one."

"Gotcha. Well, let me know what you need in the morning. I'm going to get some more sleep."

"Me, too. Thanks for everything."

"It's nothing." She spun around and headed into her garage with the broom.

She was something else. He was sure glad to have met her. Once her garage door closed, he looked over the car one more time and went inside. Tomorrow would be a long day, and he was already going off too little sleep and too much stress.

Inside, he locked the deadbolt and headed upstairs. Chris stepped out of the kitchen. "What was that all about?"

"The break-in?" Rusty asked.

"No, the lunar eclipse. Yes, the break-in."

Rusty bit back a sarcastic comment. "No idea."

"I don't like it."

"Me, neither. You'd think with a neighborhood watch like you guys have, that wouldn't have happened."

Chris folded his arms. "No. I mean I don't like what you're bringing to our home."

"Excuse me?"

"We've never had anything like that in this neighborhood until you showed up."

"So, you're blaming me for this?"

Chris narrowed his eyes. "Yeah. It was your car. You've brought this in."

"How, exactly? I flew from almost across the country, put my own life on hold, and have been taking care of your family. I've been dealing with the loss of Mandy, also, through all of this."

"You haven't seen her in years! What, like twenty?"

Rusty furrowed his brows. "She's my sister, and nothing can change that. Those kids are my niece and nephew."

"Then where were you all those years?"

"Look," Rusty said and straightened his back. "We're all tired and under stress. Let's talk about this in the morning when we're feeling better."

"I have a better idea. How about instead of that, in the morning, you pack your stuff and get out of here? Stay away from me and my kids. Take the trouble you brought with you."

Kaylie appeared in the hall. "Dad! No."

Chris didn't even acknowledge her. "I'm serious."

"Who's going to watch the kids all day?"

"They can watch themselves! Kaylie's almost fourteen. Thank you for your help, and if you'd like me to pay you back, I will."

Rusty shook his head. "Forget it."

"I don't want you thinking we owe you anything."

"You don't. You're family. Let me be here for my niece and nephew."

"Just leave us alone. We don't need anything from you. I want you gone by the time I get back from work tomorrow. Then I never want to see you again."

"You can't keep me from them."

"Watch me." Chris turned and stormed down the hall.

"Dad!" Kaylie's voice wavered. "Don't do this."

He turned and faced her. "I'm responsible for you two. It's my call, and I want him out of our lives."

"But—"

"No more. Go back to bed."

She turned to Rusty, tears shining in her eyes. "Don't let him do this."

"I'm sorry."

Kaylie turned to Chris. "I hate you! All of this is your fault, you know."

Chris spun around and stepped closer to her, stopping only about an inch from her face. "Never say any of that ever again. Do you hear me?"

"Or what?" Kaylie demanded.

"Or you'll regret it. That's what."

"What will you do to me?"

"Just do what I say!" He punched the wall next to her head. His fist went through and drywall flew in all directions.

Kaylie turned to Rusty, fear in her wide eyes. Then she looked at Chris. "I really do hate you." She spun around, went into her room, and slammed the door.

"What are you looking at?" Chris demanded. He went into his own room and slammed the door. It clicked as he locked it.

Rusty went into the guest room. He shoved the dresser back in front of the door and sat on the bed, his mind reeling.

How could he leave those kids with someone so temperamental? Mandy sure wouldn't want to, and he wouldn't be able to live with himself if something happened.

At least he had until the next evening to figure something out. He could talk with the kids and see if they felt safe. If so, maybe getting a hotel would be for the best. No reason to further ignite Chris's anger. Rusty could still visit the kids while he was at work. He'd just have to be careful none of the neighbors saw him and reported back to Chris.

He climbed under the covers and rested his head on the pillow, closing his eyes. Thoughts continued to race, despite his best efforts to shut them up. His mind took him back to the restaurant and the two glasses of wine.

Guilt punched him in the throat. What had he done? Why had he given into the temptation? Now he would have to start all over, and not only that, but go back to his meeting and admit to failure.

Twenty

~

T RAVIS HIT SNOOZE and pulled the pillow over his head. He'd spent half the night up, wooing the latest prospective client. It had been worth it in the end because Bryan Worthington had signed the contract. But it had been almost two in the morning, and by the time he got home, Angeline was already asleep.

She'd woken when he climbed into bed, and she was pissed. He never should have promised to have dinner with her that night. Not when he knew he had a meeting that could potentially go long.

His alarm went off again.

Angeline pulled the pillow off his face and glared at him. "Would you just turn that thing off?"

"I'm tired," he snapped.

"I can't imagine why." She shoved the pillow back in his face.

Travis sat up and picked up his phone. He let the alarm continue.

"Why do you always have to turn that so loud?"

"So I can hear it."

"My grandmother in Paris can hear it. And she's deaf."

Travis shook his head and silenced his phone, turning off the alarm. "I got the deal last night."

"Was it worth it?"

"Of course."

Angeline rolled her eyes. "It always is."

"I didn't hear you complaining when we signed the papers for the bungalow in Hawaii."

"Are we actually going to be there together?"

"Of course. What kind of question is that?" he asked.

"We never see each other."

"What's right now?"

"Ugh. You're impossible." She spun around, threw herself down, and pulled the covers over her.

"Women," Travis mumbled. "Can't live with 'em…"

"I heard that."

"And I don't care." He threw his legs over the edge of the super-king bed and stormed over to his dresser. He picked out his dress shirt and slacks, slamming each drawer along the way.

"Real mature."

He spun around. "Would you shut up? I didn't do anything wrong."

"No, you just broke a promise. Again."

Travis put the clothes over his desk chair and stomped over to her side of the bed. "What's your problem?"

"You are. But that isn't going to change, is it? Your real wife is the business, and I'm just the mistress. Actually, no. I'm not even that, am I? If you had one, you'd see her more than me."

"I don't have time for this."

"That's hardly news."

He took a deep breath. "What do you want? A new car? A diamond necklace? What?"

"I don't need another thing. We have more than I know what to do with that. You should know by now what I want."

Travis furrowed his brows. "What?"

"You!"

"I'm so sick of this argument."

"Then do something to change it." She sat up and glared at him.

"Or you could try being grateful for everything I do. No wife in the town has nicer things than you. Not even Camille—I make sure of that."

Angeline shook her head and swiped a blonde curl from her face. "You don't get it."

"No. You're the one who doesn't get it, and I'm sick and tired of the complaints. Do you know how many women would cut off their right arm to be in your shoes?"

"Their right arm, huh? That's pretty specific."

"Like I said, I don't have time for this." He spun around to grab his clothes.

"You mean you don't have time for me. Your wife. The woman you once couldn't live without."

"My mistake." He grabbed his clothes and stormed into the bathroom. Just before closing the door, he could hear her sobs. Again. He swore under his breath.

How had his parents managed to have such a happy marriage when Dad had spent so much time at work? Travis couldn't remember a single argument between the two of them. Unless they'd fought behind closed doors, too. Was that where he'd subconsciously learned to keep their fights?

It didn't matter. He just needed to shower and get to the office. There was no time for breakfast, so he'd have to ask one of the assistants to find him something. Not that he was in any mood to eat, anyway. Angeline had made sure of that.

Travis set the water as hot as he could stand it and got in, fuming about Angeline. Didn't she know he wanted to spend more time with her? He just couldn't afford the time now—and that was a big distinction. Later, he would have the time. But now he needed to build the clientele. Sure, he had regular ones, but not enough.

Would it ever be enough?

He shook that thought out of his head. He just needed a few more years, and then he could give her what she wanted—including the babies. But now she needed to be patient and wait. To just enjoy the fine things he'd provided for her.

Travis rinsed off and then grabbed the towel.

"Your phone keeps ringing," Angeline said through the door.

"It's on silent. How would you know? Unless you've been watching it."

"The damn thing keeps vibrating."

"So sorry to disturb your slumber." He tightened the salmon-colored towel around his waist before going back into the room.

Angeline handed him the phone. Sure enough, five missed calls.

He called Wes. "What's so urgent? I'm on my way."

"Well, you need to call Juan Fields. He's about to have a conniption fit."

"Fields?" Travis asked. "What does he want? We didn't send him anything."

"No, but he says someone else sent in something of yours."

Blood drained from his face. Travis swore. He knew exactly what that meant. Clearly, he hadn't made himself clear to Mandy's brother the other night. "Thanks for the heads up, Wes." Travis ended the call.

"What's going on?" Angeline asked, the anger mostly gone from her face.

"Just something at work. Don't worry about it." He spun around and stormed into the bathroom. This was the last thing he needed. He grumbled as he got dressed and shaved.

Wes would help him figure out a way to make the problem go away. He took a deep breath and went back into the bedroom.

"Travis, I—"

"Look, Angeline." He took a deep breath, swallowing his pride. "Just know that I want to spend time with you. I do. If I can get away tonight, we'll have dinner, okay? But please—please—don't have a fit if I can't make it happen. Things come up in this business. It doesn't mean you're not important."

"You call this a—?" She bit her lip. "Okay. I understand. Just let me know if you can make it."

"Thank you." He went over to her, kissed the top of her head, and went to the door.

Just as he turned the handle, Angeline spoke again. "I love you, Travis."

He spun around, feeling his anger toward her melt away. This had to be why Dad had always told him it was best to tell the woman you love what she wants to hear.

Travis went back over to the bed and brushed his lips across hers. "And I love you. I'll do my best to have dinner with you tonight. I promise."

She smiled, barely.

He ran his fingers through her hair. "Wear the black dress again," he whispered.

"Call me before you leave."

"I will."

Travis hurried downstairs. One of the household servants stopped him. "Would you like me to drive you to work, sir?"

And have him overhear Travis's conversation with Juan Fields? "Not today, Andrew. Why don't you prepare breakfast in bed for Angeline?"

"Yes, sir. Good day." He spun around and headed for the kitchen.

Travis double-checked he had everything he needed, hurried to the garage, and got in a car. He opened the garage door with the remote and found Juan's number in his contact list.

"Hello, Travis." Juan's tone didn't tell him anything.

"What's going on? Wes said you have some news." Travis would wait before reacting. He pulled out of the garage, pushed the button to close the door, and quickly checked for cars before pulling onto the private road.

"Someone submitted your DNA, sir. I ran it and came up with you."

"Who requested it?" Travis demanded.

"I don't have that information. They just send me the samples, and I follow the orders."

Travis hit his steering wheel. "Find out, then."

"It's not that easy."

"Make it that easy."

"I could lose my job if I get caught."

"Fine. Forget it. I'm pretty sure I know who, anyway." Travis waved and forced a smile to the guard at the neighborhood gate.

He waved back and tapped on keyboard to open the gate for Travis.

"Thank you. I can tell you it's a paternity test."

Travis swore. It was definitely Mandy's brother. "And?"

"It's positive."

The words felt like a punch to the throat. Travis had always suspected Mandy was right. The pictures of the boy she'd shown him were nearly identical to ones of him as a child. Even so, he'd managed to convince himself it was nothing more than an unfortunate coincidence.

"Sir?" Juan asked.

"I'm thinking."

"Okay, but I need to get going. My break's almost over."

"Destroy the results."

"What? I can't do that. The computer system stores everything."

"It's already there?"

"I didn't know it would find you as a match. There are ways to quietly run a search, but I didn't know. I just thought it was another paternity test for the courts."

"It's not going to go that far," Travis muttered. "Thanks for the heads up, Juan. I appreciate it."

"Sorry I can't do more."

"Wait. What kind of DNA samples did they get?"

"Let me check." Papers rustled on Juan's end. "Saliva—not a very good sample—and a nail clipping."

Travis scowled and shook his head. That was probably the entire reason those two had agreed to serve at the parties. "Thanks, Juan. If you hear anything else, let me know. And keep this as quiet as possible."

"Will do. Just like last time. Take care." The call ended.

His stomach twisted in tight knots. He had a few options. Quietly give them some money in hopes it would be enough to drop it. But if Rusty was anything like his sister, it wouldn't be enough. Not even close.

Travis could lawyer up, and he would if it came to it. But he was sick of these accusations. And if Angeline ever found out about how many he'd had... But this thing with Mandy, it was long before Angeline entered the picture. Even so, he wanted to keep her completely out of it. And besides, he'd managed to keep his attorneys out of this one so far.

He'd hoped Mandy's death would be the end of his troubles. She'd sworn that her husband knew nothing about her accusations—that he suspected nothing. Unless that had been a lie to make Travis more cooperative.

His mind bounced back and forth the entire ride to the office. The less people that knew, the better. Even though everything was supposed to be confidential at the lab, people loved to gossip about the Calloways. Always had. And it would only take one loudmouth to ruin his reputation and marriage.

He would certainly take care of the situation, but the damage would be done. There was too much to lose. He had to figure out a way to stop this before word got out.

Twenty-One

~

RUSTY THREW ALL of his stuff into the luggage and double-checked the room. Only a few hours before Chris returned from work. He carried his stuff down to the door.

"Are you leaving already?"

He spun around. Kaylie stood at the top of the stairs with a huge scowl on her face.

"No, not yet. I want to hang out with you guys until your dad gets back."

"He's a jerk."

Rusty went up the stairs and patted her back. "He's doing what he thinks is best for you guys."

"I hate him."

"Don't," Rusty urged. "You're all going through the worst time of your life. You need to stick together. I'm sure he'll come around—just give him time."

Kaylie stepped back. "I'd rather kick him in the nads."

Rusty flinched. "Tell you what. Let's give him a few days to relax. I'll try to find a hotel with a pool, and while he's at work, I'll bring you kids."

Brady came down the hall. "Really? Awesome."

"You shouldn't have to leave." Kaylie folded her arms. "It's not fair."

Rusty frowned. "Nothing about any of this is fair. Your mom should still be here and—"

"I don't wanna talk about it," Kaylie said. "How long are you staying?"

"Until he gets back."

"Can we watch a movie again?" Brady asked. "That was so much fun last night."

"Sure." Rusty ruffled his hair. "You want to set it up while I make some popcorn?"

"Yeah." Brady ran over to the remote collection and grabbed one for the TV and plopped onto the couch.

Rusty turned to Kaylie. "You want to pour some chips into a bowl?"

She shrugged and rolled her eyes. "Whatever."

"Try not to be upset. He'll calm down. I'm sure of it."

"He's such a jerk. Everything has to be his way. You'd think now with Mom being gone, he'd figure it out. Start being nicer. But, nope. Still being a first class a—"

"Why don't you get some pop, too?"

"Fine." She spun around and went into the pantry, slamming things around.

Rusty's heart ached. He hated that she was in so much pain. They got everything ready in silence.

Once they were done, Rusty put his arm around her shoulders. "I promise to hang out with you guys while he's at work tomorrow."

"Can't you just tell Dad no? That you won't go anywhere. You're family, Uncle Rusty. We want you here—me and Brady. Stay for us." She pleaded with her eyes.

He took a deep breath. "I'm going to a hotel for you guys. He's angry and needs some space. Hopefully he'll cool off in the meantime. Do you feel safe with him?"

She shrugged.

"Do you? It wasn't right what he did last night."

"You mean hitting the wall by my head?"

Rusty nodded.

"He's a jerk, but he's not going to hurt us. I wish you'd stay."

"I really think giving him a little space is best for now. Call me anytime. You've got my number in your cell, right?"

She nodded but frowned.

"If he gets to be too much, let me know. I'll drop everything and head over."

"Really?" She played with a strand of hair. "You will?"

"I promise. And remember, Laura's next door."

"Okay. And you'd better find a hotel with a good pool. Like, a slide or something. No gross, little one."

"Cool pool. Got it. Anything else?"

Kaylie shook her head. "Nope. Hope you like *Star Wars*. Sounds like Brady picked one of them."

"I love them." He grabbed the bowls of popcorn. She picked up the chips and pop. They set everything on the coffee table. "Did you guys know your mom and I used to watch the original movies all the time?"

Brady's face lit up. "You did?"

Rusty handed him a bowl. "We used to have marathons all the time. We'd invite our friends over and watch all three in a row, and in between movies, we'd act out scenes."

He looked thoughtful. "I could totally see you guys doing that."

They all settled onto the couch and Brady started the movie.

"I hate Jar Jar," Kaylie said.

"Who doesn't?" Brady asked. "I heard he's actually a Sith."

"Shut up."

"There's a whole theory. You should look it up."

As they bickered back and forth, Rusty couldn't help smiling. How many times had he and Mandy argued about pop culture?

He tried to relax and just enjoy the time with the kids, but it felt like a big countdown. Every moment was closer to Chris getting back home. Once the movie started and the kids were throwing popcorn at each other, he managed to relax and have fun with them. He caught as many airborne kernels as he could and stuck them in his mouth.

After the movie ended, they cleaned up and Rusty put some dinner in the oven.

"Are you staying, after all?" Brady asked, his eyes wide. He suddenly looked so much like Mandy, it made Rusty's chest constrict. The way his eyes got big and hopeful just like Mandy's used to.

"Sorry, kiddo. Just trying to get everything ready so you guys can have the best night possible. If I'm gone and dinner's cooking, hopefully your dad will be in a better mood when he gets here."

Brady's face fell. "You're leaving now?"

Rusty checked the time. "Unfortunately. But I told your sister I'm going to find a hotel with a nice pool and bring you guys tomorrow while your dad's at work. Sound good?"

"I guess."

"It will be. I'll see you guys in the morning. Get some rest tonight." He gave them both hugs—neither wanted to let him go. It broke his heart. Chris was going to be home soon, so Rusty left quickly. As he closed the door, he could hear Kaylie grumbling about her dad.

Rusty groaned when he saw the car. He'd forgotten about the break-in. He put the luggage and his briefcase in the trunk. He'd need to return it to the rental place to get a new one.

Laura came over from her garden. "Are you moving?" she teased.

"I'm going to find a hotel and give Chris some space."

Her face fell. "A hotel? I have plenty of spare rooms. Save yourself some money and stay here."

He glanced up to the house and saw the kids watching him from a window. He'd promised them the pool. "I don't want to put you out."

"You wouldn't. I swear."

"I'll think about it. I need to get this back before the rental place closes for the night."

"Want me to go with you?"

He did, but that was the problem. "Thanks, but I need to get this returned and then find a hotel with a big pool that the kids will love."

Laura's eyes lit up. "I know great one not too far away. Let me lock the house, and I'll show you."

Rusty couldn't help feeling excited at the prospect of her going with. "All right."

"Hold on." She hurried into her house and returned with her purse a minute later.

He waved to the kids before climbing into the car and driving off. Hopefully his absence would make life easier for the kids when their dad got home.

When they got to the main road, traffic was bad.

"I should have taken care of this before rush hour," Rusty complained.

"You needed your rest," Laura said.

That much was true. "I just feel bad about leaving the kids. They really didn't want me to."

"Sucks that their dad is such a jerk. We may be able to save one of them from him, though."

Rusty turned to her. "Did you get the lab results back?"

"Not yet. I'm going to call in the morning if I don't hear back by then. What are you going to do if Travis is Brady's dad?"

"I have no idea. The last thing I want to do is separate them. They need each other."

Laura frowned. "Light's green."

He turned his attention back to the road and drove through the inter-section.

"Turn here. It's a shortcut when traffic's this bad."

Rusty took a sharp right and followed her directions, barely paying attention. What *would* they do if they found out Brady was Travis's? Would Chris even want to continue raising him?

Soon, he pulled into the parking lot and had to put it all out of his mind. By the time he had a new car, he also had a headache.

"Want me to drive?" Laura asked.

He rubbed his temples. "If you don't mind. I haven't seen that much paperwork since I purchased my house."

"No kidding," Laura said. "Let's hope this car stays in one piece."

"Does the hotel you were talking about have a private parking lot?"

"A parking garage. You have to have a hotel key card to get in."

Rusty sighed in relief. "Sounds like a secure place."

"It's one of the best around here."

"You've stayed there?" he asked.

"Yeah, when my house was being renovated. Oh, turn left up ahead."

He followed her directions for a few miles until he pulled in front of a tall, gorgeous building. It was going to cost a fortune, but with any luck, he would only be there a few days.

After checking in, he realized Laura still needed to get home. "I should get you home. You're probably starving. It's past dinnertime."

"We can order in. They also have a couple wonderful restaurants—my treat this time."

"If you insist." He smiled, glad to have her company a little longer. He looked around the beautiful lobby. "Where are the restaurants?"

"There's a buffet down to the left. We'll overeat for sure. The food is divine. Down the other way is a French restaurant."

"Where do you want to eat?" he asked.

"Depends." Her eyes sparkled. "Do you want to go for a dip after?"

He arched a brow. "You want to go for a swim? We don't even have suits."

"I stuck one in my handbag." She held up her small purse, which had to contain an even smaller swimsuit.

Rusty's heart raced. "I don't have one."

"There's a gift shop down the way." She tilted her head to the left. "They have plenty."

He swallowed. "Let's try the buffet and see how we feel after."

She smiled. "Sure. Sounds like a plan."

They made their way to the buffet, which had such a heavenly array of scents. It made Rusty's mouth water.

Laura insisted on paying and then grabbed a plate. "Where do you want to start?"

"I'm not sure." He stared at the rows of food. "I think I'll wander and see what strikes me first."

"Good plan. I think I see lobster. That's where I'm going to start."

"Okay. Find you in a few minutes." They parted ways and Rusty walked along, finally choosing steak and vegetables. He found Laura, and as they made their way to a table, his phone rang. With the heavily-loaded plate, he couldn't balance that and the phone.

Laura talked about the food as they settled into their chairs and started eating. He knew he should check to see who had called, but with his stomach rumbling as it was, he wanted to eat first. There was no way he could handle anything as famished as he was, anyway.

He emptied the plate quickly, barely taking the time to savor the tasty food. Just as he picked up his water, the phone rang again.

"I'd better get that. What if it's the kids?"

Laura nodded, her mouth full of food.

Rusty pulled out the phone and accepted the call. "Andy? Is everything okay? I told you only to call if there's an emergency."

"Sorry, boss, but there is."

"What's wrong? Did one of the trucks get into an accident?"

"No, they're fine."

Rusty sighed in relief.

"But I just received word that your house is on fire."

He nearly dropped the phone. "My house?"

"The fire department's there now. Someone saw, and called here, knowing you own the place."

Rusty's heart sank. "I'll catch the next plane."

"If you need a place to stay—"

"I won't. Talk to you soon." Rusty ended the call.

"What's wrong?" Laura asked, her eyes wide.

"My house is on fire." His voice sounded like someone else.

"What?" she exclaimed.

"I need to get back home." He put his face in his hands, trying to think straight. "I'll need to return the rental car... can you drive me to the airport?"

"Whatever you need."

He looked up at her. "Can you check on the kids when Chris is at work? I promised them a swim."

"I'll take them swimming."

Rusty stared at her. "How could this have happened?"

His phone alerted him of a text. It was from a blocked number.

I warned you to leave well enough alone.

Twenty-Two

R USTY PAID THE lot attendant and headed for his pickup truck. His stomach had been churning acid since he'd heard about the fire. In all the time it had taken to return his rental car, book a flight, and then sit through it, he'd done nothing but worry.

Had his whole house burned down? Could it have been a small outdoor fire? Or had he lost everything? All pictures and memories of his family? His heart constricted. What if the only reminders of them he had were the few items in his office at work?

He'd thought through everything. At the very least, he was sure he'd stored all his digital pictures somewhere online. It was just a matter of figuring out where. He couldn't think straight. In a way, it felt like losing his family all over again—except that he didn't know if he had lost their stuff.

If anything remained, he promised himself to take pictures of everything to at least have those. The boys' artwork. Lani's blankets and scarves—and everything else she'd crocheted. She'd been so talented, she had sold a lot online. But she had also been humble. She hadn't opened the shop until her friends convinced her she would be doing the world a service.

Rusty found his truck and opened the door. It was stuffy from having sat in the warm sun all the time he'd been away. He started the engine and opened the windows. Once he got on the freeway, enough air would get in to make it breathable. He didn't have time to wait.

He slid on his bluetooth earphone and called Andy.

"Hey, boss. Are you in town?"

"Yes. Do you know the extent of the damage?" Rusty asked.

"No one will tell me anything. I tried."

"I appreciate that."

"Like I said, if you need a place to stay—"

"I won't. Go home, okay? It's getting late." Rusty went around a slow sedan.

"My shift isn't over."

"Okay. Thanks."

"My offer stands."

"I'll keep that in mind. See you tomorrow."

"Goodnight."

Rusty ended the call, eager to get home. There were too many traffic lights and slow drivers. It would take forever to get home. He went around another slow vehicle.

"Relax," he told himself. It wasn't like he would be able to undo any of the damage by getting home faster. In all likelihood, the fire department was long gone, having already put out the blaze. Whatever damage was done—or not done—was already set in stone.

Images of charred remains plagued him. He thought of all the precious things possibly lost. Lani's jewelry. Parker's favorite teddy bear. Tommy's cherished train set. The...

Tears blurred Rusty's vision. He wiped them away. No matter what happened, his memories were there. Nobody could take those from him. It didn't matter what shape the house was in. Things were just things, anyway. He'd already lost what was most important—them.

That was why the things were so important. Those were all he had left of them now.

If he even still had them.

He cleared his throat and focused on the road.

"Stop thinking," he ordered himself. Not that it mattered. Images of his fears shot through Rusty's mind, despite his best efforts.

Finally, he reached his turn. It wouldn't be much longer until he finally saw the extent of what was lost.

The air smelled of smoke. And not from a campfire or a safe fireplace. The stench made his stomach lurch. It was the odor of his home. The memories he held so dear.

A lump formed in his throat. The moment of truth was coming. He stopped and flicked the blinker on. All he could see was trees and bushes. Soon, his house—or what was left of it—would finally be visible.

His heart raced as he turned. It felt like a mile-long move, but in all actuality, only took a moment. He turned into his driveway and hit the brakes, jolting to a stop.

Rusty stared at his home as more tears blurred his vision. Relief washed through him. His house still stood, but a hundred feet away, his unattached garage was almost completely destroyed. It mostly held random things from his towing business. If he thought he could fix one of the trucks himself, he brought it there. Or if they didn't have room for something in the office or the storage areas, it went there.

It was a catch-all of sorts that badly needed to be organized. Well, not anymore. The fire had taken care of that. The garage was just his work stuff. It could all be replaced. But all of his family's stuff would still be there. Safe.

He gave way to the tears and rested his head on the steering wheel. He shook. Their memories were still intact. His sobs washed away all the unfounded fears. Once there was nothing more left in him, he sat up and glanced over the house again. It was still in perfect shape.

Rusty cut the engine and ran to where the garage door had been. Wrapped around what was left of the doorframe was some yellow tape. *Police* tape? A notice was posted next to it.

He grabbed the note, shone a flashlight on it, and read the small print.

They wanted him to call the station.

Clearly, they had to have suspected arson. Why else would the cops be involved?

He swore. They were stomping on his last frayed nerve.

Rusty considered walking around to look at the damage, anyway. Would he really be breaking the law by entering his own property? He shone the flashlight, barely able to see anything. From what he could tell, everything was ruined. At least it was insured.

And better than that, it was completely set apart from the house. No connecting wires or anything like that. Any melted wire would result in the power being shut off in the house if they were connected.

He glanced over at the house, noticing his porch light still on. He was tempted to just go inside and take a load off. But he couldn't put off the cops.

Rusty grumbled and called the number on the paper. He explained who he was, and the lady on the other end told him he needed to go to the station. He told her he'd be right down.

The sooner he got this over with, the sooner he could get inside and wrap his arms around his family's things.

Rusty walked back to his truck, the feeling of defeat squeezing him. He picked up a rock the size of his fist and squeezed. He narrowed his eyes, staring at the charred remains of his garage.

How *dare* someone do this to him? Stupid arsonist.

He squeezed the rock tighter, a couple sharp edges digging into his flesh. He aimed the rock at the rubble, imagining Travis Calloway's face. That man had the means to make this happen from clear across the country. Rusty pulled his shoulder back, aiming at the charred mess. His arm released and moved forward.

At the last moment, he turned his body and threw the rock into the woods. He heard the sound of it hitting a tree and then bouncing into another, until all went silent. He picked up another rock and chucked it. Then another and another.

Finally, he climbed back into his pickup and headed for the station.

Halfway there, his phone rang. It was Andy, probably wanting to know how badly burned the house was. Rusty ignored the call. He was in no mood to talk to anyone. The only reason he was going to speak to the officers was because he didn't want to commit a crime by entering his own building.

Once he reached the police station, he again explained who he was. The officer behind the desk took him to a room with a long table and what had to be a two-way mirror.

"Is this going to take long?"

"No idea. Just wait, please."

Rusty frowned, but didn't reply. This was the icing on the cake of a horrible week. He wanted to ask what else could go wrong, but didn't dare. Things could always get worse. Always.

After about twenty minutes—which felt like hours—the door finally opened. A tall man with dark hair and dark circles under his eyes came in.

"Rusty Caldwell?"

Rusty nodded.

The man sat across from him. "Detective Fleshman. I'm sorry about your house."

Rusty nodded again. He was going to say as little as possible. Who knew what kind of incriminating evidence had been planted? He might need to lawyer up before the night was over.

Fleshman pulled out an iPad and slid his finger across the screen. "Where were you when this happened?"

"Across the country."

"Oh?" Fleshman arched a brow. "What were you doing there?"

Rusty flinched. "Helping my dead sister's family."

The detective's eyes widened. "Your sister just died?"

"It's been one hell of a week."

"Sounds like it. I hate to add to it, but the fire department believes your garage fire was no accident."

Rusty rubbed his temples. "Arson."

"They haven't ruled it yet, but it looks that way. There will need to be a full investigation."

Wonderful. "What do you need from me?"

"I have some questions for you."

"Then I can go home?"

Fleshman slid his finger around the screen again. "You can return as long as you stay away from the garage."

"No problem."

The detective looked up from the tablet. "Do you know anyone who would have reason to do this?"

Aside from his brother-in-law or the CEO of Clockworks? Rusty shook his head. If either of them had cops knocking on their door about this, they might decide to up the game. Torch his house. Hit his business, maybe. Or worse, go after the kids or Laura.

Detective Fleshman asked a long list of questions, tiring Rusty out all the more.

"Just one more." Fleshman held Rusty's gaze. "You can't think of anyone who would have reason to do this?"

"You already asked me that."

"I'm asking again."

Rusty sighed. "Come to think of it, I did receive a couple semi-threatening texts."

The detective titled his head. "Did you happen to save them?"

"I think so." Rusty pulled out his phone and scrolled through the texts. He showed Fleshman the latest one. The detective took a picture of it with the iPad. Rusty scrolled through until he found the first one. The one Laura had also received. Fleshman took a picture of that one, too.

"No phone calls?"

Rusty shook his head. "Just the anonymous texts."

"Do you know what they mean? They're definitely threatening. What you're supposed to stay away from?"

"Got me." Rusty shrugged. "I figured it was a wrong number."

The detective studied his tablet's screen. "The last one was sent after the fire."

"I got it driving home."

"We'll contact your carrier and see if we can find out the source of them."

"Can I go home now?" Rusty asked.

Fleshman slid his finger around the screen again. "Looks like it. Remember, don't touch anything near the fire. It's still an active investigation."

"As long as I can sleep in my own bed."

"Shouldn't be a problem. The damage was contained to the garage from what I have here. It was far enough away from the house that it wasn't affected." The detective got up and opened the door. "Have a good night."

Rusty snorted. "Right. You, too."

The drive home went by in a blur. Could Travis or Chris really be behind the arson? He didn't have any other enemies. Rusty had always made friends everywhere he went—except for the drunks that didn't want to be towed. He'd been sworn at and even assaulted, but nothing that ever resulted in a real issue. Many times, he even received a thanks or an apology the following day.

By the time he pulled into his driveway again, his body ached. He couldn't wait to climb into his own bed and fall asleep.

But first, he needed to get home. He grabbed his luggage and the new locking briefcase, set the truck alarm, and headed for his front door. The air inside had a slight smelled of smoke. There were some air filters somewhere. He would need to find them and then plug them all in.

He'd been lucky, and he knew it.

Rusty turned around and headed for his room. Everything seemed to be in its place, each item right where he'd left it. Pictures hung on the walls as if nothing was wrong. Images of a happy family. If he didn't know better, he'd think that happy family was sleeping within these very walls.

At least no one had bothered his home. Chills ran through him. That probably meant this was only a warning.

Twenty-Three

~

*B*ANG! *CRACK!*
Rusty sat up, pushing the covers away. He reached for his nightstand, opened the top drawer, and pulled out the revolver.

Scratch! Bang!

Someone was just outside his room, hitting the wall. He scrambled out of bed and readied the gun. It could very well be the same person who had destroyed his garage. He would take them out. Self defense. No one would question it for a moment.

He crept to the window and lifted a blind just slightly.

Nothing.

Crack!

Whoever it was, he was right underneath the window. Rusty stood on his toes and peered down as far as he could. All he could see was brown. It looked like hair.

He braced himself and prepared his voice to be as deep and loud as possible.

"Get out of here!"

The person below him scrambled to his feet and roared. The fur-covered body turned and faced Rusty, making eye contact. It took him a moment to realize it was a bear. Not a person.

Rusty's heart pounded like a jackhammer, nearly bursting through his chest. The bear hurried away. Rusty leaned against the wall and slid to the floor, trying to catch his breath. He released his hold on the revolver and set it on the carpet next to him.

"Stupid bear," he muttered and gasped for air. He should have known better. Wildlife came up to the house all the time. That was one reason

161

they had built such a tall, strong fence around the kids' play area out back.

Once his heart and breathing had returned to normal, Rusty got up and returned the weapon to its place. He sat down on the bed and allowed his body to go limp. It was still early, but there was no way he would fall back to sleep after that. He leaned back, his head landing on the soft comforter. The one Lani had picked out just before…

Rusty ran his fingers through his hair. The familiar curls were already beginning to return from the too-short cut. He reached for the items he'd brought to bed with him the night before. Parker's favorite brown teddy bear—kind of ironic. Tommy's train plushy that he'd gone to bed with every night. The last blanket Lani had made.

He held them close and took in the scents. They still smelled like his loved ones—barely. It was a miracle the smells had held on so long. Or maybe it was just his imagination at this point. It had been so many years. The boys had never even known they'd had cousins on Rusty's side.

His chest tightened. He pushed the items aside and sat up.

"I'm not going there today—not getting upset." He shook his head. Today would be all about taking pictures of everything that had belonged to Lani and the boys. Everything. If it took him all day, he'd make sure that no matter what happened to all the stuff, he would at least have pictures uploaded somewhere safe.

Rusty's stomach growled. He'd start after a quick breakfast. Then he'd be set for the task. He opened the fridge. Moldy strawberries sat in a bowl on top. What else had gone bad? He didn't want to know. Probably more in the drawers.

He grabbed the bowl and dumped the fruit into the garbage. Then he went into the freezer and found some breakfast burritos he'd frozen a while back.

He put them on a plate and into the microwave. Then he started a pot of coffee and wandered down the hall to use the bathroom. He stopped in front of a picture of him and Lani. Her gorgeous, perfect smile. Her head was turned just slightly, looking at Rusty. An adoring expression covered her face.

Guilt punched him in the gut.

What had he been thinking, allowing himself to have feelings for

Laura? He'd promised to love Lani for the rest of his life. Well, technically until death do them part. He frowned. Never had he been able to imagine himself growing old with anyone else. He hadn't wanted to. It was Lani or nothing.

Laura's face popped to mind. Or Laura?

How could he even think that? No.

Rusty gazed into Lani's eyes in the picture. He was taken back to a conversation they'd had years earlier. Before they'd even talked about having kids. They'd given each other their blessings to move on if they died.

"But you didn't mean it, did you?" he whispered, still staring at the picture.

Lani just continued to smile, staring lovingly at Rusty.

"You couldn't have." He turned and walked away, the image of Laura replacing the one of Lani in his mind.

Rusty turned and punched the wall. His fist went through, leaving a hole.

"I can't do this. I just can't." He belonged here. In this house. Near the memories of his *family*. He couldn't allow himself to forget them. They deserved to be remembered. Thought about often. Never forgotten.

He went into the bathroom, rubbing his sore knuckles. He was probably lucky he hadn't broken anything. Barely scratched his skin, in fact. It would bruise, sure, but nothing more.

When he came out of the bathroom, a familiar picture of the boys faced him. They gave him their sweet smiles—the same ones they'd given him thousands of times, always melting him.

What would *they* think of him nearly moving on? Starting to look at someone else the same way he'd always looked at their mom? Or caring about two other kids? Kids who would be about their age. Almost like he was replacing them all.

Rusty grabbed onto the doorway and leaned against it. He was a traitor. Not only that, but a falling-off-the-wagon traitor. He'd had a drink. Just like the guy who had killed them all.

Maybe it was time to give his old sponsor a call. Or time to have a drink. What did it matter? He'd already broken his streak. His chip was worthless now. He would have to start over from ground zero.

May as well have a drink if that was his plan. He'd thought he could handle just a drink. How many times had he heard *that* story in a meeting? He should have known better.

Rusty glanced up at the picture of the boys. "I'm sorry."

He went into the hall, heading for the one place he could find something to drink. Lani's wine collection. He'd never been able to toss it. Swore he'd never touch it. And he never had. Not during all his tough days. But this, this was too much. At least it would help him to feel a little better.

Halfway down the hall, he stopped. The wine collection was in the garage. The burned up, destroyed garage where he was less likely to see it on a regular basis. He turned toward a wall and balled up his fist. He aimed, staring at the wall, his eyes narrowing. But then he loosened his hand and turned around.

Punching holes in the walls wasn't going to solve anything. Not that the wine would, either, really. But it would feel a lot better than bruising his fist some more.

He went into the kitchen. Maybe Lani had stuck some wine in one of the cabinets. He'd never gone through them, and some were pretty deep—the perfect place to hide a bottle for a romantic night. And she'd loved to plan those. Candle-lit dinners with mood-setting music in the background. A perfect meal with a bottle of wine. She knew what drink went with what meal.

She'd been able to drink without getting drunk. But then again, back in those days, so had Rusty. Lani never knew this kind of pain, though. Hadn't even lost a grandparent, much less the ones closest to her. He was glad she never had go through anything like that, but he had.

And if he was going to show up at a meeting and admit defeat, he may as well make it worth it. Have a real story to tell.

Rusty lowered himself onto the floor and opened the nearest cabinet under a counter. He pulled out pots and pans of every shape and size. Then he found fancy serving dishes and platters he hadn't seen in years. Some, he swore were from before the kids.

But no wine. Not yet, anyway. Would she have bothered storing any drinks way down there? Where he could barely reach? She had been tall, too, but not as tall as him. Lani would have practically had to climb inside the shelving to get anything way in the back.

He reached way into the back, finally finding the end of the storage. He pulled out some plastic storage containers. No wine. The containers needed to go—no wonder they were so far in the back. They'd probably been shoved back as new things had been added in. He returned the rest and went to another cabinet, again finding no wine.

Maybe he should go to the store and pick some stuff up. Then he could grab a beer instead. Maybe something harder.

And leave his house alone for someone to torch as soon as he was out of sight?

Rusty shook his head. He was desperate, not stupid.

He needed to get pictures of everything. That had been the original plan, and he needed to stick with it. Get pictures and store them safely online. It was too early to get drunk, anyway. Especially for someone who planned on sobering up. Again.

Or did he want to? Did it even matter? His family was gone and he couldn't help Kaylie and Brady—not really. Their dad wouldn't let him near them.

Did he even have any right to try? He'd never been there for them their entire lives. Not once had he tried reaching out to their mom—his sister. His flesh and blood. Even after he went through the same struggles.

Part of him hadn't wanted to talk to Mandy—that would have meant admitting where he'd gone wrong. Following their parents and abandoning her when she needed them most. How could he have looked at her after betraying her?

Everyone was better off without him.

Anyone who got close to him died. The evidence was plentiful. Lani. Parker. Tommy. Mandy.

Laura and the kids were better off with him staying away. He would do them all a favor staying home.

Rusty stood and stretched his legs. Where was his phone? It took better photos than his camera. And the sooner he got everything cataloged, the sooner he could have a private party for one.

He went back into the bedroom and found the phone sitting on the nightstand. The battery was almost dead. He'd been so stressed the night before, he hadn't thought to check.

Rusty found a cord and plugged it in.

He sat on the bed and rubbed his temples. How much was one man supposed to take? He was going to snap soon. That was why he needed something to drink. It would relax him. Then he could think clearly. Not like now. His body ached. Fatigue had him by the throat.

Maybe he just needed a nap. A nice long one. Then when he woke, the phone would be ready to take pictures.

Rusty leaned back and rubbed his temples. His tense body started to relax, and before he knew it, he fell asleep.

Some time later, a loud knock sounded from the front door, waking him.

Twenty-Four

RUSTY SHOOK OFF the sleep fog and climbed out of bed. The pounding on the door continued. Or was it from his head? He was pretty sure he had a headache.

The banging continued.

"I'm coming!" He ran his hands through his hair and stumbled. It was probably a good thing he hadn't had anything to drink. He was already a mess.

He made it to the front door and stood tall. Who could it be? The cops? Had they found the arsonist already?

Rusty opened the door and stepped back. He did a double-take. "Alyssa?"

He vaguely recalled her saying she'd watch the place after she followed him home the night he found out about Mandy's death.

Alyssa Mercer stood on his front porch, next to a young man a little taller than her with dark hair past his ears. He resembled her. It was probably her son. He was definitely too young to be her husband. And he appeared to be checking Rusty out, too. Some first impression.

"What's going on?" Alyssa asked. "Your shed is destroyed."

"Garage." Rusty rubbed his eyes. "Arson, apparently."

Alyssa's eyes widened. "Are you okay? No offense, but you look terrible."

"My sister just died and someone lit my garage on fire. I think I'm entitled."

"Hey, I'm the last one to judge. Do you need anything?"

A drink. A really hard one. Rusty shook his head.

"Can we come in?"

He stepped closer to the door. "I'm here now. Thanks for checking in. I don't want to keep you two."

Alyssa glanced at the young man. "Sorry, I forgot to introduce you. This is my son, Alex. Alex, this is Rusty."

"Nice to meet you," Alex said. He held out his hand.

Rusty took his hand and shook it. "Likewise. I hope this visit didn't take you away from anything important."

Alex shook his head. "Just picking my classes. I'm starting at the U in the fall."

"That should be fun. Well, I don't want to keep you guys."

Alyssa caught his gaze and frowned. "I feel like we should do something for you. You just don't seem yourself. I mean, obviously you're having a hard time. What do you need? We can run to the store."

"Really, I'm fine. It's just a headache."

"Do you have any painkillers?"

He opened his mouth to say yes, but realized he wasn't sure.

"That's it," Alyssa said. "We'll drop by the grocery store down the road. Need anything else while we're there?"

Just alcohol. He shook his head. "I've got everything else."

Alyssa handed Alex a set of keys. "Can you pick up some aspirin? I'm going to make him something to eat."

Rusty put up his hand. "Really—"

"I insist. After all you did for me when I was at the end of my rope, it's the least I can do for you." She came inside.

Alex glanced at Rusty, shrugged, and turned around. A few moments later, a car door opened and the engine started.

Alyssa closed the door behind them. "Okay, now that Alex isn't here, will you tell me what's really going on?"

Rusty sighed. "I told you. My sister died and someone set my place on fire."

She gave him a knowing look. "There's more to the story than that. I can tell something else is wrong."

He really didn't want to admit to falling off the rails. The man who towed drunks had turned to liquor himself.

"What is it? How can I help?"

"You've done plenty, thanks."

"Don't want to talk? Okay, I'll just make you something to eat, then."

He shook his head, but didn't say anything. Maybe she'd feel better after he ate, and then leave.

In the kitchen, Alyssa gestured toward the table. "Sit. It's my turn to take care of you."

Yawning, Rusty sat.

She opened the fridge. "Oh, these have to go."

Had he forgotten to toss the strawberries? He put his face in his palms. "I haven't had time to—"

"Don't worry about it." She turned around, holding an armful rotten food. "You look like you could use some more rest. Why don't you go to bed? I'll let you know when the food's ready."

"But I don't want you to be—"

"Nonsense. Go."

"Was I this pushy?"

The corners of her mouth twitched. "Worse, but in retrospect, that's what I needed. You'll thank me later. Trust me."

"Okay." He got up and headed out of the room. He stopped and turned around. "Thanks, Alyssa. I appreciate it." Even if he was annoyed, it was true.

She smiled. "It's my pleasure. Get some rest."

Rusty went to his room, sat on his bed, and took a deep breath. As tired as he was, he didn't feel like lying down. He needed to get started on taking pictures. He'd just start in there with Lani's stuff. Then he'd get the rest of the house after Alyssa left. Hopefully Alex would pick out extra-strength painkillers. The pain in his head was squeezing tighter every minute.

He looked around for his phone. It was on the nightstand, still plugged in where he'd left it. He grabbed it. The battery was full. Good, but even if it wasn't, he would have still unplugged it.

Where to start? Rusty glanced around, his gaze landing on the closet. His heart nearly leaped into his throat. He hadn't gone near Lani's side in… ever? He wasn't sure he'd even looked in. It was a habit to pretend her stuff wasn't there next to his. Some things were harder to deal with, and her clothes were one of them for some reason. Something he'd never been able to face.

Rusty took a deep breath and stood in front of the closet door. He opened her side and studied the clothes hanging exactly as she'd left them. Mostly color-coded and sorted by season. It was exactly her. And it was going to break his heart all over again. He scanned her shoes lining the floor beneath. They were arranged in the same pattern—color and season, with the practical shoes in front and the pretty ones in back.

He reached for the nearest clothes. Something in the back corner of the closet caught his attention. Some long dresses nearly blocked it from view, but him pulling hangers off had disturbed them, revealing whatever was there. He slid the clothes back and kneeled.

It looked a basket of some kind. He leaned over the shoes and pushed the long dresses out of the way. It was a large picnic basket, and he'd definitely never seen it before.

Carefully, he grabbed the handles and brought it out. It was painted reddish-brown and was high quality. And heavy. His heart raced, wondering what could be inside. What had Lani been doing with it?

He set it on the bed and opened the top. Two bottles. One of wine and the other champagne. Two wine glasses. Some plates, flatware, and nonperishables. Were they supposed to go on a picnic? It was hard to remember so far back, especially with everything being a blur around the time of the crash.

There was something else in there. A paper. He pulled it out. An envelope with what felt like a greeting card inside.

Rusty's hand shook. He nearly dropped the card. What was inside? Why the picnic supplies? He opened the sealed card, shaking, and managed to give himself a paper cut on this thumb. He pulled the card out. It had a picture of a happy couple in love.

His heart nearly jumped out of his chest as he opened it. The inside read *Happy Anniversary*. Hearts were drawn in Lani's handwriting. On the left side of the card was a personal note. Rusty's throat closed up. He slid to the carpet and stared at the writing. His hand shook too much to read the writing.

He took several deep breaths and rested the card against his knee.

Dear Rusty,

You've given me everything I ever dreamed of—and far more! I never knew life could be so wonderful, but you showed me paradise on earth. Love grander than I ever imagined. Then along came those two wonderful boys, partly you and partly me. All perfection. I really couldn't ask for anything more.

His vision blurred from tears. He wiped them away, but even more replaced them. They fell faster than he could keep up with. His life with Lani and the boys really had been perfect. But then it had been snatched from them all. Oh, how he wished he'd been in that car. Either to save them or go with them. It didn't matter which. Living without them was the worst fate. And to make matters worse, back at Mandy's, he'd acted like they had never even existed.

Footsteps sounded down the hall. Rusty scrambled to his feet and locked his door.

Alyssa knocked. "Are you okay in there?"

Rusty cleared his throat. "Just resting."

"Alex is back, and he needs to get back to the house. The food has another hour before it's ready. Will you be able to get it? Sorry we can't stay."

He wiped his eyes and took a deep breath. His eyes felt swollen. Oh, well. He opened the door.

Alyssa's eyes widened when she saw him. "Are you okay?"

"Allergies," he lied. "I came across some dust."

She didn't look like she believed him. "Do you want me to come back? I'm sure Chad—"

"No," Rusty said. "I just need to take care of some things. I'll be fine. I promise."

Alyssa tilted her head, looking unconvinced. "Okay. But if you need anything—anything at all—please call me. I can't imagine what you must be going through, losing your sister after losing your family." She frowned and patted his arm. "Oh. Here's the painkillers." She dug into her purse and handed him a bottle of ibuprofen.

"Thanks, Alyssa. For everything."

"Call me. Anytime."

He nodded. "I will."

She squeezed his arm. "Take care of yourself. I might check in on you later."

Rusty could tell by her expression that she was worried. He tried to force a smile, but it didn't work. "I'll be fine. I always am."

Alyssa frowned and then turned around. A minute later, he heard the front door close.

He sighed in relief. More tears came. He hadn't been expecting to find anything new from Lani. Especially nothing like that. He cleared his throat again and sat next to the basket, waiting for the tears to stop. He picked up the card and read the rest of the handwritten note.

Lani wrote about some of the best times they'd had together as a couple and as a family. His heart both swelled with love and shattered into pieces as he read the words. The note was too short—why couldn't it go on forever? He wanted more new time with Lani. But it ended all too soon.

I just want you to be happy always and forever.

All my love,

Lani

Rusty rested his head on his knees and sobbed like a baby. It was too much. How could he be happy ever again? Misery was his destiny. Loneliness. Fatigue. Anything but happiness.

He'd managed to survive. To get by. To make himself feel like he was righting the wrong of their deaths by towing drunks. Saving others. But to what end? His family was still gone and nothing could bring them back.

Rusty set the card next to the basket, grabbed a framed picture of Lani, and put it next to the card.

"Let's have that wine, sweetie." He dug into the basket, finding a corkscrew, and opened the bottle of wine. He poured it into the two glasses and set one next to Lani's picture.

Rusty took a sip, but then paused. "Wait." He raised his glass. "To happiness." He waited for her to raise her glass. "No? Not anymore, huh, babe?"

He downed the whole glass and then looked into Lani's eyes. "If I could go back in time, I would. I'd do anything to keep you three out of the car that night. Anything at all." He frowned and poured more wine for himself. "You should have some. It's good. But you already knew that—you picked it out."

Before long, the bottle was empty, leaving only Lani's untouched glass. He leaned back against the bed and closed his eyes. The alcohol felt good running through his system. He finally felt relaxed.

"How about that champagne?" Rusty didn't wait for a response. He drank her glass and then opened the champagne bottle and poured some into each glass. "Hopefully you guys are happy wherever you are. If there's anything in the great ever-after." He tapped her glass, careful not to spill it. His reflexes weren't up to their normal speed.

Rusty drank half the bottle before looking back into Lani's eyes. "What do you guys think of me spending time over at Mandy's? With her kids and neighbor. I went out with Laura, you know. It was fun. She's nice and pretty. Really pretty, actually. But in a different way than you. You're classy down to your core. She's... a free spirit. You'd like her, though." He sighed. "I'm some husband, huh?"

He poured himself another glass, spilling some onto the carpet.

"That was a waste," he muttered.

An alarm went off somewhere. His eyes widened. It wasn't another fire, was it? He scrambled to his feet, tripping over them. He stumbled down the hall, and it was only when he was almost to the kitchen and smelled something mouth-watering that he remembered Alyssa had made him something to eat.

Rusty tripped over the floor as he entered, catching himself on the wall. He stood tall, trying to gain his bearings. The room was moving around him. At least the tears had stopped. He felt better.

Mission accomplished.

Now to turn off the timer. He walked slowly, carefully and then reached for the off button.

Finally, blessed silence. Now to get the food out without burning himself or dropping it. Maybe he should have waited on the alcohol until after he'd eaten. That would have been the smart thing to do. But he didn't care. He felt better, and for the time being, that was all that mattered.

Twenty-Five

~

L AURA'S FINGER HOVERED over the call button, but once again, she canceled the call. Rusty would call when he was ready. She couldn't stop worrying about him, though. Had he lost everything in the house fire? Or had the fire department been able to put it out before there was any real damage?

Did he have someone to talk to? Laura would be freaking out of if her home had been destroyed. And there was no way it was a coincidence. Not with everything else going on around here.

She scrolled over to the latest text that had come in earlier.

Watch out, or you'll be next.

What if someone did try to set her house on fire? She went to a window that overlooked the house next door. Was Chris behind all this? If he was, he'd be stupid to light up her house. Flames spread quickly, jumping from one home to the next, especially in the summer heat in Florida. Their entire block could be gone before the fire department arrived.

Okay, maybe that was a bit of an exaggeration, but with Chris's home so close, he'd be stupid to recreate Rusty's fire.

What else did whoever was behind all this have planned? More texts? Rumors?

Laura had already had enough dirty looks and rude comments. In fact, she didn't even know what rumors had been spread. She and Rusty had been so busy with other things, neither had checked.

It was obvious that it went beyond gossip about Travis freaking out on Rusty. Yes, that would raise a few eyebrows, but people acted like they were criminals. And it was so strange how Lisa had acted when Laura and

Rusty had taken the samples in. Usually, Lisa would do anything for Laura.

Chills ran down her back just thinking about the glares and comments around town. People were truly disgusted by them. Sure, she was used to being an outcast, but this had been taken to a whole new level.

Laura needed to sit. She went into her office and turned on the laptop. Maybe she could find something online. One of those annoying local gossip blogs had to have something.

She'd been avoiding them, preferring not to know what people were thinking. But it was becoming increasingly clear she needed to know as much as she could. Maybe she could even find something that would give a clue as to what was coming next.

It was at least worth a try. The computer finally loaded. She typed in her password—she was so shaken it took her four tries. It took a moment for everything to load, but soon she had several local blogs in the tabs.

Laura started with the most popular one. There was nothing about either her or Rusty on any of the recent posts. Some news about a couple big deals Travis Calloway had in the works. Some kids had broken into the high school and messed up the cafeteria. A missing teen had been found alive and well at a college party a few towns over. A popular couple was getting a divorce. Rusty's car break-in.

At least now she was getting closer to the party. She scanned some more posts until she saw the headline.

Mandy Oates's Brother Kicked out of Calloway Party—You Won't Believe Why.

Laura scanned the article, at first seeing exactly what she expected. A blown out of proportion account of what had happened that night. It made Rusty look like a drunken fool—as though he'd been the one to break the glasses. Travis, of course, looked like the town hero.

Then on the third paragraph, Laura froze. She blinked a few times and had to re-read the opening lines several times to make sure she hadn't read it wrong.

Rusty has been hiding a horrible truth. He actually fathered one of

Mandy's children and is desperate to lay the blame on someone else. This week, it's Travis Calloway.

Laura shook her head. Was that what people really thought? That Rusty and Mandy had...?

Her stomach lurched at the thought.

It couldn't be true, could it?

No. Not only was it physically impossible—Rusty and Mandy hadn't even seen each other since before Laura and Chris met—but it was also ludicrous. There was no way either one of them would even consider what the article was accusing them of having done. Rusty was a stand-up guy. How could she doubt him, even for a moment?

Rage surged through Laura. She wanted to defend both of them, her best friend and Rusty. How dare they publish such horrible lies?

It certainly explained why Lisa wouldn't help them, and why she had glared at Rusty when they came in with the paternity test.

She closed her laptop. If there was more, she didn't want to know. They were better off without the knowledge of whatever other rumors had been floating around. That one was bad enough. What could be next?

Travis obviously had something to hide. He had to be behind the rumors. It was the only thing that made sense. Mandy had been after him for money. Rusty was trying to clear her name. And Travis had the influence to get anything posted that he wanted.

Laura leaned back and closed her eyes. They really needed those results back. Not that they could entirely undo the damage already done, but at least they would have proof. Mandy had been sure it was Travis, so that had to—

A clinking sound came from the lower level.

Laura's heart nearly leaped into her throat. Pulse racing, she scrambled from the chair. It sounded like someone was trying to open the downstairs door.

Mind spinning, she went into her coat closed and grabbed a baseball bat. She had it there for an occasion such as this, though she'd hoped never to use it. The sounds continued.

If the person managed to open the door, the alarm would sound and alert the security company. But by the time they called the police and they arrived, she could already be dead.

She reached into her pocket. Where was her phone? Had she left it somewhere? She'd almost called Rusty.

The living room. That's where she'd left it. Clutching the baseball bat, she hurried into the couch and found her cell phone.

Thunk. The familiar sound of her downstairs door hitting the wall beside it. It was open. Someone was now in her house.

Her fingers shook as she dialed 9-1-1.

"What is your emergency?"

"Someone's in my house," Laura whispered, backing away from the stairs. "They broke down my door, and are inside."

"What's your address, ma'am?"

Laura backed up more and whispered the information into the phone.

"Can you repeat the last part?" asked the operator.

She took a deep breath and repeated herself, speaking closer to the receiver.

"Thank you. Please stay on the line. I'm going to—"

"Just hurry." Laura ended the call and stuffed the phone in her pocket.

Footsteps sounded downstairs. The intruder was walking around the downstairs area. Doing what? Looking for something?

Laura's pulse drummed in her ears. It made it even harder to hear what he was doing. She squeezed the bat as hard as she could and took several deep breaths. The rushing blood quieted.

There was no way she could make it to the front door unseen. He kept pacing near the stairs, probably going through her things. By the time she reached the door, he would have enough time to grab her and drag her wherever he wanted.

One thing she wasn't going to do—hide and cower. She looked around for anything else that could be used as a weapon. There were no guns or pepper spray in the house.

Knives. She had a whole set in the kitchen. Laura crept over, needing to pass the stairs. She turned to look. A man dressed in black stood there.

Laura screamed. The sound echoed around her.

"You weren't supposed to be home."

"And Rusty's house wasn't supposed to catch fire. Things change." She clutched the bat, ready to swing.

He pulled up a sleeve and revealed a large pocket knife. He flung it open and held it out.

"I'm not afraid to use this!" Laura readied the bat.

He lunged for her, aiming the blade at her throat.

Laura swung, hitting him in the hand. The knife flew out of his grip. He reached for it, and Laura took advantage of his distraction and hit him across the head. It wasn't like the shows she'd seen. He didn't crumple to the ground. Instead, he turned to her, nostrils flaring, blood dripping down his face.

He jumped at her, his face contorted into a tight scowl. Laura moved to the side and swung the bat again. This time, he grabbed it and aimed for her. She looked around and grabbed a half-full wine bottle from her rack.

"I'm not here for a date," he sneered.

Laura hit him across the face. It didn't shatter, as she'd hoped. The intruder stumbled back, swearing and grasping his nose, which gushed blood. She turned and smashed the bottle against the table. This time, it shattered and sent the sticky liquid in all directions.

She held up the sharp container. "Don't come near me. I'll do more than break your nose."

Sirens sounded outside. Laura breathed a sigh of relief.

The intruder swore. Without warning, he lunged for Laura and wrapped his arm around her neck. His blood dripped onto her hair and dress.

She gagged, unable to breathe, and tried to pull his arm off. He dragged her out to the living room and stopped near the front window. The intruder swore again. "They're stopping here."

Laura jammed the broken bottle into his thigh. His arms released her. Gasping, she ran toward the stairs. He ran toward her, knocking her over just before she fell down the flight. Laura kicked him off and ran down, stumbling over a couple steps. Grumbling, he grasped at her just as she turned the doorknob.

"Not so fast." The intruder wrapped his hand around hers. "You're not going anywhere."

She struggled against him and they fell down the next flight of stairs. Laura landed on top of the intruder. Something crunched and he let out a yowl. They rolled down until they reached the bottom. She jumped up, but he didn't move—just lay there moaning.

Laura stumbled to the back door and opened it. The sounds of sirens filled the air.

Twenty-Six

~

BRADY STARED AT Kaylie, disappointment in his eyes. "Why hasn't Uncle Rusty come by?"

Kaylie shrugged, wishing she knew. "Maybe he's busy."

"With what?"

"His car? Finding a place to stay? I don't know."

"He said he'd take us swimming."

"I know. He will, okay? He's not our babysitter."

Brady frowned. "He kind of is."

"Look. I'm almost fourteen. You'll be twelve soon. We don't need a sitter."

"Well, I'm hungry." He threw the game controller on the couch. "I'm not even allowed to cook."

"I am, and it's time you learn."

"What will Dad say?" Brady's eyes grew wide with fear.

"He'll be glad we can take care of ourselves. Come on." Kaylie's stomach grumbled. She went into the kitchen. It was already after three. No wonder they were so hungry. They'd had a bowl of cereal for breakfast earlier, but had been holding out until Uncle Rusty came by for lunch. She spun around and glared at her brother. "I said, come on."

Brady muttered something, but got off the couch. "I'll just have more cereal. I don't care."

"I do. I'm hungry. We can at least have some mac and cheese."

He shrugged. "Do you know how to make it?"

"Yeah. I've made it before. Besides, there are directions, dummy."

Brady narrowed his eyes. "Quit calling me names."

"It's what siblings do." Kaylie spun around and found a box of shell-shaped noodles and thick cheese sauce. Organic. "Grab a pot and fill it with water."

"No."

She turned and faced him. "No?"

"You heard me."

"Why not? I thought you were hungry."

"I am, but I'm not doing anything until you say you'll be nicer to me."

Kaylie rolled her eyes. "Are you serious?"

"That's exactly what I'm talking about."

"We're supposed to bicker and pick on each other."

Brady folded his arms. "Says who?"

"Says everyone in the history of brothers and sisters."

"That doesn't mean—"

The front door burst open. Brady spun around and Kaylie moved to see around him. Dad slammed the door and ran his hands through his already-messy hair. His eyes darted back and forth, not seeming to notice either of them.

"What's going on?" Brady asked.

Kaylie stepped beside him. "Yeah, Dad."

He glanced up at them, an expression of fear on his face.

"What's wrong?" Kaylie exclaimed.

"They're coming for me."

"What?" Brady's voice cracked.

"Who?" Kaylie asked.

Dad shook his head. "I don't have time to explain. Where's Rusty?"

"You kicked him out, remember?" Kaylie narrowed her eyes.

He swore. "Right. Well, you're going to have to call him. He's back on duty."

"What's going on?" Brady demanded.

"It's a long story. I don't have time to explain it. Just don't answer the door unless it's Rusty." Dad hurried past them and down the hall, slamming his bedroom door.

Brady turned to Kaylie. A tear sat at the edge of his eyelid, about to fall onto his face. "Wh-what's going on?"

She put her arms around him and held him tight. "I have no idea, but we'll call Uncle Rusty, like Dad said to."

"But why does he look scared?"

"I have no idea." Kaylie rested her head on his for a moment before stepping back. "I tried calling Uncle Rusty earlier, but he didn't answer."

"What are we going to do if he can't watch us and Dad can't?"

"Mom always said we could go next door to Laura."

"But Dad doesn't want—"

"I don't think he has much of a choice. If we can't find Uncle Rusty, we'll go there."

"What if she's not there?"

Kaylie took a deep breath. "You worry too much."

"I can't help it. I wish Mom was here."

A lump formed in Kaylie's throat. "Me, too. She'd know what to do." Though, Kaylie had a feeling that if Mom were there, none of them would be in the situation to begin with. Everything seemed to go back to her death.

"Why can't we have a funeral for her? She deserves one. A nice one."

Kaylie nodded. "We'll ask Uncle Rusty, 'kay? I'm going to call him now." She ran down the hall to her room, where her phone was charging.

Dad was yelling behind his door. He kept pausing, but it was hard to tell if he was on the phone or just venting to himself.

She hurried into her room, unplugged her phone, and found Uncle Rusty's number. "Come on, pick up," she begged.

Brady came in. "Did he answer?"

Kaylie shook her head, listening to the voice message. "Uncle Rusty, we need you. Call me back, or just come over. But hurry!" She ended the call.

She and Brady went into the hall. Something broke against the wall in Dad's room.

Brady turned to her, wide-eyed.

Sirens sounded outside. Dad let out a stream of profanities from behind his door.

Brady ran to the living room. "Oh, my gosh!"

"What?" Kaylie ran over to him.

"Look." He pointed out the window.

Police cars pulled into their driveway. A fire truck and ambulance parked in front of Laura's house.

Brady and Kaylie exchanged wide-eyed glances before turning back to the front yard. More police cruisers pulled up. Some into Laura's driveway and another into theirs.

"Don't open the door," Dad ordered.

Kaylie whipped around. He stood by the stairs, a backpack slung over his shoulders and two more bags in his hands.

"Dad?" Brady asked.

"Stay in here." He started down the stairs.

"What's going on?" Kaylie asked.

"No time to explain. Just stay where you're at."

"But... but..." Brady shook and tears ran down his face.

Kaylie put her arm around him. "It's going to be okay."

Dad's footsteps echoed down the stairs, past the front door, and down the bottom level.

Brady just continued trembling in her embrace.

The sliding glass door downstairs squeaked as it opened and then slammed shut.

"Where's he going?" Brady whispered.

"I have no idea."

Someone banged on the front door.

Brady jumped. "What do we do?"

Kaylie peeked outside. "Dad said not to answer it."

"Should we?"

"Open up!" More pounding. "Police!"

"It's the police," Brady said.

"I know. But..."

The cops continued banging on the door. "We know you're in there!"

Brady shook harder. "I don't want to go to jail."

"They're not going to put you in prison. We didn't do anything wrong."

"What if Dad did? Can they make us pay?"

"This isn't the middle ages. Come on. We better answer it."

"Open up!"

Brady took a deep breath and then nodded. He wiped his eyes.

"We'll be okay. I swear."

"I don't believe you this time." He slid his hand in hers, like when they were younger.

Kaylie squeezed his hand and then they walked slowly to the front door. She felt like they were headed for their execution.

She swallowed and then opened the door. Three officers stood in front of them. Surprise covered all of their faces.

"Where is Chris Oates?" demanded the tallest one.

Brady turned to Kaylie, his eyes bigger than she'd ever seen him.

She turned back to the police. "He's not here. Did you try his work?"

"Excuse us, we need to get by."

"Don't you need a search warrant or something?" Kaylie asked.

The tall one stepped forward, forcing her and Brady out of the way. The first two ran up the stairs.

"Come on in," Kaylie mumbled.

The third officer stopped and looked back and forth between Brady and Kaylie. "Why don't we go outside?"

Brady clung to Kaylie.

The cop gave a reassuring smile. "We're here to help you."

Listening to the other two stomp around upstairs, Kaylie doubted that. They were there to find Dad. But why?

"Follow me," said the officer.

Brady looked at Kaylie. She nodded, and they went outside. It seemed like emergency vehicles lined the street, but it was really just their house and next door. Cops swarmed Laura's front yard.

"What's going on?" Brady whispered.

Medics carried someone on a stretcher through Laura's yard.

"No!" Kaylie released Brady's hand and ran next door. Had Dad hurt her? Was that what all this was about?

Laura wasn't on the stretcher. It was a guy. Fear pierced Kaylie, worried that it was Uncle Rusty. He was friends with Laura. But the injured man was shorter and had longer hair.

Relief washed through her. Brady appeared at her side. "Who's that?"

"I have no idea. Where's Laura?"

More medics came around from the other side of the house. They were helping someone in an orange and brown dress. Laura.

Kaylie ran over. Blood was spattered over her shoulders and a big round stain sat near her middle.

"Laura!" Kaylie exclaimed.

She looked over. "Are you two okay?"

"Yeah. You're bleeding!"

Laura shook her head. "It's not my blood."

A cop came up to them. "We'll need your dress for evidence."

"Right now?" Laura asked. "Or can I go in and change?"

"You can go in with some of our officers."

A couple more police came over to them. They looked at Kaylie and Brady.

"Where's your mom?" asked one.

Kaylie scowled. "Dead."

"Oh, right. The suicide from last week."

"She didn't kill herself!" Brady screamed. "I wish everyone would stop saying that."

"We'll have to take you two into custody."

Kaylie's heart raced. "What do you mean?" She grabbed her brother's arm.

"Your dad's going to be booked downtown." The officer flicked his head toward their yard.

Dad was in cuffs, surrounded by cops. Kaylie's heart sank.

"We're going to jail, too?" Brady asked.

The officer shook his head. "No, but you're going to have to enter foster care. I'm sorry to say, but you'll probably be separated. Not many people are willing to take on two teens."

Brady clung to Kaylie.

"He's eleven." She glared at the cop.

"I'm just saying the chances of you two staying together aren't good."

"They can stay with me," Laura said.

"You licensed for foster care?"

She shook her head.

"They have to go with a blood relative, otherwise the foster system. Are you a relative?"

Laura shook her head again and her face fell.

"Uncle Rusty!" Kaylie exclaimed.

The officer glanced around. "Your uncle's here?"

"Not here, here," Kaylie said. "But he's in a hotel nearby. He was staying with us before. He can come back."

"Rusty, you say?" The cop scribbled notes onto a pad of paper. "Same last name as you?"

"Russell Caldwell," Laura said. "He's their mom's brother."

The cop wrote more down. "If he agrees to take care of you kids, and we see proof of identification, you two can stay with him."

"He will," Kaylie assured him. "He flew all the way out here just to help us out."

"Then you may be in luck." He glanced at Laura. "In the meantime, you should get cleaned up."

She glanced down at her bloody dress. "Yeah, I should."

"Someone have Russell's number?"

"I do," Kaylie and Laura both answered.

Twenty-Seven

~

RUSTY SAT ON the couch in the family room—another part of the house he tended to avoid. A large photo of his family stared at him. Everyone was smiling and happy. Somehow the photographer had managed to get both boys looking directly into the camera while smiling. It was something Rusty had rarely been able to do.

He stared at their features, wondering what they would look like if they were still with him. Both would be handsome young men, that much was certain. They'd both inherited much of their mother's features. Everyone always said that if they weren't two years apart, they could have been twins. He'd only ever been able to see their differences, but now, somehow, he could see what everyone meant.

"So, I told your mom about Laura." He leaned back against the cushions. "The nice lady who lives next door to your Aunt Mandy. Have you met her up there? I bet you guys would love each other. It's too bad I never made sure you guys all met here."

Rusty sighed, feeling defeated. He'd made so many wrong decisions. If he'd been with them that night... If he'd only swallowed his pride and reconciled with Mandy...

So many regrets. Too many mistakes.

Everyone he cared about was dead.

Not everyone. Laura's beautiful smiling face came to mind followed by Brady's mischievous grin and Kaylie's spunky laugh. He really did love those kids. And Laura... he definitely had feelings for her.

Part of him wanted to go back and make sure they were all okay. Between the texts and the vandalisms, he had real reason to worry about Laura. And those kids with Chris, especially if he'd hurt Mandy.

Rusty leaned his head back against the top of the couch. No, they'd all be better off if he stayed away. They would just end up hurt—maybe even killed. It was obvious that was what happened to those he cared about. And besides all that, if he stayed away, maybe the murderer would leave everyone alone.

Everyone would be better off if he stayed away. He sat up and looked back at the picture of his family. If only he could see them one more time. Or even be with them forever. Like it was supposed to be, before that drunk loser took everything from him. From all of them.

But was he any better than the drunk? He was right back there. Except for one major difference. He wasn't stupid or cruel enough to climb behind a wheel. He wouldn't take another person's life.

He studied each one. Lani. Parker. Tommy. Maybe joining them was the answer. It wasn't like he was doing any good here. He'd just brought more trouble to Laura and those kids. Laura wouldn't have gotten involved with Travis's parties. The DNA testing. And maybe Chris would have been more relaxed without Rusty around.

Going there had been a bad idea all around, for everyone.

Rusty stared into the eyes of each family member in the picture. "I'll see you guys real soon." He turned around and headed for his room. The gun was still there. It would bring him to his family.

He stumbled into the bedroom and stared at the picnic. Two empty bottles, two empty glasses. A picture of a beautiful woman and a card declaring her love for him.

Yes, it was time to complete the family. Bring them all together where they needed to be.

Rusty sat on the bed and opened the drawer in his nightstand. He stared at the loaded gun. It would only take a moment and everything would be made right.

He reached for it and paused. What about his parents? He didn't even know how they were handling Mandy's death. Would they be able to survive losing both of their children in the same month?

Sure, his dad was a bit of a jerk, but he wasn't heartless. For the most part. And his mom… She was kindhearted. Her only fault, really, was going along with Dad because she thought that was what a good wife should do. Rusty was certain she had longed to reconcile with Mandy years ago.

At least she would have Dad. They could get through it together. They'd held each other up after losing the only grandkids they knew.

Maybe he should leave them a note. Then he would know to reach out to the kids. They could focus on them rather than Rusty and Mandy.

He found a pad of paper and a pen. For a moment, he thought about how to word the note, then he scribbled it down and set it on his pillow. If Travis really was Brady's father, then Rusty's parents might have to raise the boy. Chris would have no rights, and it was obvious Travis wanted nothing to do with him.

Rusty picked up the revolver and cradled it, studying it. His pulse raced, sounding like a drum in his ears. Would this really take him to his family, or was he just kidding himself? If nothing else, it should protect Laura from more threats—or worse.

He slid his fingers around to the trigger and took a deep breath. He thumbed the cylinder and released the latch. He cupped his left hand around it and checked for the bullets. Three. Two more than he would need. He slid the cylinder closed and wiggled it. It was all set. He just needed to…

Take a deep breath.

"I can do this," he muttered.

His cell phone rang, startling him. He dropped the gun and scrambled to catch it. His fingers wrapped around the handle just before it hit the ground.

Rusty put it on the bed next to him and looked at the phone. It was Laura. She'd be better off without him. He ignored the call and set the phone back down and reached for the revolver.

The phone rang again.

"Give it up." He glanced at the phone again. This time it was Kaylie.

What if something was wrong? Had Brady gotten hurt?

He picked up the phone. "Kaylie?"

"Uncle Rusty!"

"What's going on?"

Kaylie gasped for air on the other end. "My dad—they just took him to jail. The cops want to send me and Brady to different foster homes. They—"

"Wait. What? Say that again."

Kaylie repeated herself. He hadn't heard wrong. His heart dropped to the floor. "Why do they want to separate you?"

"Because there's no relative to take care of us. You've got to come over right away."

He took a deep breath. "It might take a little while. Is there someone I can talk to?"

"Yeah, but where've you been all day?"

"I had some stuff to take care of. I thought Laura was going to tell you guys."

"Looks like something came up."

"What do you mean?"

"I better let her tell you. Hold on."

Shuffling noises sounded through the phone. "Rusty?" Laura's voice was strained.

"What's going on over there?"

"It's a long story." She sounded out of breath. "I need you to talk to the officer, and tell him you'll be right over to take care of the kids."

"Right over?"

"I've got to get this blood off me. They want my dress for evidence."

Terror choked him. "What do you mean? What happened?"

"I'll tell you when you get here. Here, talk to the officer."

More shuffling noises. "Is this Russell Caldwell?" asked a deep male voice.

"You can call me Rusty. Can you tell me what's going on?"

"Your brother-in-law is heading downtown to be booked and if a relative can't take them, we will need to contact DHS."

"I'll be there as soon as I can."

"Bring your identification."

"Where will the kids be?"

"At the station."

"Can't you leave them with Laura?" Rusty exclaimed.

"She's not a relative. And she will need to be questioned herself."

"For what?"

"Just get over here. If you're not here by dark, I'm going to have to put them in foster care."

"Please, Uncle Rusty!" Brady begged in the background.

Rusty swore. "I'll be there. Tell them not to worry." He ended the call and opened the browser app and searched for available flights. The soonest one was on a crappy airline with a reputation for not keeping the planes in good condition. It would have to do. Otherwise, he wouldn't make it before dark.

He barely had enough time to make it and get through security. If traffic was decent.

Rusty ran through the house to make sure nothing was plugged in that shouldn't be—the last thing he needed was another fire. Then he threw some clothes into a suitcase and ran to his truck. Just as he put it in reverse, a police cruiser pulled into his driveway.

"Are you kidding me?" Rusty unrolled his window. "Can I help you?"

"We need to look at the crime scene."

"You don't need me here, do you? I need to get to my niece and nephew."

"Go ahead. We'll call you if anything comes up."

Rusty pulled out of the driveway, sending gravel flying behind him.

Luckily, traffic was light. He made it to the airport with a few minutes to spare. Parking and security went without a hitch. He'd even managed to pick a suitcase that was small enough to be carried on the plane. Finally, things were going right. For however long that lasted.

He sat by a window and watched planes land and take off. He could barely concentrate, though.

What had happened to Laura? Why was she covered in blood? Had Chris attacked her? Travis? Could that be why Chris was in jail? Or had he been found guilty of killing Mandy?

How were the kids doing? Probably scared out of their minds.

A flight attendant called for everyone to board the plane. Rusty rose and grabbed his luggage. His mind raced until he got in his seat. Fortunately, he was next to a window. With any luck, he would either end up with no one next to him or someone who didn't feel like talking.

He just wanted to get back and take care of Laura and the kids. They needed him—and he wanted to be the one to take care of them. He shuddered at the thought of what would have happened if they'd called five minutes later.

Rusty had been wrong. They weren't better off without him. And he definitely wasn't better off without them, either.

The intercom crackled overhead and a tired-sounding woman told everyone to head to their seats and wait for further instructions. Rusty buckled himself in and relaxed. It looked like he'd have the row to himself after all.

A bronze-toned, bleach-blonde twenty-something sat next to him. She flashed him a wide smile, showing off unnaturally white teeth. "Phew. Barely made it."

Rusty forced a smile.

She shoved a bright yellow bag into the overhead compartment and sat, leaving the seat in between them empty. Hopefully that was a good sign.

Rusty pulled out his earbuds, hoping she'd catch the hint.

"I'm Haley." She held out a hand.

He slid the earbuds in and shook her hand. "Rusty."

Haley looked him over. "Are you an active guy?"

"Yeah. I'm pretty tired, though. I'm going to get some shut-eye before we land. Big night ahead of me."

"Really?" She arched a perfectly trimmed brow. "I have something that can help you."

Rusty gave her a double-take. "Come again?"

Haley smiled and dug into her purse. Its pattern had multi-colored C's pointing in every direction. She pulled out a brochure of some kind. "Have you heard of Aphro-Deity?"

"Can't say that I have."

Haley grabbed his arm. "You're going to love it!" She flipped through her brochure and stopped at a page near the middle. "These are all totally amazing aphrodisiac products. We've got lotions, vitamins, energy drinks, shakes, shampoos, and so much more. Even bronzers." She looked him over again. "The ladies won't be able to keep their hands off you with a deeper tan. And then you'll have the stamina of an eighteen-year-old." She winked. "I think I have a sample of vitamins in here, too."

Rusty glanced around for an escape. The plane was already going down the runway. And all the other seats he could see were occupied. The only empty one sat between him and Haley. Great.

A flight attendant came by and asked Haley about something to drink. While she was distracted, Rusty slid the earbuds into place, leaned back against the seat, and closed his eyes.

"So, as I was saying," Haley said, her voice barely audible over the music in Rusty's ears. "Hey, there's no way you're asleep. Rusty. Rusty!"

He faked a snore and let his head rest on his shoulder. She grabbed his arm and shook. He let his body move back and forth, but gave no indication of being alert. Finally, she gave up.

Would he be able to get to the kids before dark? What had happened to Laura—why was she covered in blood?

Barely an hour earlier, he thought he'd had nothing to live for. But now he knew better. There were three people who he cared very much for. That much was certain.

And now he had Lani's blessing. He couldn't get the line from the card out of his mind: *I just want you to be happy always and forever.*

Holding Laura, Brady, and Kaylie would make him happy. Seeing them, and knowing they would all be okay. And caring about them wasn't dishonoring Lani or the boys. In a way, maybe that was doing exactly the opposite.

Twenty-Eight

~

L AURA STOPPED PACING and went to the window again. Rusty was due
to arrive with the kids soon. She didn't know what his newest rental
car looked like, so that didn't help matters. Her nerves were shot—and
that was after drinking both a relaxing tea and some wine while trying not
to pace.

The edge of the sky was growing dark. What if he didn't get to the
station in time?

It was anyone's guess when—or if—Chris would be out of jail. If they
suspected him of Mandy's murder, he wouldn't be getting out anytime
soon. Especially if he was guilty. But even if he wasn't, the police probably
had no idea Travis most likely was.

Her stomach twisted in knots. Mandy would have been sick at the
thought of her kids in foster care.

Where was Rusty? Had his flight been delayed? Why hadn't he called?

A car drove down the road. She jumped and watched it, but it didn't
slow.

Laura went back to pacing. The television played an old rerun of
Friends, but she couldn't focus.

The familiar sounds of a car pulling into the driveway sounded next
door. She ran over to the window and saw a red sedan. It looked like
Rusty and Kaylie in the front. Laura sighed in relief before finding the
remote. She turned off the TV and ran outside.

Rusty and the kids were just getting out of the car.

"You got them in time," she exclaimed.

"We had to wait forever," Kaylie complained.

"They wouldn't let us see Dad, either." Brady frowned.

"At least you get to sleep in your own beds tonight," Rusty said. He turned to Laura and wrapped his arms around her, holding her tight.

The embrace surprised her, but she melted into it. "How's everything back home?"

He rested his head against hers. "I was lucky. The fire was only in the garage. It could've been a lot worse."

"I'm glad to hear that. Are you guys hungry? I've got some dinner in the oven. It's ready, just warming."

"I'm starving," Kaylie said.

"Me, too," Brady said. "Please, Uncle Rusty."

"Of course." He let go of Laura and stepped back. "How are you doing?"

"Just been worried about you guys."

"Any... news?"

Laura shook her head. "Lisa said the results would be ready in the morning."

"What results?" Kaylie asked.

Rusty patted her shoulder. "Don't worry about it. Let's just get something to eat."

They all hurried inside. Laura got the food from the oven while everyone washed up. They devoured the meal, leaving only empty pans and plates. The kids went to the living room and watched TV while she and Rusty cleaned things up.

"Did you learn anything about why Chris is being held?" Laura asked.

"They wouldn't tell me anything. I was lucky just to get the kids. Do you know how hard it is to prove you're an uncle?"

"Pretty hard?" she guessed.

He put a plate in the dishwasher. "I had to have my parents fax over both my and Mandy's birth certificates, showing we have the same parents. Then they had to look up her social security number to verify her name change." He lowered his voice. "I thought for sure they were going to put the kids into foster care, but it all worked out."

"So, what's the plan?"

Rusty shook his head. "I wish I knew. I'll just try to keep things as normal as possible for them. Once you hear back from the lab, we can decide our next move."

Laura nodded, thinking. "What if Travis is the father?"

"I think we should take it to the cops."

"Hopefully they'll believe us."

"What could be clearer than DNA?" Rusty asked.

"They might question how we got it. And they're not going to want to accuse the town's most powerful man of murder."

His eyes narrowed. "If he did it, they don't have much of a choice."

"I'm on your side. I'm just saying that politics around here…"

"They'll probably question Chris first, anyway. Especially with him already in custody. If he isn't the father, he's automatically a suspect."

Laura closed the dishwasher and started it. "Should we go to them with what we have already? Did you bring Mandy's paperwork back?"

He nodded. "It's in the trunk, but I'm not going back to the station tonight. I need to get the kids home and into bed. They won't like going to sleep so early, but they're exhausted."

"Aren't we all?" Laura sat at the table. "I can take it down for you. Then I can come over after they're asleep."

He wrinkled his forehead. "Won't they question how you got it?"

"They don't need to know about the bank box. I'm her best friend. Who's to say she didn't give it to me for safekeeping?"

Rusty didn't appear convinced.

"Look at it this way, they'll be able to question him tonight. Get it out of their system so that when we get the other results tomorrow, they can go straight to…" Laura paused, seeing a shadow move just outside the kitchen.

"What?" Rusty asked.

Laura pressed her finger up to her mouth and rose. She crept to the doorway and stepped out. Kaylie stood by the wall. Her eyes widened like saucers when she saw Laura.

"What are you doing?" Laura asked.

"I… I had to go to the bathroom, but then I heard what you were saying."

Laura pulled her into the kitchen. "What do you think you heard?"

Kaylie's eyes grew wider, and she stared back and forth between Laura and Rusty.

"Kaylie?" Rusty asked.

"Do you… you think Dad isn't our dad?"

Laura turned to Rusty, sure her eyes were as wide as Kaylie's.

Rusty took a deep breath. "This is something I was going to discuss with you kids later, once things were sorted out."

"Who's our dad?" Kaylie clutched the back of a chair, staring at her uncle.

He peeked out into the living room and then stepped closer to Kaylie. "Your dad is your dad, but it appears he's not Brady's."

Color drained from her face and she sat. "Does that mean he's still my brother?"

Rusty sat and put his hand on top of hers. "Of course. You both have the same mom."

"But who…?"

He looked at Laura, his expression begging her for help.

She scooted closer to Kaylie and put her hand on Kaylie's arm. "That's what we're trying to figure out. Your mom started the whole process, but didn't get a chance to finish it."

Kaylie's face paled even further. "Does Dad know?"

Laura and Rusty exchanged a glance. "We're not sure," Laura said.

"So, he might have…? I mean, Mom might not have killed herself?"

Neither Rusty nor Laura replied.

"Is that why he's in jail?"

"We don't know," Rusty said.

"But that's why they kept asking him questions, right?"

"Honey," Laura said, "they always suspect the spouse. Your dad could be completely innocent."

Kaylie rested her head against the table.

Laura arched a brow, trying to ask Rusty silently what to do. He shook his head, obviously not knowing the answer.

Kaylie sat up. "Are you going to tell Brady?"

"As soon as we know more," Rusty said.

"But you already know Dad's not…"

Rusty shook his head. "That's all we know so far. There's so much going on, I don't think right now is the time."

"When?"

"Maybe later, after we watch a movie and have some ice cream. We all need to relax, and besides, he's only eleven. It's going to be a lot for him."

Kaylie let out a long, slow breath. "But if he's not Dad's, can he still raise him? Will Brady have to move away?" Kaylie's eyes shone with tears.

"There are too many unanswered questions now," Laura said. "But your dad is the legal parent of both you guys. And if the other guy hasn't stood up to take responsibility after all this time, chances are good he won't now. I can't imagine you two will be separated."

A look of relief covered Kaylie's face.

Laura glanced at Rusty. "Why don't you get these two home, like we talked about? Then I can take that paperwork."

He nodded and then turned to Kaylie. "You won't tell him without me, will you?"

Kaylie shook her head, her eyes wide. "No way."

"Good. I think we need to tell him together." Rusty got up and went into the living room. "Come on, Brady. It's time to go home."

Laura followed them outside. The kids headed for their front door. Rusty and Laura headed for his rental car. He opened the trunk and reached in, appearing to unlock the briefcase.

"Are you sure you want to go down there by yourself?" He turned to her, holding the manila envelope they found in the lock box. He opened it and rifled through the papers.

"I don't mind. You need to focus on the kids. I feel horrible that Kaylie overheard us."

He frowned. "You and me both. But I suppose it's for the best. She can process it and help her brother when he hears the news."

"That's one way to look at it. She is pretty protective of him."

Rusty nodded and handed her half a dozen papers. "These are the ones you'll need. If Chris is guilty, maybe they can get to the bottom of this before we get the results."

"What do I tell them if they want to know who the father is?"

"I wouldn't drop his name, not until we know for sure. We've already seen what he's capable of."

Her stomach twisted in knots remembering her blood-soaked dress that now belonged to the police as evidence. "You mean kicking you out of his party?"

"My garage fire. The threatening texts—those stopped once I got on the plane back home. You haven't gotten any more, right?"

Laura nodded. "But the guy from earlier."

Rusty slapped his forehead. "Oh, crap. I completely forgot to ask you about that. I'm such a jerk. Honestly, I was worried about that. It's just that with everything else... I'm so sorry."

She shook her head. "Don't worry about it. I've been trying to forget, myself."

He pulled her close. "What happened?"

Laura cleared her throat. Tears threatened. "I was inside, trying to work, but I couldn't focus. I was worried about you and the kids. Angry about Mandy. Then I got thinking about how everyone has been treating us, so I got online to see if anything had been published."

Rusty squirmed. "And?"

She took a deep breath. "It seems Travis not only wants to make you look bad, but also get the focus off himself."

"What do you mean?"

Laura really didn't want to say it, but she had to. She blurted out, "A popular local blog claims you fathered Brady."

His eyes widened and then his face paled. "You didn't believe it, did you?"

"No." At least not once she started thinking straight. "I know you'd never do that."

He played with a sleeve of his t-shirt. "Once we prove Travis is the dad, we'll make sure they retract that."

She frowned. "Good luck. It's not a paper—just a gossip blog."

"Well, when the news comes out, I'm sure everyone will figure out the truth. If he fathered Brady, obviously I couldn't have." His expression softened. "Tell me about the attacker."

"It was just after I read the gossip column that I heard something downstairs." Tears blurred her vision and she began to shake.

Rusty rubbed her back. "You don't have to talk about it."

"I need to. I grabbed a baseball bat from my coat closet and called for help. I wanted to run outside before he saw me, but I couldn't." Laura shook harder. "Everything is such a blur, but I fought back and protected myself. I'm safe and he's going to jail once he gets out of the hospital, so I guess that's all that matters."

Rusty ran his hands through her hair. "I'm so sorry I wasn't here."

"You couldn't help it. You had to take care of your house."

He scuffed his toe and rubbed the back of his neck. "Still, I wasn't there for you. I'm sorry." He met her gaze and looked away.

Laura's heart nearly jumped into her throat. She was the one who had been attacked, but now she found herself wanting to comfort him. She really did care for him—enough that she wanted to let go of her fears and reservations. To trust him, despite her poor track record with men.

Rusty glanced up and met her gaze.

She took a deep breath. "To tell you the truth, what really has me shaken is that the whole thing brought back some traumatic memories."

"Oh?" Concern covered his face. "What?"

Laura closed her eyes. Rusty's hand rested on hers. His other arm rested on her shoulders. She held her breath and trembled. He kissed the top of her head.

"I've had trust issues since my dad took off on us. I've always been with guys who were bad for me one way or another. One yelled at me all the time. Another broke things to scare and control me. The last one... I thought he was going to hit me. I really did. That was when I swore off men forever. Until I met you."

He was quiet for a moment. "I'm realizing a lot of things today, too, and I'm still sorting them out. It scared me down to the core when I heard you'd been hurt. Just know that the last thing I would ever want to do is to hurt you."

Laura's heart swelled. She turned and brushed her lips across his. Rusty reached around and pulled her close, bringing his hands to the small of her back. His mouth covered hers, with a gentle force. The scent of his woodsy cologne engulfed her. She relaxed in his embrace and drew into the kiss.

Twenty-Nine

T RAVIS SET DOWN the phone, careful not to show the raging emotions fighting to emerge. Anger. Rage. Fury. And worst of all, fear.

Angeline arched a brow. She scooted closer to him. It made the family room feel suffocating.

"Everything okay?" she asked.

Why was it always so hard to hide things from her? "Fine."

"Okay." Her still-raised eyebrow told him she didn't believe it.

"It is." He picked up his glass of wine and took a long, slow sip. It did nothing to relax him.

The lab results told him what he had already known. He'd fathered Mandy's second child. Sure, he knew it could have been the husband. What was his name? It didn't matter, but soon he'd find out. Once Rusty got a hold of the results in the morning, Travis was sure to hear from all of them.

Would they want him to pay up? Take the kid? Or worse… did they suspect him of harming Mandy?

The husband was already in jail.

"Did you hear me?" Angeline asked.

Travis blinked a few times and stared at her. "What?"

"What's gotten into you lately? It's like you're in your own little world."

"I have a lot on my mind. You know I have several big deals I'm juggling. Everyone wants me all the time." Including Angeline. Including Mandy's family.

"Seems like more than that, Travis. Do you want to talk about it?"

And hurt her with the knowledge that he had a kid out there already?

Multiple kids, in fact. But the other women had happily kept quiet about everything. Not Mandy. He'd underestimated her.

She'd underestimated him, too.

"You used to be able to tell me everything," Angeline said, staring into his eyes. "Don't you remember? Before we married, every free moment you had, we spent it together. One thing you said you liked about me was that I'm a good listener. I still am, you know."

He nodded. "Of course you are." But her patience would only go so far. And he'd given her so much in the prenuptials—he'd really been in love, and ignored the advice of his attorneys.

Travis couldn't afford to divorce her. And if he was completely honest with himself, he didn't want her to leave, either. Not that his actions showed it with how little time he'd spent with her since they'd married. He knew how badly she wanted his time.

"Do you want to take a vacation?" he asked, his heart racing.

"Of course." Her eyes lit up. "When should I plan for?"

"I mean right now. Leave as soon as we can. Take the private jet and head anywhere you want. Where do you feel like going? The summer home in Italy? Our new place in Hawaii? Somewhere else altogether?"

Angeline's mouth gaped.

"All of them? Spend a few days at each one?"

"I… what's brought all this on?"

His stomach knotted. "Why are you questioning a good thing?"

"You can't blame me for being surprised. I had to fight for this dinner with you. Now you want to fly out on a long vacation—right now?"

"I thought you'd be happy."

"Of course. I'm just not prepared."

"Each place has everything we need. We can send for luggage. I thought you enjoyed being spontaneous. And you want to spend more time together, right?"

She tilted her head and studied him. "What's going on?"

"Nothing. I'm just trying to spend some time with my wife. If you don't want to…"

"I do. But I've got the gala tomorrow. I've put so much into it, Travis. I can't miss it."

He frowned. Another day? In the morning, Rusty would get the test results. Find out that Travis fathered that kid.

"Can't we leave the day after tomorrow?" Angeline asked.

Travis pulled her close and nestled her neck. He trailed kisses from her shoulder up to her ear.

"You're not answering my question," Angeline said.

Travis unbuttoned her top two buttons as he kissed along her jawline, stopping to nibble her mouth.

She kissed him back and her body started to relax. But then she stopped. "What's going on?"

"I just want to spend more time with you." He threaded his fingers through her hair.

"Why are you so eager to get me out of town?" Angeline backed up and studied him.

"It's not like that." His pulse raced. The room seemed to heat up. "I just want some time with you. I've been thinking a lot about what you said earlier."

"Why?" She started to look suspicious again.

"Can't a man want a vacation with his wife?" He brushed lips across hers and then deepened the kiss as he simultaneously pulled her closer, pressing her against him.

"Of course, but tonight?"

"Yes."

"I told you, I can't."

Travis backed up and slammed the table. "I can't believe you, woman! You beg for time with me. Plead. Threaten. Everything. Finally, I offer it to you, and what do you do? Question me!"

Angeline's eyes widened and then her brows came together. "Of course! After the way you've been acting. And don't call me woman."

"I'll call you whatever I feel like. Start packing. I have calls to make."

She shook her head. "You're really something else. You ignore me all this time, and then just expect me to say 'how high?' the moment you say 'jump.'"

"I'm giving you what you want!"

Angeline stood up and glared at him. "I want to know what's going on. You can't blame me for being curious."

"Suspicious is more like it. Damn it. Just pack your things. I'll meet you in our room after I make some calls."

"No."

He stared at her. "No?"

"I realize you're not used to hearing that word—maybe no one has ever said it to you. But I am. No. I'm not going anywhere with you right now. The gala is important to me, and I'm not going to drop it."

They stared each other down. Travis was in too much shock to think of a response. His mind spun out of control.

His phone rang. He pressed ignore without even checking to see who the caller was.

"Now you're ignoring calls?" Angeline asked. "What's going on?"

"I'll tell you when we're on the plane."

Her brows came together. "Tomorrow night?"

Travis hit the table again. "No! Tonight. I'll meet you in our room in an hour."

"I told you no. I have a lot to do to get ready for tomorrow evening."

"What's wrong with you?" he demanded.

"Me? What's wrong with *you*?"

Travis spun around and stormed to the doorway. He turned back and glared at her. "Be in our room in an hour."

Angeline's mouth formed a straight line, but she didn't say anything.

"One hour." He left the room and checked the missed call. Wes. Another one from Juan at the lab. What more could he possibly want?

He went into his home office, locked the door, and returned Juan's call. "More bad news, I assume?"

"The phone rang while I was packing up for the night, and I didn't answer it because I need to get home."

"Can you get to the point? I'm in a rush."

"Sorry. I checked the message, and it was the cops. They want the results."

Travis swore. "You haven't told them, have you?"

"Of course not, but my boss already sent the results upstairs for the morning. It's locked, and I don't have a key."

"But they know about the paternity test."

"Yes."

Travis took a deep breath. "Okay. I appreciate you letting me know."

"Sorry I can't do more. My hands are tied."

"I understand, and I'll deal with it."

"If you need anything—"

"I don't. Everything's covered. Talk to you later." Travis ended the call and slunk into the soft leather sofa across from his desk.

What would he do if Angeline refused to go with him? Would he go without her? He had his own business to take care of—stuff far more important than a stupid gala.

The phone rang again. Wes.

"What?" Travis demanded.

"Did you talk to Juan?"

"Yes." Travis toyed with his tie, loosening it.

"Are you heading out of town?" Wes asked.

"Angeline won't go. Not yet."

"The gala. Camille won't stop talking about it. Go without her. She'll meet you after it's over."

"That pretty much blows my cover, don't you think?" Travis exploded. "A romantic getaway without my wife?"

"No, it doesn't. You're going ahead of time to set things up personally. Makes you a hero."

Travis rolled his eyes. "Makes me a loser. What did you find out about Caldwell?"

"Rusty's back in town. He's either staying at his sister's place or with the skank next door. He's been to both houses since arriving. He's got the kids."

"And the police are onto me."

"All they'll find is you fathered the kid. He's what? Twelve? That doesn't prove anything other than that you slept with Mandy thirteen years ago. They can't pin her death on you. We made sure of that."

Travis slid his tie off, balled it up, and threw it across the room. "No chance they can figure out we hired him?"

"I took every precaution. Even more than I needed to. They can't link us to her killer."

"Except that now they know about the paternity."

"Which doesn't mean you killed her. The husband's in jail for it. Seems everything fell into place nicely there. They have some solid evidence against him—so I hear." Wes laughed. "Don't worry, Travis. It's not coming back to you. We hired the best of the best. They took care of it and even got someone else to take the fall. What more could you ask for?"

"How about a cooperative wife?"

"You wouldn't want a timid little mouse, and you know it."

"Fine. So, what should I do? I can't think." Travis rubbed his temples.

"That's why you pay me the big bucks." Wes laughed again.

"Would you stop that?" Travis exclaimed. "There's nothing funny about any of this."

"You'll be the one laughing when all of this is over. Just go on with everything like business as usual. If you really want a vacation with Angeline, start planning. If you have any meetings set up over the next couple weeks, have your secretary change them to virtual meetings."

"The police are going to question me."

"You've done nothing wrong. They can't prove ties between you and the killer. Repeat that to yourself. It's true, and you need to believe it. Worst case scenario, you'll have to fess up to Angeline about this and pay some support."

"To whom? The mother's dead!" Travis got up and kicked his desk. "They're going to send the kid here. His dad's in jail."

"Maybe the uncle will take them on. He lost his family, remember? Look, they can't *force* you to take the kid. It's a free country, and you pretty much run this town. The cops practically work for you."

"Until I break the law."

Wes laughed. "You do that nearly every day. They've never held you accountable for a thing. You won't be connected to Mandy's death. My man left no evidence of a break-in and the drugs aren't supposed to be detected."

"Then how do the cops know she had drugs in her system?" Travis shouted.

"How the hell do we know? She was a former druggie, right? Probably fell off the wagon."

Travis released a string of profanities. "Is that the backup plan? She was a druggie, what, fifteen years ago?"

"Hey, they won't connect it to you. And even if they do, you have connections. People cower in fear from you."

Travis paced. "I should have listened to my gut. It was a bad idea to have her killed. How did I let you talk me into it?"

"Excuse me?" Wes asked, no longer laughing.

"You heard me."

"Don't turn on me," Wes exclaimed. "Why didn't you just pay that chick off?"

"She wouldn't take a lump sum." Travis kicked his desk again as he paced the large office. "Not like the others. No, she wanted monthly payments. And that's neither nor there, so get off my back."

"Look. We both need a break. Let's just sleep on this. Everything's going to be fine. After all these years, I'm sure you can easily give up your parental rights. Maybe you can pay off the uncle or the husband. I'll look into it."

"Then double-check that *nothing* leads back to me."

"Fine."

"Great. Talk to you then." Travis ended the call. Things were going from bad to worse faster than he could keep up. Angeline. Wes. The test results. The cops.

The cops. That was it. Wilson had been promoted to Lieutenant recently. Travis pulled out his phone and found Wilson's number.

"Calloway," Wilson said. He sounded less than thrilled to hear from Travis.

"Look, you remember Candy?"

Silence. "Hold on a moment. I need to close my office door… Why are you bringing the hooker up again, Travis?"

"I need you to remember what I know. What it can do to you."

"Why?" Wilson demanded.

"Because something might cross your desk that you need to forget about it. Accidentally destroy, perhaps."

Wilson swore. "I just got this promotion, and now you want me to put it on the line?"

"Or I could tell the captain about Candy. Didn't you see her friend—?"

"Fine. You have my word. Consider it taken care of."

"Thank you. Have a wonderful day." Travis ended the call.

Unfortunately, murder was something Wilson might still choose not to ignore. Travis needed to do everything he could to make sure the information never even reached the police station.

He couldn't afford to sit around and wait for Wes. Look where that had gotten him. Mandy's murder was supposed to go smoothly. Travis wasn't supposed to have to give her or that kid another thought ever again. Yet look what had happened. Where he was now.

A broken nail he'd clipped off and left on his plate at the last party would be his undoing. He'd been too distracted and he'd made a mistake. One little mistake. And it was going to cost him. Either by pissing off Angeline or worst case, him going to jail for being behind Mandy's death.

It was time to take matters into his own hands. Rusty would be going to the lab the next morning to pick up the results. Travis could talk to him man to man. And if that didn't work, then he would simply kill him. If the cops were going to arrest Travis for murder anyway, he may as well be guilty.

Thirty

~

RUSTY CHECKED HIS face in the mirror. He'd been awake for hours after a restless sleep. The cops were looking into Travis, or at least that's what they'd told Laura.

He wasn't convinced, though. Not with the way everyone in town worshiped Travis.

After one last glance in the mirror, he went into the hall and peeked in on the kids. Both were sleeping soundly. They would probably be out for hours still. It was early—far before they ever got up. He could run to the lab when it opened and be back before either one had any idea he'd ever left.

The previous night had been awful. Poor Brady had been crushed at the news of Chris not being his dad.

Rusty couldn't get Brady's reaction out of his mind. First, the boy's smile faded until his lips pressed tight. He slowly shook his head, his eyes shining with tears. Brady got up and paced until Rusty led the three of them onto the couch.

"H-how could this happen?" he asked, rocking himself.

Kaylie slid over to him and put her arm around him. "It doesn't change anything. Does it, Uncle Rusty?"

He moved over to the other side of Brady and put his arm around him, too. "You're still part of this family, and everyone is going to keep loving you just as much."

Brady turned to Kaylie, his mouth shaking. "You're still my sister, right?" Tears spilled onto his face.

Kaylie's eyes shone. "Of course. Like I said, nothing's going to change. Nothing."

Brady sniffled. "Thanks. Uncle Rusty, I hope you're right."

Rusty's heart shattered into hundreds of tiny pieces. A lump formed in his throat, and tears of his own stung his eyes. He wrapped both of them in an embrace. "I love you guys. I'll always be here for you, and you know what, Brady? No matter what biology dictates, your dad is your dad. He loves you. I don't want you to worry about any of this. But you need to know, just in case people talk about it."

A car horn sounded outside, bringing Rusty back to the present. He left a note on the kitchen table on the off chance that one of them woke before he returned. Then he locked up and went next door.

Laura answered, wearing a powder blue, lacy robe. "What's going on?"

"I'm going to the lab. I want to be there when they open."

She yawned. "I told you, they can fax me the results."

"I know, but I want the originals."

"The cops are already looking at Travis as a suspect."

"Right. But I want to bring them a certified original copy."

"Now it's certified?" She arched a brow.

"Whatever it takes for them to pay attention."

"You don't think they believed me?"

"It's not that," he said. "Travis has a lot of power around here. If they have any reason to doubt, I'm sure they'll take it."

"Well, let me get dressed and go with you."

Rusty shook his head. "I want you here in case the kids wake. Brady was really shaken last night."

Laura frowned. "Poor kid. Are you sure, though?"

"Yes. I want to get this taken care of as quickly as possible. Plus, I need to figure out what's going on with Chris. How long they're planning on holding him. I need to know what to tell the kids—what to do with them. I can't leave my job forever. I'm the boss."

"Okay. Just let me know what you need. I'll keep my phone on me."

"Thank you. For everything." He wrapped his arms around her, pulling her close. Holding her gave him confidence, and he needed all he could get at this point.

She squeezed him back. "It'll all work out."

"It's already starting out to be a good morning." He leaned his head against hers and took in her scent. She smelled fresh, like the ocean.

"Yeah. No one slashed your tires."

"Don't give anyone ideas." Rusty brushed his lips against her, letting the kiss linger. He pulled himself away. "I'll see you soon."

She ran her fingers along his jawline. "I can't wait."

Rusty gazed into her eyes. Part of him wanted to stay with her all day and hide from all the problems. But he needed to take care of everything, and the faster the better. He brushed his lips across hers and spun around before he could talk himself into staying. He hurried to the car.

"Bye," Laura called.

"See you soon." He kept his attention on the car, got into the car, and started the engine.

Would proof of Travis's paternity actually do anything? If there was even half a chance, he needed to give it his full effort. Not only to clear Mandy's name, but to give the kids full certainly that their mom hadn't killed herself. And that their dad hadn't killed her. Or at least the dad who had raised them. If Travis was behind her death, then that would at least be easier on Brady than Chris, who felt like his dad.

Maybe after dropping the paperwork off at the station, he should look into counseling for the kids. If anyone would need it, it would be those two.

And he needed to call his sponsor.

Rusty focused on the roads, trying to remember the turn he needed. So much had happened since going there last. He nearly missed the turn, and the tires squealed in protest as he took it.

Finally, the parking lot came into view. It was nearly empty. He recognized a few vehicles from the other day. He parked near the front and as he made his way around the lot, he noticed a car parked just around the building on the other side.

It stuck out like a sore thumb. A shiny, dark teal Jaguar convertible.

Any other day, he would admire it and maybe even snap a picture. He hurried inside and up to the office. "Hi, Lisa. Do you remember me from the other day?"

Lisa grimaced. "I sure do."

His stomach twisted in knots. "Well, if you saw the results, you know

I was falsely accused."

"If you say so."

"I just need the results."

"Sure." She turned to her computer and typed on the keyboard. "They haven't even been filed away yet. Hold on."

Lisa got up and went back into another room.

Rusty glanced around, eager to get away. Chills ran down his back and he shivered. It felt like someone watched him.

She returned with a stack of papers and a stoic expression. "Do you want me to interpret the results for you?"

"They're positive, right?"

"Yes, but I can show you—"

"I just want the originals. I don't need details."

She handed them to him. "Here you go."

Rusty shook his head. "Are you able to certify these?"

"I can sign them for you."

"And that'll do it?" he asked.

"I work here, don't I?"

He shoved the papers on the desk.

Lisa grabbed a pen and signed each page. "In case you have any other questions..." She scribbled a phone number on a sticky pad, removed the sheet, and attached it to the pile of papers. "But this should do it."

Rusty took the papers, pulled off the sticky note, and put it in a pocket. "Thanks."

Lisa mumbled something he couldn't understand.

He hurried out of there. The chills hadn't disappeared. He followed the maze-like hallway, got into the elevator, and they finally let up. Once back on the ground floor, they returned again. This time with the hairs on the back of his neck standing.

Rusty stopped and looked all around. He was alone.

It had to all be in his head. He flipped through the pages. Maybe he should have had Lisa make copies just in case. But it was too late for that now. He wasn't going back up there. He would just stop off somewhere and make copies before going to the station. He'd seen an office supply store in town not far from there.

His phone. Rusty pulled it out and snapped pictures of each page.

He went outside. A movement on his left caught his attention. He flinched. "Travis?"

Rusty almost hadn't recognized him. Travis had more than a five o'clock shadow and dark bands under his bloodshot eyes.

That explained the Jaguar around the other side of the building.

Rusty's stomach dropped to the ground. "Is everything okay?" He glanced around, not seeing anyone else. There was no way Travis would show up alone. There had to be others hiding somewhere.

Travis narrowed his eyes. "We need to talk."

"Sure." Rusty kept his voice steady. "I apologize about the other night. I've kept my word and stayed away."

"Because you've been out of town." Travis folded his arms.

"How'd you know that?" Rusty asked.

"I just do." Travis's gaze shifted to the stack of papers in Rusty's hand. "What do you have?"

"These?" Rusty asked. "Just something for my sister and my nephew."

"You don't know what you're getting yourself into. Give those to me."

Rusty stepped back. "I'll just hold onto them. Excuse me."

Travis held up a fist. "You need to hand those over. Now."

"No." Rusty stared at him, showing he wouldn't be easily intimidated.

"Why does everyone keep saying that to me?" Travis's face reddened. "Hand over the papers."

"I said no."

Travis stepped closer, holding his fists higher. "Do you have any idea what my attorneys will do to you for stealing my DNA?"

"Stealing?"

"Of course! Hand them over and I won't press charges."

"What are you so afraid of?" Rusty demanded.

"Afraid?" Travis exclaimed. "Calloways fear nothing."

"Then let's talk about these results. Work something out."

"What's there to work out?" Travis demanded. "I already spoke with Mandy, but that wasn't enough for her."

Rusty flinched. "What do you mean?"

"It doesn't matter. Just give me the papers, and you'll never have to worry about me again. If you don't, you'll have much more to worry about than you ever thought."

"You don't scare me."

Travis's nostrils flared. "You have no idea who you've crossed."

Rusty narrowed his eyes. "The almighty Travis Calloway—the man who thinks he can get away with murder."

"I didn't touch Mandy!"

"No, but you're behind the murder."

Travis's eyes went wild. He lunged for Rusty.

Rusty moved out of the way. "Thought we were going to discuss this."

Travis grabbed Rusty's shirt. "You just accused me of murder."

"These papers"—Rusty held them up and wiggled them in Travis's face—"indicate you have motive."

Travis threw himself against Rusty, knocking them both to the ground. Rusty's head hit a small, sharp rock. It dug into his scalp, cutting the skin.

He shoved Travis off. "Don't add assault to conspiracy to murder."

"Are you an attorney now?" Travis jumped to his feet.

"Just a humble tow truck driver." Rusty rose, also. He felt his head. Blood pooled in his hair.

Travis laughed. "You're as pathetic as your sister."

Rusty's fist met Travis's jaw. It made a cracking noise upon impact.

Travis punched Rusty in the eyeball. "Don't like me talking about your whore sister like that?"

"Now you've done it." Rusty dropped the papers and grabbed Travis's collar, squeezing tightly. Travis gagged and then spit in Rusty's eyes. Rusty was forced to let go of Travis to wipe the saliva. "Now you've given me your DNA. Can't claim I stole anything."

Travis stepped back, squatted, and scrambled for the papers.

Rusty shoved Travis from behind. He flew forward, landing on the pavement. His face hit the sidewalk.

Rusty kneeled and flipped Travis over. "Why did you do it?"

"You don't have any proof. Just that I slept with her, and last I checked, that isn't a crime." Travis reached for Rusty's shirt.

Rusty moved out of the way and sat over Travis. He clenched his fists and hit Travis on one side of the face and then the other.

Travis kicked him off, but Rusty recovered and punched him in the chest. Again, and then again. Travis blocked the next one and threw Rusty onto the pavement. Rusty landed on his side, the edge of the sidewalk digging into his ribs. He groaned and pushed himself to sitting. Travis came over and punched him alongside his head.

Rusty's ears rang as the next hit came, this time to his nose. Blood gushed out. It got on Travis's shirt as he completed the swing, leaving a red trail along his arm. Rusty grabbed his shirt again and shoved him against a tree.

Travis reached for him. Rusty had had enough. He balled up his fists and hit Travis in the right cheekbone, then the left. Travis's skin swelled with a purple hue.

Everything Travis had done ran through Rusty's mind, fueling his fury. He continued hitting Travis, not stopping when blood dripped down his face and onto Rusty's hands and shirt. Finally, Travis slunk to the ground and moaned. He reached for his face.

"Leave us alone," Rusty ordered. "Even if you manage to destroy the papers,"—he glanced over to where they lay scattered—"the proof is in the lab."

Travis looked up and glared at Rusty. "And I know people in that building. How do you think I knew to meet you here? I'm not letting you take those to the cops." Travis narrowed his eyes and crawled toward the papers.

"If you had nothing to do with Mandy's death, you wouldn't be concerned about them."

"Except her kid." Travis rose and dusted off his clothes. He smeared his blood on his shirt. He grabbed Rusty's collar. "And that's a big problem."

"He's your son, too." Rusty shoved Travis away and then he stepped back, fixing his own shirt. "Was that the matter? You didn't want to take responsibility for your actions?"

"It's not my fault she didn't use protection. That was her responsibility. I'm not going to let this destroy my marriage."

"Why not just pay the support? I'm sure you could afford it, and

Angeline would never know."

Travis narrowed his eyes when Rusty said her name. "Keep her out of it."

"Like you kept my sister out of it? Just tell me the truth, are you behind her death?"

"What, you got wires on you?"

Rusty patted his shirt. "Nothing. I just need to know for myself—closure."

Travis furrowed his brows and stepped closer. "I have nothing to admit. Let me take the papers, and you drive away with your house still standing. You think the garage fire was bad? You haven't seen anything yet, pal. Stay out of my life."

Rusty shook his head. "You're unbelievable. How do you expect to keep getting away with this stuff?"

"I get what I want. One way or another." Travis went over to the papers and picked each one up, not taking his gaze from Rusty. He walked back over, his shoulders and head held high. He fixed his shirt and then stared into Rusty's eyes. "And if you want to blame someone for Mandy's death, try yourself. Some big brother you were. Where were you when she needed you?"

Rusty gasped. He clenched his fist and hit Travis across the face as hard as he could. Travis stumbled back, grabbing his cheek. He glared at Rusty, but didn't move toward him.

Travis fixed his collar. "One thing I remember Mandy talking about. It wasn't that her husband was overbearing." He shook his head. "In her most vulnerable moment, she told me how much she missed her older brother. That she'd adored him as a child, but he'd let her down."

Rusty stumbled back, feeling his words worse than any physical hit. He backed into a tree and used it to steady himself. His breathing became labored.

Travis turned around and went to the car, squealing the tires as he left the lot.

Once Travis was out of sight, Rusty pulled out his phone and found the sticky note. Fingers shaking, he called Lisa. "This is Rusty. I'm going to need you to fax all those results to the police station. Now."

Thirty-One

~

RUSTY STEPPED OUT of the car, still in a daze over what Mandy had told Travis. Laura ran out of her house and stopped before reaching him.

"Oh my gosh. What happened to you?" she exclaimed.

Rusty reached up and felt his sore face. Everything hurt, especially his nose. "Travis showed up at the lab," was all he could say.

Her eyes widened. "You… you got into a fight with him?"

"I did."

Laura stepped closer and rubbed the side of his jaw. "Let me get you some ice."

Rusty wrapped his arms around her. How could he live with himself after what he'd done to Mandy?

Laura held him tight. "I'm so glad you're okay. I've heard of guys walking away from a fight with him in a lot worse shape."

Rusty doubted that. Travis had hit him where it really hurt.

"It's not just him. He always has people around him."

"Not this time."

"He didn't?" She stared at him.

Rusty shook his head.

"Did you take the papers to the station yet?"

"He has them."

"Travis?" she exclaimed.

"I called Lisa and had her fax the results over to the cops."

Laura glanced over at Mandy's house. "What about Brady? If Travis is the father…?"

"One thing at a time."

"Let's get you cleaned up, then." Laura took his hand, led him to her house, and had him sit at the kitchen table. She handed him ice and cleaned up the blood while he moved the ice around to the various sore places on his face.

Rusty closed his eyes. He'd forgotten how nice that was to have someone take care of him.

"Done," Laura said. "You'll need to change your shirt, though."

He glanced down and saw the big red splotches.

"I have something that probably fits you. My brother left some stuff last time he visited."

"If you're sure." He headed to the bathroom to look at his face. He was pretty messed up, but once the swelling went down, he would be fine. Maybe just a couple small bruises.

"Here you go."

He turned around. Laura held out a black denim shirt with large red flowers and bright green leaves spread across the shoulders and chest.

"Thanks... I think." Rusty took it, closed the bathroom door, and changed shirts. He found Laura in the kitchen and handed her his bloody shirt. "Mandy would ask if I had a cowboy hat to go with this one." The corners of his mouth twitched, though tears blurred his vision. Or would his sister have been too hurt by his absence to make any jokes?

"You okay?" Laura asked.

He shook his head no. "I miss her so much, and I really blew it by not reaching out to her."

A pained expression covered her face. "Oh, Rusty. She adored you. Never said a bad thing about you. I swear."

Rusty shook his head.

Laura laced her fingers through his and led him to the kitchen and she handed him more ice. "Use that while I get some food ready."

A few minutes later, she put two bowls of what looked like oatmeal—but with a different texture—covered in berries and cinnamon.

"Thank you." But he couldn't bring himself to take a bite. "The kids are going to be up soon. I need to figure out what to tell them about all this."

"Maybe we should find out what Chris plans first," Laura said. "What if he doesn't want Brady?"

Rusty frowned, his heart aching. "Then he has no parent."

Laura patted his hand. "But a kind-hearted uncle."

"I don't want to split the kids up."

"Might not have a choice. Would you take Brady back to your home?" The question seemed to hold so much more than it asked. Her eyes were intense as she studied him.

He swallowed. "Like I said, I wouldn't want to separate them."

"But you have your entire life across the country."

Rusty nodded. And all the memories of his family. "I think I need more ice."

She pulled some out of the freezer and they sat in an awkward silence.

What *would* he do? Everything was back home, but now all the people he cared about were here. He couldn't abandon Brady. He wouldn't separate the siblings. And he didn't want to leave Laura. But here, he had no source of income. Nowhere to live.

A knock sounded on the front door. Laura rose. "I'll get it."

"After someone attacked you? Travis is still on the loose. No way." Rusty put the ice down and went to the door and opened it. Brady and Kaylie stood there.

Kaylie stared at his shirt. "Yee haw."

Rusty had forgotten about the borrowed shirt. "You don't like it?" he teased.

"It's great, if you're going to the rodeo."

"Maybe we are."

The kids exchanged a worried glance. Rusty moved aside and let them in.

"Are you guys hungry?" Laura asked.

"We just had cereal," Kaylie said. "What's going on?"

"Let's have a seat," Rusty said. They all went to the living room and sat on the couch. "It looks like your dad might be coming home today."

"What?" Brady exclaimed. "Does he know…? Will he still…?" Tears filled his eyes. He wiped his face. "I'm such a baby."

"No you're not," Kaylie said. She wrapped her arms around him. "And if he won't let you stay, I'll go with you."

"Really?"

"Of course."

"But where?" Brady asked.

Kaylie looked at Rusty.

His heart raced. He swallowed. "I'll take you kids if you need me to."

They both jumped up and threw themselves against him, knocking him against the back of the couch.

A car sounded outside. Laura got up and peeked through the blinds. "Looks your dad's home" She lifted the blind higher.

The kids exchanged a worried glance.

"I'll go next door with you," Rusty said.

Kaylie shook her head. "He doesn't like you, Uncle Rusty."

Rusty stood taller. "I can handle him."

Laura met Rusty's gaze. "If you need me, just let me know."

He nodded and guided the kids downstairs. By the time they got outside, the taxi was already gone and Chris wasn't in sight. He had to already be inside.

"You guys ready?" Rusty asked.

They nodded. Brady's eyes shone again.

Rusty put an arm around him. "Everything will be okay. I promise."

"H-how do you know?" Brady sniffed.

"Because no matter what, Kaylie and I are here for you. If I have to sell my house and business and move my life here, I will. You guys are more important than any of that."

Brady leaned his head against Rusty's chest.

"Are we ready?" Rusty asked.

"He'd better be ready," Kaylie grumbled.

"Let's hear him out, okay?" Rusty said. "We know he didn't hurt your mom." Given the lengths Travis had gone to with everything else, it only made sense.

"Doesn't change the fact he's been a jerk for so long." Kaylie stepped back and glared at her house.

"I want to hear what he has to say first." Rusty headed for the front door and the kids caught up with him. He turned the knob. It was unlocked. They went inside, their footsteps echoing on the tile.

Upstairs, Chris sat at the kitchen table. His head rested on his arms, his face buried. He shook.

"Dad?" Kaylie asked.

Chris lifted his head. His hair stuck out in all directions, he had a bruise near one eye, and dark circles under both. He glanced at all three of them, not saying a thing.

"Are you okay?" Kaylie whispered.

He stared at Brady. "Do you know?"

Brady stepped closer to Rusty and nodded.

"Travis Calloway." Chris shook his head. "I never would have guessed. But it makes sense—only he could pull it all off."

"What do you mean?" Kaylie asked.

"You guys should sit." Chris waved his hands toward the other kitchen seats.

Kaylie sat next to him. Rusty took the chair across from him and Brady sat as close to Rusty as possible without sitting on his lap.

Chris stared at Brady, his expression soft. "This doesn't change anything."

"Wh-what do you mean?" Brady asked.

"You're my son no matter what anyone says. I'll fight the courts with my very last penny if I have to. No one's going to take you from me."

Brady dissolved into tears. Chris got up and wrapped his arms around the boy. Rusty scooted over to give them space.

Kaylie didn't look convinced. "Then why have you been such a jerk lately?"

Rusty shook his head, trying to convince her to change her tone.

"And by lately," Kaylie continued, narrowing her eyes, "I mean since before Mom died. Like way before that."

"Kaylie," Rusty said.

"No," Chris said. "I deserve it. I had plenty of time to think while sitting in that cell. Will you two hear me out?"

Brady nodded fast, his eyes wide.

Kaylie frowned, folded her arms, and leaned back against the chair. "Fine."

Chris took a deep breath. "More than a year ago, I came across your mom's diary. We weren't getting along, and I read it in hopes that it would tell me why she seemed to hate me."

"Because you're a jerk." Kaylie glared at him.

He nodded. "But I wasn't always. You remember that."

She looked away and shrugged.

"I remember," Brady said.

Kaylie shot him a dirty glance.

Chris kissed the top of Brady's head. "I wasn't trying to pry by reading it—I just wanted to know what I could do differently. I thought she was mad about something minor. Then I found out about Travis Calloway." He paused. "My world fell apart in a single moment. I knew we had problems. What marriage doesn't? But I didn't realize they went back before Brady was born." He took a deep breath and paused. "I tried to come to terms with everything. I waited, hoping your mom would tell me what was going on. She didn't, and it infuriated me. That's why I started getting temperamental."

"Why didn't you just talk to her?" asked Brady.

"And admit to reading her diary?" Kaylie raised her chin. "Why not? That's what you did."

Chris took a deep breath. "You're right. I should have fessed up. But I was scared."

"Of what?" Kaylie snapped. She leaned over the table and glared at him.

"Of losing your mom. Your brother. If she left and took you guys with her, I was afraid she might have been able to keep him from me if I wasn't his natural father." He turned to Brady. "You have no idea how much that scared me. It has every day since I found out."

Kaylie glared at him. "So you just decided to be mean to all of us? Is that it?"

"I wasn't trying to. Like I said, I was terrified of losing your brother. She could have decided to walk out of my life at any moment." He paused. "That and the threats."

"What do you mean? That doesn't make any sense." Kaylie leaned back and folded her arms.

"I was receiving anonymous threats. Now it all makes sense. Travis was behind it all." Chris ran his hands through his hair. "I even told the cops about the threats, but they wouldn't listen. Those detectives kept interrogating *me* about the calls and messages I received. Never once did they bother actually looking into everything."

"What do you mean?" Brady asked. "Why wouldn't they believe you?"

"Travis knows almost everyone on the force—that's common knowledge. He had to have convinced someone to make me seem as guilty as possible. There's no other reason I can think of to explain why they refused to look into any of the threats I received."

"I believe you, Dad," Brady said.

Chris embraced him again.

Rusty pressed his palms against the table. "But why'd you take the journal from the guest room?"

Chris flinched and titled his head back slightly. "What?"

"Mandy's diary. It was in my room. I found it and was reading it. Then you took it."

"I didn't take it. Mandy moved it, and I never saw it again."

"It was me," Brady whispered.

"You?" Rusty asked.

Brady looked down at his hands and nodded. "I usually hide my candy under the guest mattress."

"You already knew about Travis?" Chris asked.

"No. I didn't read it. I just wanted to have something of hers near me. It's under my pillow if you want it. I'm sorry."

"Don't be," Rusty said. "It's fine. You know what? I think you guys need to talk alone. I'm going to head next door for a while."

"Wait," Chris said.

Rusty turned to him.

"I owe you a big apology."

A knot formed in Rusty's belly. He slid a thumb through a belt loop.

Chris took a deep breath. "I was worse than rude to you, and you didn't deserve it. You dropped everything to fly out here across the country and help us out. I was feeling every emotion under the sun, and I took it out on you. I know it was for the kids and not me, but I can't thank you enough. For everything. I hope you can accept my apology."

"Of course." Rusty held out his hand, and they shook.

Thirty-Two

~

RUSTY ADJUSTED HIS tie and glanced around the wake. Flowers. There were so many of them. It was as if each guest had brought multiple bouquets. And there were plenty of guests. Mandy probably would have been surprised if she could have seen it.

Kaylie ran up to Rusty, her ankles wobbling in the black heels. She adjusted the length of her black dress. "Uncle Rusty, I want you to meet my best friend. She's over there. Come with me."

Someone bumped into Kaylie, messing up her hair. The lady paused and hugged Kaylie. "I'm so sorry for your loss, sweetie. Your mom was a wonderful person. The service was beautiful."

"Thanks." Kaylie glanced at Rusty and rolled her eyes. The woman walked away.

Rusty arched a brow and fixed the flower clip in her hair.

"Thanks." Kaylie patted her hair. "That woman used to always talk bad about Mom behind her back. So did a bunch of other ladies. I don't know why they're here."

"Maybe they feel guilty."

She shrugged. "Maybe. Come meet my friend. She's over by the dessert table."

"Actually, I have someone I'd like you and Brady to meet first."

"Who?" She played with her wrist corsage.

"Your grandparents."

Kaylie's mouth gaped. "Our...? You mean Mom's parents? They're here?"

He nodded. "Where's your brother?"

She looked around. "He was with Dad a minute ago."

"He might like to meet them as well."

"Okay. I'll go grab them." She ran off, disappearing among the crowd.

Rusty still hadn't adjusted to the change in the townspeople's attitudes toward Mandy and the kids since the papers proclaimed her a victim of murder rather than having committed suicide. Not only that, but everyone seemed to have forgotten all about the wild claims of Rusty fathering Brady.

He turned around and nearly bumped into Laura.

"How are you holding up?" she asked.

"It's nice to meet so many of Mandy's friends."

Laura gave him a knowing look. "How many of them would she have called a friend?"

"The good thing is that the kids say they've never been treated better."

"It's too bad that it took this."

Brady, Kaylie, and Chris came up to them.

"We get to meet our grandparents?" Brady asked.

"They're right over here." He turned to Laura. "Why don't you come with us? I'd love to introduce you to them."

She smiled. "I'd be honored."

Rusty took her hand and led them all to the table where his parents sat. He still couldn't get used to how much silver they both had in their hair or the added wrinkles. They reminded him of his own grandparents. It had definitely been too long since he'd allowed himself to see them.

He made the introductions. His parents shook hands with Laura and Chris, but gave hearty hugs to Brady. Kaylie hung back for a moment, but then threw her arms around them.

As his mom sat down with the kids, his dad came over to him. "Thanks for giving us the jewelry. I never thought I'd see my watch again—or your mother's necklace."

"And I still can't believe Mandy hung onto them all that time."

"Me, neither. Thanks again for insisting we come."

Rusty patted his back. "Don't mention it. Go spend some time with your grandkids."

Chris came over to Rusty and smiled, but then it disappeared. "I really wish I would have insisted Mandy reach out to you guys. It's obvious how much Brady and Kaylie need you three in their lives."

"We're here now," Rusty said. "And I'm not going anywhere."

"Right." Chris nodded. "How's your new house?"

"It's working out well. Once I get fully unpacked, I'll have you guys over. The kids are going to love the pool."

"They haven't stopped talking about it since you told them."

Rusty grinned. "That doesn't surprise me. They haven't stopped asking me when they can use it."

"Anytime they want to come over is fine with me," Chris said. "I have another few days off work, but then no more days off until the end of the year."

"They're welcome anytime," Rusty assured him.

Some people came up to Chris, and he turned to them.

Laura squeezed Rusty's hand. "So, when do I get to the see the new place?"

"I still have a lot to pack."

She nudged him. "I can help with that, you know. Girlfriends are good at that stuff."

Rusty's heart raced. Girlfriend?

Laura watched him, obviously feeling out his reaction. He smiled. "Well, when you put it that way, how can I refuse? I might put you to work, though."

"I'm not afraid to get my hands dirty."

"You haven't seen the shape of the guest bathroom yet."

His parents waved them over to the table. The six of them talked for a while until the room started clearing out.

"We should get going," said his dad. "We tire easily these days."

"How long are you staying?" Brady asked.

"A few days. We were hoping to spend some time with you guys."

Rusty rose and helped his mom out of her seat. "If I can swing it, I'll have my housewarming before you leave."

Laura nudged him. "I'm going to help you clean. We'll be ready tomorrow."

His eyes widened. "I don't know about that."

"Okay. Two days." Laura put her hand to her chin. "Five o'clock.

Everyone comes to his new pad. Can you be there?"

"We'll be there," Rusty's dad said.

"Us, too." Kaylie smiled.

They all said their goodbyes and then Laura followed him to his new place. It was only about five minutes from Laura and the kids.

His heart raced as he unlocked the front door. "It's a mess."

"You should have seen my college dorm."

Rusty laughed.

"Or even my house before I hired Cindy."

"Just promise not to judge me."

"You have my full respect after wearing my brother's shirt."

He shook his head and a grin tugged at his mouth. "I was hoping you'd forgotten about that."

She brought a hand to her mouth. "Uh, oh."

Rusty's stomach dropped. "What?"

"You didn't want me posting that picture on Facebook?"

His mouth gaped. "You didn't…"

She slapped his arm and laughed. "I'm just kidding. Let's get inside. I want to see the bachelor pad."

"Okay." His heart nearly leaped into his throat. It wasn't so much about the mess as it was about… the room.

He had put all of the important items that had belonged to his family into one of the spare bedrooms. The pale green walls were covered with the boys' artwork. Two shelves and a desk held many framed photos of their happiest moments. The twin bed was covered in blankets Lani had made—the top one, a beautiful pine-colored blanket she said reminded her of their woods. The bed had Parker's and Tommy's favorite stuffed animals resting on the pillow.

Another shelf held a mixture of their favorite books. Mostly picture books and early readers since the boys had been so young. Maybe one day, Rusty would be able to sit and read through them again. It was a bit much to even see the spines with the titles.

Of course, other rooms had their things. Pictures in the living room and hallway. Photo albums in the living room. All of their collected furniture and other household items. But the one extra bedroom—the one he'd spent the most time on. That was why the rest of the house was such a wreck.

Rusty gave Laura the grand tour, purposefully staying away from the bedrooms until last. He stayed quiet as she checked out the photos along the way. Finally, she picked up one frame. It held a picture of the family at a picnic not long before the accident.

Laura smiled sadly. "You guys look so happy here."

He nodded, feeling a lump in his throat. "We usually were."

She set it down and wrapped an arm around his back. "You've really had more than your share of heartache."

"That I have, but I've been blessed again. Sitting there at the table with you, the kids, and my parents earlier. It was…" He struggled to find the right wording. "I can't explain it."

"You don't have to." Laura moved her hands around his neck and kissed him lightly on his lips, tickling them. Rusty's pulled her closer and took hungry possession her mouth, allowing the raw emotions of the day to sweep him away in her embrace. She responded, kissing him back with equal passion.

After only a few moments, Laura pulled back and cleared her throat. "Why don't you show me where I can start cleaning?"

He swallowed and eyed her form-fitting black dress. "In that?"

She touched his mouth with her finger. "I always keep a set of clothes in my trunk. I'll be right back."

"Don't you want to see the rest of the house?"

Laura tilted her head. "You seem hesitant to show me the rest. It isn't a big deal."

He cupped her chin. "I really do have the best girlfriend, don't I?"

She reached around his waist and pulled herself closer. "I think so." She gave him a quick kiss before heading outside.

Rusty leaned against the wall and took a deep breath. Part of him wanted to show her the room. More than part, actually. He hadn't shared that part of his life with anyone. No one had entered any of their bedrooms at home since right after Lani, Parker, and Tommy's funeral. And this was home now.

It was strange to think of the only house they'd all had together as anything other than theirs. But the house back in Washington was home to the new renters. And luckily, they didn't mind the construction until the garage was rebuilt.

Not that Rusty really needed a new garage—even if he were to return to Washington, which he wasn't. He'd sold the towing business and now worked with Laura, expanding her consulting practice into a firm. They had rented some office space and hired a few consultants.

A twinge of guilt ran through him thinking about the house he'd left behind. It had been the right decision. He needed to be near Laura and the kids. Not that it had made leaving the house much easier.

He almost hadn't been able to let go of the key when handing it over to the renters. But when he watched their two kids scamper off toward the backyard, his heart warmed, knowing the long-abandoned play set would finally get some use. The home would have a family again, like it was meant to.

The front door opened and brought Rusty back to the present. Laura came in, wearing a brown camisole and cutoff shorts. It was strange to see her in anything other than a dress, but he liked it. She would look beautiful in anything.

Rusty stepped away from the wall. "You could've gotten dressed in here, you know."

She shrugged. "It was quicker in my car."

"I hope none of my neighbors saw you."

"Nope. I was careful. Where should we start?"

He slid his fingers between hers. "First, I want to show you something." His pulse raced in his ears, drowning out whatever she said. He squeezed her hand and led her down the hall and to the room. "This is much more than a spare room."

Rusty opened the door and took a deep breath. He may as well find out now, rather than later, before things got really serious, if she thought he was crazy for the… shrine to his family.

Laura stepped in, still holding his hand. "Wow," she whispered.

He braced himself for more. He probably was a little over the top for this room. Would she be able to handle this side of him?

She let go of his hand and walked around the room, gazing at everything but touching nothing. Finally, she turned to him. "You really did have such a beautiful family. I can't imagine how much you miss them. It must have felt like your whole world ended."

The lump in his throat grew exponentially. Tears threatened. Maybe this had been a bad idea. He nodded, careful not to blink.

"I can't even imagine what you've been through." Laura shook her head and wandered some more until she came to the bed. She stared at the stuffed animals.

"Those were Tommy and Parker's favorites." His voice cracked. Tears blurred his vision. He wiped them away before she could turn and see.

Laura studied them for a minute before coming over to him and wrapping her arms around him. "Thank you for showing me."

"I hope you don't think I'm crazy."

"Never." She leaned her head against his. "I don't know what I would have done if I'd gone through all that."

He ran his fingers through her hair. "I pushed everyone else away. We used to have tons of friends, but I couldn't deal with it. I couldn't let anyone in—literally or metaphorically. Not until I met you and the kids."

She looked at him and ran her fingers along his jawline. "I'm honored. Thank you for trusting me."

"I didn't think I could love again…"

Her fingers paused near his ears.

Maybe he shouldn't have said love. He cleared his throat. "But I want to risk it. You're definitely worth it."

"Oh, Rusty." Laura pressed her palms against his cheeks and gave him the sweetest, yet most passionate kiss. She pulled away and stared into his eyes. "I love you, too. And I won't break your heart. I promise to handle it with care." She slid her fingers through his and led him out of the room.

The breeze from them walking past knocked something over in the room.

"Hold on a moment." Rusty went back inside. Resting on the floor, he found the anniversary card Lani had left for him in the picnic basket. He slid it open, re-read the handwritten note, and held it close to his heart for a moment. Then he slid it in between two of Lani's favorite books and went into the hall, closing the door behind him.

Thirty-Three

One Year Later

TRAVIS STARED AT Angeline through the window and grabbed the phone next to him. She picked up the one on her side and balanced the baby in her other arm.

"You grow lovelier every day. And look how big Travis junior has grown since last week." Travis smiled, meaning every word. Sure, he'd been upset about the news at first. More upset when Angeline had admitted to quitting the pill. But now, his family was all he could think about.

"He's really growing fast." She snuggled the baby, her face lighting up.

Travis tugged on the ugly orange suit. "I can't wait to get out of this thing. You got confirmation from your friend about the jury's decision, right?"

"Shh." She narrowed her eyes. "Don't let them think you're involved with anything illegal. That might be all they need to keep you in there."

"Did you?" he insisted.

She shook her head and popped a pacifier in the squirming baby's mouth. "No. Just that they came to a decision. Wes promised me he's taken care of everything. And tomorrow, you'll be a free man. We'll finally be a family."

"I'll finally get to hold our son. The first thing I'm going to do is take you on that vacation. It's long overdue."

Angeline smiled sweetly. "I've already packed. The flight is booked. We just have to wait for the judge to read the victory."

"Exactly."

"Calloway," said the prison guard behind him. "Time's up."

Travis kissed his first two fingers and pressed them against the window. Angeline did the same.

"See you tomorrow." She blew him a kiss.

"It's a date. A victory celebration for three." He hung up and turned around, eager to get back into his cell.

The clock indicated they had another twenty minutes before that would happen. The guard led him outside to the yard. Travis found an empty spot along the building and leaned against it, trying to blend in.

It didn't work.

Three inmates sauntered over to him.

"How's the Lady Killer?" Bulldog asked, folding his arms. He stood taller than the rest and could cause a total eclipse of the sun on his own.

"Innocent until proven guilty," Travis said.

The three laughed.

"Yeah, I ain't done nothin', either." Deuce's lip curled, exposing several gold teeth.

"Tomorrow's your big day, isn't it?" asked Maverick.

"Yeah." Travis glanced to the side and took a few steps away, hoping they'd take the clue.

"I don't think Lady Killer likes us," Bulldog said.

Travis stepped forward and stared. "Stop calling me that. I never touched anyone."

Bulldog pulled up his shirt, exposing a razor tucked into his pants.

"Where'd you get that?" Travis exclaimed. And more importantly, what was going to do with it?

"Don't matter none. Keep your space, Lady Killer."

Travis stepped back to his place against the wall. He glanced away again.

"You think you goin' free?" Deuce asked, rolling up his sleeve. "Lady Killer."

He turned and stared at him. "Look, I don't care what you or anyone says. I never touched her. When she died, I was out of the state."

"Never touched her?" Maverick asked. "Why you in here, then?"

"Yeah, why?" Bulldog stepped closer.

Deuce narrowed his eyes. "You know what we do to guys who hurt women and children?"

Travis swallowed. "Guess I'll never know."

Maverick snorted. "You got that wrong. Don't he, boys?"

"I have to get ready for court." Travis edged away from them.

"That's what you think." Deuce grabbed his collar. "Don't walk away when we're talking to you."

Travis narrowed his eyes and clenched his fists. "Let go of me."

"Why? You got someone on your side?" Deuce looked around. "I ain't seein' no one coming to help you out."

"Just let me go. They're going to call us in soon."

"That just means I gotta make this fast."

Bulldog and Maverick laughed.

"I can pay you off," Travis said. "Any amount you wish."

"You can't buy your way out of trouble in here, pretty boy."

"What about your families? Couldn't your girlfriends use some new jewelry while waiting for you out there? Or your moms?"

"Wait," Maverick said. "My kid needs braces. Can you—?"

"Shut up," Bulldog warned.

"You got enough for braces?" Maverick asked.

Travis breathed a sigh of relief. "Yeah. All the orthodontic care you need."

Deuce hit Travis across the face. A ringing sounded in his ears.

"You losers aren't getting a dime now."

All three piled on top of Travis, hitting him on all sides. Something sliced deeply into his flesh, just above his elbow. Warm blood ran down his arm.

"Stupid Lady Killer," someone muttered just before another fist slammed into the side of his head.

Travis blacked out.

Thirty-Four

RUSTY THREW A towel around his neck and rose from the reclining pool chair. He took Laura's hand and helped her up. "It's almost time."

She squeezed his hand. "It's going to be okay."

He readjusted her new engagement ring and gazed into her eyes. He tried to smile. It didn't work.

Laura wiped something from his face and turned to the pool. "Come on, kids! It's time to go inside."

Kaylie and Brady stopped splashing and climbed out of the pool. Laura threw them each a towel and they all went inside. She turned on the TV.

"Hurry up and get dressed," Rusty told the kids. He grabbed his blue V-neck from the dining room chair and slid it on.

Laura rubbed his shoulders. "You didn't have to." She kissed his ear.

He kissed her cheek. "Once this is over, I'll be able to relax."

"Let me mix you some lemonade."

"I just want you near me."

She took his hand and led him to the couch. "I'll be right back."

The kids came back, dressed.

"Did it start?" Kaylie asked, suddenly serious.

Rusty shook his head.

"Where's Dad?" Brady asked. "He said he'd be here."

A car sounded in the driveway.

"And he's here," Rusty said.

"I'll get the door," Laura called, coming out from the hall. Now wearing a brown and green flowing dress, she smiled at Rusty. She went to the front door. Rusty followed a few steps behind.

"Good to see you again, Chris." Laura wrapped her arms around him.

"You, too." He put his arms around her and then stepped back.

"Mandy would have liked this," Rusty said.

Chris frowned. "Unfortunately, it took her death for it to happen."

"The important thing is that it did. Let's hurry. The coverage is about to start."

Chris grabbed his stomach. "I don't know if I'm ready for it."

"Me, neither," Rusty said, "but we need to watch."

Soon, all five of them were gathered on Rusty's sectional, fixated on the television. After a few too many commercials, a local journalist appeared in front of the court house. Behind her was a crowd gathered outside, but not allowed inside.

Laura grabbed Rusty's hand and held it between both of hers. The kids both scooted closer to Chris. Rusty and Chris exchanged a nervous glance. He knew they were both thinking the same thing—had Travis's expensive attorneys managed to help him get away with murder?

Everyone thought it would take a lot longer for the trial to start, but his attorneys made it happen faster than any other in the state's history.

Now was the moment of truth. The jury had deliberated. Handed their decision to the judge.

Would Mandy receive justice? Or would her killer roam free?

Rusty peeked over at Brady. His arm was linked with Chris's. Despite finding out about the biology of their relationship, they had grown especially close over the last year. Kaylie said she'd never seen them get along better.

Brady looked over and met Rusty's gaze. He held up his hand and crossed his first two fingers.

They'd need a lot more than luck, but Rusty raised his hand and crossed his fingers, also. He turned his attention back to the screen. The journalist was going over the major details of the trial. All stuff Rusty knew by heart. He and Laura had followed the case closely. Almost obsessively.

It had been enough of a distraction that between focusing on that and going to the local AA meetings, he hadn't touched alcohol since that day in his room with the picnic basket. He'd come clean to Laura about his problem, and she'd been more than supportive, giving up drinking herself. Also, his new sponsor had been a real help getting Rusty to come to terms with his conflicting emotions—feeling as though he was betraying his family by loving Laura and the kids.

The woman on television wouldn't stop talking. She needed to get inside so they could hear the judgment. Rusty squirmed in his seat.

Laura patted his hand. "Relax, sweetie."

Relax? Not until Travis Calloway was handed a life sentence without the possibility of parole.

Images from the trial flashed across the screen, including ones of Rusty on the stand. Then Chris. Finally, Laura and the kids. Rusty's stomach churned acid. It still angered him that Kaylie and Brady had been brought into it. They knew nothing about Mandy's relationship with Travis. At only twelve and fourteen, they shouldn't have had to be witnesses on a murder trial.

But they had been there the morning Mandy was discovered. And they knew their mom and her life well—minus anything to do with Travis. If he was convicted, they would be able to feel like they played a part in their mother's justice.

"Come on," Chris muttered.

"They sure like to drag things out," Rusty said. His stomach continued churning.

Finally, the screen showed the inside of the full courtroom. They'd been invited, but neither Rusty nor Chris wanted to put the kids through that. They both agreed a fun swim in the sun beforehand would be the best thing for them.

The worst scenario would be having to face Travis—in person—if he was set free. Though Chris was in anger management, he didn't trust himself if that was the outcome. Rusty wasn't sure he trusted himself, either, even though he'd already been given the chance to let his fist meet Travis's face.

The camera stopped on Travis, whose face was bruised, and then it focused on the judge. He spoke about the heinousness of the crime committed. The seriousness of murder. Of trying to cover it up.

Was that a sign? Rusty dared not get his hopes up. It was probably just the judge's opinion. The jury's decision sat on his desk, unopened.

He picked up the envelope.

Laura squeezed Rusty's hand. Or was it him squeezing her hand?

Brady leaned against Chris. Kaylie brought her hands up to her face, squeezed tightly together. "Please, please," she whispered.

The judge opened the envelope. It seemed to take forever. Finally, he pulled a piece of paper and unfolded it.

Rusty held his breath. He was tempted to close his eyes. He'd seen the slimy lawyers at work. They could have convinced the jury that Travis was not guilty.

Silence rang in Rusty's ears.

"Hurry up," Brady said.

The judge unfolded the paper a second time and stared at it. He looked up at the camera with no expression on his face.

Rusty wanted to jump up and yell.

The judge handed the paper to the foreman.

"The verdict is…"

Laura squeezed his hand.

"Guilty as charged. Travis Calloway is sentenced to life in prison without the possibility of parole."

A female sob—probably Angeline—sounded. Then cheers broke out in the courtroom.

Rusty's body went limp with relief. He leaned back against the couch and stared at the ceiling for a moment.

"Yes!" Kaylie exclaimed. She and Chris high-fived each other. "Brady?"

Brady's eyes were wide.

"Mom has justice now," Kaylie exclaimed. She held up her palm for Brady to hit.

Rusty's heart went out to his nephew. He'd just watched his biological father sentenced to life in prison. For murdering his mother. He was probably conflicted and confused—at best.

"Let's get some air, buddy." Rusty leaned over and patted Brady's shoulder.

Brady nodded. The two of them went out back and sat at the edge of the pool, letting their feet dangle in the water. Rusty didn't say anything. What was there to say? Nothing could change anything for the boy. He'd never get the chance to meet his birth father if wanted to. It had to be a hard hit. Just as it would have been if Travis had been declared innocent.

"Sometimes life puts us in no-win situations," Rusty said.

Brady kicked his feet, splashing water onto his bare legs. "I'm happy that Mom's killer is going to pay." He sighed. "But I'm sad, too."

Rusty put his arm around Brady. "You have every right. Your mom was taken from you. And by your birth dad."

"What am I supposed to feel?"

"Anything. Feelings aren't wrong."

Brady leaned his head against Rusty's shoulder. "I love my dad… but part of me wishes I could know Travis. I'm a horrible person."

"No you're not. You're an amazing young man with more on your plate than you should have to deal with."

"You really think so?" Brady asked.

"I know so."

"How did you deal with your family dying?"

Rusty took a deep breath. "Not very well. I pushed everyone away for a long time. It wasn't until I met you guys and Laura that I let anyone in. Actually, losing my family is why I never came out to see you guys before."

"Did you feel bad?" Brady looked at him and tilted his head.

"You bet. I almost didn't come back when I went home because of the house fire."

Brady's eyes widened. "Really?"

"But then when I heard you guys were in trouble—that you needed me to keep you out of foster care—I realized how much we needed each other. And you know what else I figured out?"

"What?" Brady stared at him with a deep-seated eagerness in his eyes.

"That it's okay to love many different people. Even if it feels like you're betraying someone."

Relief covered his face. "You mean it's okay that I want to meet Travis?"

Rusty nodded.

"Even though he killed Mom? And my dad would hate me for it?"

"He would never hate you." Rusty's heart broke, realizing just how much Brady was holding in. "Never."

Tears ran down Brady's face. "Thanks, Uncle Rusty."

Rusty wrapped his arms around Brady and pulled him close. "Anytime, kid. And I mean that. Don't keep these worries to yourself again. Got it?"

Brady nodded.

They sat out there for a while, until Brady sat up. "I guess we should go in there and celebrate. Do you think Mom knows?"

Rusty ruffled his hair. "I'm sure of it. In fact, I'll bet she's up there with your Aunt Lani and your cousins, having a huge celebration."

A wide smile spread across his face. "I like that. Mom has them, and we have you."

He kissed the top of Brady's head. "And one day, we'll all have each other."

Brady wrapped his arms around Rusty and squeezed.

Rusty sniffed the air. Something sweet made his mouth water. "We'd better head inside. I think they're waiting for us."

"I can't wait to see what Aunt Laura made. It smells delicious."

They went inside to the kitchen where Laura was setting a large plate of desserts on the table. She gave Rusty a wide smile. "Why don't we take this outside?"

Everyone carried the sweets and drinks out front, where Rusty's porch swing had its new home. Laura arranged the food on the table next to it.

Chris's phone rang. "It's my new boss. I'd better take it." He hurried inside.

Rusty sat in the middle of the bench and spread his arms across the back. Laura sat next to him. Brady popped a piece of chocolate in his mouth and sat on the other side of Rusty. Kaylie squeezed in next to her brother.

Rusty's heart swelled. Family filled his bench again.

**If you enjoyed *No Return*, you'll love Gone—
the story where we first met Rusty.**

About

Macy Mercer only wants a little independence. Eager to prove herself grown up, she goes to a dark, secluded park. She's supposed to meet the boy of her dreams who she met online. But the cute fifteen year old was a fantasy, his pictures fake. She finds herself face to face with Chester Woodran, a man capable of murder.

Distraught over his own missing daughter, Chester insists that Macy replace his lost girl. He locks Macy up, withholds food, and roughs her up, demanding that she call him dad. Under duress from his constant threats and mind games, her hold on reality starts to slip. Clinging to her memories is the only way of holding onto her true identity, not believing that she is Chester's daughter. Otherwise she may never see her family again.

Preview of Gone

SITTING IN HIS warm truck across from the park, Chester Woodran watched her walk across the open field. An overhead light turned on as she passed under it in the dusk. Her long, dark hair swished back and forth behind her. She wandered around the playground, walking between the climbers and slides until she stopped in front of the swings.

He had spent hours watching her. Studying her. He knew her almost better than she knew herself.

The moment of truth would arrive soon. She'd come a few minutes early, but he wouldn't deviate from the schedule. He would act exactly on time. He'd laid the groundwork. He wasn't going to let her change a thing.

Chester pulled out his phone and scrolled through the pictures, stopping at his favorite. It was the girl in the park for sure, although he couldn't see the details of her face up close yet. He would have to wait a few minutes.

From the phone, her light brown eyes shone at him. Her shy, almost insecure face smiled sweetly.

His heart sped up at the thought of many weeks of work coming together at long last. The waiting was about to end.

Clenching the steering wheel with all his might, he took several deep breaths to calm himself. Every precaution had been taken. Prepared with painstaking care. There was no chance of anything going wrong so long as he stayed with the plan.

The alarm on his digital wristwatch beeped. He turned it off and then leaned back into the seat, adjusting his over-sized glasses.

It was time.

More Information.

stacyclaflin.com/books/gone

Also from the Gone saga…

Dean's List

Every marriage has secrets. Some are deadly.

Lydia Harris knows her marriage to Dean has problems, but when she finds a box of news clippings he took great pains to conceal, the problems go from disappointing to dangerous. Nation-wide murders… in cities where he has traveled. She doesn't want to believe him capable of such violence, so she searches for clues to explain the hidden clippings.

As the evidence begins to mount, Lydia is torn. Dean seems to be trying to rekindle their lost spark, and she yearns for what they'd once had. But can she look past her own feelings to uncover the truth, or will she be next on his list?

Pick up this nail-biting psychological thriller today!

stacyclaflin.com/book/deans-list

Exclusive deleted scenes and bonus stories

The collection *Tiny Bites* contains three short stories from the Gone saga and a couple never-before-seen, exclusive deleted scenes.

Researching

Chester Woodran is a man at the end of his rope. He's lost everything, including his family. He wants to replace his daughter. This is the story of how he goes about finding a *new* one.

Desperate

Macy Mercer has been bullied at school for years because of her weight. Now thin, her reputation remains. Lonely and desperate, she seeks approval online, but will it only make things worse?

A Very Dysfunctional Christmas

Macy's family is barely surviving in the wake of her disappearance. Christmas only makes things worse. Will they ignore the holiday altogether, or manage to find some joy despite their worlds falling apart?

Read the stories and deleted scenes today.

stacyclaflin.com/books/short-stories

Other Books

The Seaside Hunters series

The Transformed series

Transformed Standalone Books

Haunted
Coming Soon

Visit StacyClaflin.com for details.

Sign up for new release updates and receive three free books.
stacyclaflin.com/newsletter

Want to hang out and talk about books? Join My Book Hangout and participate in the discussions. There are also exclusive giveaways, sneak peeks and more. Sometimes the members offer opinions on book covers, too. You never know what you'll find.

facebook.com/groups/stacyclaflinbooks

Author's Note

Thanks so much for reading *No Return*. I've been wanting to tell Rusty's story since we first met him in *Gone*. I've really enjoyed getting to know him through his own story, much as I did with Lydia in *Dean's List*. Some really interesting characters have come from the Gone saga, and I'm excited to write at least a couple more. Luke and Alex will get their own stories. Perhaps others, too?

Feel free to let me know your thoughts. I'd love to hear from you. The easiest way to do that is to join my mailing list (link below) and reply to any of the emails.

Anyway, if you enjoyed this book, please consider leaving a review wherever you purchased it. Not only will your review help me to better understand what you like—so I can give you more of it!—but it will also help other readers find my work. Reviews can be short—just share your honest thoughts. That's it.

Want to know when I have a new release? Sign up here (stacyclaflin. com/newsletter) for new release updates. You'll also get a free book!

I've spent many hours writing, re-writing, and editing this work. I even put together a team who helped with the editing process. As it is impossible to find every single error, if you find any, please contact me through my website and let me know. Then I can fix them for future editions.

Thank you for your support! I really appreciate it—and you guys!

CPSIA information can be obtained
at www.ICGtesting.com
Printed in the USA
LVOW12s0325101117
555747LV00004B/300/P